MY FRIENDS
GEORGE AND TOM

JANE DUNCAN

M

First published 1976 by
MACMILLAN LONDON LTD
London and Basingstoke
Associated companies in Dublin Melbourne
Johannesburg and Delhi

SBN 333 19896 4

Printed in Great Britain by
NORTHUMBERLAND PRESS LIMITED
Gateshead

For all the members of the Reachfar Family

'I HAVE to go home,' I had said to my friend Sashie de Marnay in his house on a West Indian beach in November of 1958. 'I am coming home,' I had written to my family in Scotland that same day and, 'I am going home,' I told Mr Arden in London in early January of 1959.

At that moment in London, 'home' was the only place that had any reality in my mind. Already the West Indies, St Jago, Sashie and the way of life in his house on the beach were four thousand miles away in memory, just as they were in physical fact, while the London I had found was a London very remote from the city I had known twenty and more years ago. In those young days, the London I knew was the London of offices, small flats and bed-sitters, a London of theatres, concert-halls, dancing and boy-friends, a city seemingly created for the enjoyment of light-minded young women like me, but the London to which I had returned was very different and frightening to a woman of nearly forty-nine who had lost youth's ability to live inside the moment. And the imposing offices of publishers Canterbury Arden & Company were not designed to give peace of mind to a diffident woman who had, to her own amazement, had three novels accepted by the firm. I was overawed and terrified by the office building and its denizens who seemed to me to be expending far too much care and attention on, to be expecting far too much of, these three novels I had written. Overawed and terrified as I was, I was at the same time fascinated by this strange new world, but I was old enough to have recognised my own slowness of wit, knew that I had to have time to acclimatise to all this strangeness and I wanted to run for home like a rabbit to the dark security of its burrow.

In the bleak early light of the January morning, though, as the train, hours behind time, laboured through the snow up to the Slochd summit on its way to Inverness, I suffered a sort of mental calamity. Where was 'home'? The question reared up as black, stark and grim as the Grampian Hills on either side of the railway line, semi-obscured yet menacing as the hills were, behind a screen of wind-blown snow. Home, Reachfar, the little croft on the Ross-shire hill-top used to be real, but it no longer existed, except as a memory, a country of the mind, half-hidden now by the weather of the years as the hills beyond the carriage windows were half-hidden by the snow. Home, now reduced from a comforting mental concept to hard concrete fact was Jemima Cottage in Achcraggan, a place never loved as I had loved Reachfar, and of which I had no clear mental picture.

Huddled against the cold among the grey blankets of the sleeper berth, I had a momentary sense of belonging nowhere until the phrase 'Home is where the heart is' came into my mind. I was here, making this journey because, from St Jago, my heart had gone out to George, my uncle, and Tom, our friend who lived in the cottage at Achcraggan. Tom and George needed me, the only people left in the world who truly needed me, and as I recognised this the train attained the summit, took on a new, more hopeful sound and the water of the stream beside the railway began to flow north instead of south, giving a sense of fresh departure. It would not be too long now before the train came to Inverness, and George and Tom would be at the end of the platform as they had always been, long ago, when I came home from Cairnton for the school holidays. It would be different, of course, I told myself, striving for reality. My father was no longer alive to receive our telegram of my safe arrival; Reachfar was no longer there to receive us as the trap drove into the

8

yard from the moor, but Tom and George would be there, my heart persisted, insisting on comfort and refuge.

I stepped out into the deep snow and looked down the long curve of the station platform. In that time of 'always', Tom would have been at the far end of the barrier, which could be seen from this angle, but he was not there now. While the porter collected my luggage, I fought the panic in my mind. Many times, in the years of the war, I had arrived at Inverness with no Tom or George to meet me. I was nearly forty-nine years old, I told myself and able to make my way to Achcraggan without help. But were they ill? What had happened? Suddenly, walking as erect as ever, although soon now he would be eighty years old, George came round the curve of the long disgorging train. His head high, his eyes searching from side to side of the crowded platform, he was coming towards me and I raised my hand high above the people around me.

'So here you are, Janet,' was his greeting. 'Your train is a long way late. You have had a long cold journey. Come down to the hotel and we'll have a dram.'

'Where is Tom?' I greeted him.

'At the funeral,' he said. 'It was but right that one of us should go.'

'What funeral? Who?'

'Young Alasdair the Doctor,' he said.

Stunned, I followed him into the lounge of the hotel and watched the porter pile my luggage in a corner. Young Alasdair the Doctor was – had been – exactly my own contemporary and he and I had fought and played our way through the years of early school. I had last seen him at my brother's home in Aberdeenshire some two and a half years before. 'The funeral,' George had said. 'It was but right that one of us should go,' but the one who had gone to the funeral was even older than George although I did not know by how many years, while Alasdair had been only forty-eight. 'It is in the nature of things and nothing to be sad about,'

9

George said when a waiter had placed our drinks on the table, 'when an old person goes but it is hard to do with when a young person goes.'

And now I was invaded by the sense that nothing is for 'always'. I had not come home to the people and the place which form the always of the mind but to people and a place that were 'the same only different' in the language of my childhood. This was no longer the time of my childhood when the people around Reachfar lived, in most cases, to the long fulness of their years.

'It was his heart, the doctor from Fortavoch said,' George was telling me. 'There was an accident to one of the men that are turning Poyntdale House into a hotel, and when Alasdair had seen to him, he got into his car to leave and just collapsed and died, it seems.'

Yes. This was the middle of the twentieth century when my husband, who had been nicknamed Twice, could die of heart disease at the age of forty-eight, just as my friend Alasdair could die at a similar age of heart failure.

'Anyway,' George said, 'when we get home you will see Jock and Roddy as well. They came up for the funeral. Even in the worst, there is a little that is good.'

'How do we get – home?' I asked.

'I have Little John the Smith and his car with me. John and Young John are at the funeral, of course. Little John has gone to buy spare parts for the garage while he is in the town here. I told him we would wait here for him.'

'How old is Little John?' I asked, feeling my way towards this new community I had entered.

'Eighteen or nineteen. Do you mind on Big John the Smith that was the precentor in the church?'

'Of course I do!' I felt an uprush of indignation as I used to do as a child when it seemed to me that George or Tom were questioning my memory or my mental capacity. 'And I remember his whisky bottle in the cupboard in the corner of the smithy.'

'Big John – he died a year or two back – was the great-grandfather of Little John and here he is.'

I looked at the young man crossing the hotel lounge towards us and corrected my former thought of 'new community' to 'new yet old community'. Little John was six feet tall and a burly reincarnation, it seemed, of his great-grandfather.

'You won't know John, of course, Janet,' George said.

I held out my hand and as the young man took it, he said, 'But I know about *you*. Last night, my grandfather was telling us about the day you and Alasdair the Doctor climbed on to the church roof.'

It is ageing to realise that one's small part in community history is old enough to be handed on by a grandfather to a grandson and as the car drove through the white country-side under the pale blue sky, by the pale grey sea, the past seemed to become more and more remote while the present became more and more unreal. It was on a day like this that Alasdair and I had searched among the snow for Miss Violet Boyd; the sky and the sea had been darkening towards evening as they were now, when at last we found her, dead, hanging from the rafters of Jock Skinner's abandoned croft house. That day was far away but yet more familiar than the sky and sea beyond the windows of the car, and Jock Skinner's old house more clearly outlined in the mind than the clutch of council houses, seen with the eyes at the road-side, as we entered the village of Achcraggan.

*   *   *

'Well, here we are, Janet,' George said as the car stopped at a little iron gate. 'You must be glad to be home after all your travelling.'

'Mercy,' said Tom in the open doorway of the house, 'we thought you were never coming! Jock and Roddy were thinking they would have to leave without seeing you. They have a long drive home. Come in to the fire. Leave those cases at the bottom o' the stairs, Little John. Can you wait for a droppie tea? No? Well, off you go and many thanks for bringing her.'

Years of time and thousands of miles of distance were wiped out as the door of the house closed and I was surrounded by the men of my family. There was comfort in the attitude of George and Tom that this homecoming was no extraordinary or unusual thing, but the most natural happening in the world.

'I'll make some tea,' Tom said. 'Sit down at the fire there. Shona sent us up a big basket of scones and a sultana cake and a ginger cake.'

'Sit down yourself,' my brother said. 'I'll make the tea.'

'I want a drink of water,' I said and followed him through to the scullery and there, watching him fill the kettle, I said, 'You haven't told any of them anything?' and added before he could reply, 'So you haven't? That's fine. But this is going to take a bit of explaining.'

The reference was to my novels which had been accepted for publication. I felt that George and Tom were going to find it very strange that, at my time of life, I had turned into a writer. Roddy, Jock's and my brother-in-law, was a writer of some renown but George and Tom never mentioned this, skirted away from the fact as if it were something of embarrassment to Roddy as well as to themselves, as they used to ignore the fact that old Maggie the Tinker was a cripple, the victim of a deformity that it was not polite to mention.

'They will be all right,' Jock said comfortably.

'Look how they are about Roddy,' I said.

'That is different.' Jock poured hot water into the teapot and swung it to and fro, looking down into it. 'Roddy is not a part of themselves. Tom and George can always take in their stride any calamity that happens to themselves.' He looked up and grinned.

'How did things go in London?'

'All right, I think. I felt a perfect fool – it was all so strange – but all the people at Canterbury Arden were terribly kind and Mr Arden himself is a nice dry sort of person and he has an old sister that I am dotty about.'

'It all sounds very family.'

'It was and just as well. You well know that I am not the cold business type.'

The kettle boiled, he made the tea and I helped to put cups and saucers on a tray. 'I brought a bottle of whisky up,' Jock said. 'It's in the sideboard cupboard through there. Get it out tonight after Roddy and I have gone and confess your sins to George and Tom. Shona and the kids talk of nothing but you and what you are going to do, and so on, and I can't keep your comic secret much longer.'

'I'll do my best. How are the kids?'

'Livelier than ever. Will you carry that tray with the grub?'

While we had tea, my family behaved typically. Nobody spoke of my husband's death, of the more recent death of Alasdair, or of my homecoming. The trend of the conversation was directed unobtrusively by George and Tom, who were men of the earth and who knew, without knowing that they knew, that the human mind needs time to grow into acceptance of important events like the deaths and homecomings of the dearly loved. They did not talk of these things. They accepted that they had happened, then raked over them the trivial happenings of the day-to-day, the present and past, as they would have raked earth over sown seed, in the faith that the acceptance, like the seed, would grow and become part of the future.

'George,' Tom said as I poured the tea, 'I have it *now* who that young fellow is who was at the funeral with Sandy Leeks. He is a breed of old Willie Oxypaw.'

Jock and I began to laugh, amused as we always were when Tom or George produced some of the old idiom of the district which, in this year of 1959, was dying out. Our brother-in-law, Roddy, who had been a member of the family for only about a year and who had been born in the West Indies and educated at a public school, opened his dark eyes wide as, I thought, his writer's memory noted the phrase.

'George and Tom,' Jock explained to him, 'often speak of the former men of this district as if they were pedigree bulls.'

'Indeed,' said George, 'one or two o' them *were* bulls although not much pedigree about them. But you are right, Tom. Yon fellow was an Oxypaw as sure as Janet is a Sandison.'

'Oxypaw?' Roddy questioned, now that he could get a word in. 'Leeks?'

'Oh, byenames,' my brother explained again. 'George should have said that the fellow was an Oxypaw as sure as Janet is a Reachfar.'

And now it had to be explained to Roddy that Willie Gordon, who would have been either the grandfather or the great-grandfather of the fellow in question, had been given this name because, each evening, his daughters would give him his choice of a bedtime beverage in the words: 'Tea or Oxo, Pa?'

'And what about the Leeks?' Roddy enquired.

'He is that chap Cooper, the Achcraggan schoolmaster that we spoke to,' Jock said. 'He is a breed of old Leeks who used to have the greengrocer's shop.'

'That's right,' Tom confirmed. 'Old Johnnie Leeks. Mercy, George, do you mind on old Johnnie's father, though, that was the whipper-in at the school for a while?'

'Fine that. He must have been the worst-tempered man in Ross-shire.'

'We-ell,' said Tom judicially, 'he had a fair puckle things to try his temper when you think on it, like you and Donald Boatie rowing along about ten yards from the beach shouting impudence at him when you should have been in the Dominie's history class.'

'I don't know how it was,' George told Roddy apologetically, 'but I never *took* to the schooling, like.'

'And it wasn't that George was thick in the head,' Tom assured Roddy now. 'Donald Boatie that used to slip the school with him was as thick in the head as shit in a bottle but George was never thick. I think myself that there was too many words in school for George's liking.'

'Words?' Roddy enquired.

'Yes. People speaking and preaching at you all day. Words only make a muddle o' things half the time whatever.'

'I am rather in favour of words myself,' Roddy said.

'But you are speaking about words written in books,' Tom continued. 'That is different. Now, myself, I can speak everlasting if I put my mind to it but I am right glad that Janet is home so that George and I needn't write letters any more. I think you have to be cleverer than us to put words on paper that make sense and if you can write words in such a way that this publisher man that Jock was telling us you have spends good money printing them into a book, they must be more sensible words than the nonsense that people will be speaking most o' the time.' Tom now frowned gravely at Roddy. 'Mind you,' he continued, 'I do not understand hardly anything of what you write but that is because you are writing of people whose like I have never come across. I daresay there are people like that fellow you have in this last book that wanted to sleep with every woman he laid eyes on but I have never seen them around Achcraggan.'

'Well now, Tom, I am not so sure,' George said. 'Andra Bull the Unctioneer did want to sleep with every woman he laid eyes on when you think on it and he did get a fair number o' them into the family way too, if you cast your mind back.'

'Well now,' Tom told us all with satisfaction, 'that is what I meant when I said George wasn't thick. It is myself that is thick. That fellow in the book was a rich, good-looking young man o' the town and I never thought o' likening him to old Andra Bull that had a belly on him like a fifty-shilling pot but at bottom the two o' them was just the same as each other. And it just goes to show, as I said before, that all these words people will be speaking is a lot of nonsense. Words that get spoken and words that get written down are two different things.'

'If you are all finished for the moment with the higher flights of literary criticism,' Jock said, 'it is high time that Roddy and I were on our way. The Glens of Foundland will be impassable with drift by now and we'll have to go the long way home round the coast.'

'Aye, it is time you were off,' George said.

We all stood up but Jock said, 'You stay by the fire, Janet. You are going to feel the cold,' and when they had all gone out to the car, I realised that, although my face felt flushed with the heat of the large fire, my feet and legs were like blocks of ice. A hot bath would help, I decided, and in the next moment, like an icy deluge, came the memory that Jock had filled the tea kettle from a white enamel bucket in the scullery and there came the other memory that, the last time I was home, George had told me that the water tank at the cottage here had burst and that, now, all the water had to be carried from the pump on the Shore Road outside.

In the few minutes while Tom and George saw Jock and Roddy into the car, I looked round the dimly lit, over-furnished little room, remembered the bright suite of rooms I had left on the sunlit Caribbean beach and felt that I was totally incapable of organising my life in any logical or sensible way, but George and Tom came back into the room, to stand side by side, looking at me as if I were a dream come true.

'My, my,' Tom said, 'but it is grand to have you back!'

'It is that,' said George. 'Tom, boil the kettle and we'll fill the bottles in her bed again.'

While George went upstairs for the bottles, I followed Tom to the scullery. As he poured water from the dipper into the kettle, some of it splashed on the floor. 'Dang it,' he said, 'you can hardly see the nose in front of your face in here at night.'

I looked up at the dangling electric bulb in the blue porcelain shade. 'That bulb is far too weak,' I said.

'Is there different strengths of them then?'

'Of course there are. You know that.'

'I do not, at least not till this minute.'

'But there has been electricity in the district since just after the war,' I protested. 'You had electric light at Reachfar.'

George arrived, carrying two rubber bottles. 'What are you two fighting about and you just home?' he asked.

'Herself,' said Tom, pointing the kettle at me, 'says there's different strengths of these electric bulbs.'

'Mercy, do you tell me that now?' said George. 'So *that* is why the lights down here are not as bright as they were at Reachfar? I thought it must be because this is the coast instead of the hill, like the wireless not being so strong down here.'

'Herself' Tom had called me, a title never used for anyone since my grandmother died. I felt so proud that I did not dare to think about it. It was easier to argue about electricity.

'You must have changed bulbs at Reachfar,' I said loudly. 'They don't last for ever.'

'Not us,' George said firmly. 'If a light went out, we got Dickson the Ironmonger to come up and sort it. Young Murdo Dickson is an electrical engineer. Tom and me are not engineers of any kind. Why are the bulbs here different from the Reachfar ones?'

'So that Jean could save maybe sixpence in every three

months on the electricity bill,' I said. 'The stronger the bulb, the more current you use.'

'Dang it, Tom,' George said, 'I wish we had known that. Every time she got in a rage, we could have put a stronger bulb in one o' the lights. *That* would have sorted her!'

Jean was my mean, ill-tempered stepmother who had lived with George and Tom at the cottage until the previous August.

'Where *is* Jean, by the way?' I asked.

'God knows,' said George, 'and maybe He cares but we don't. Some weeks back, we heard that she had fought with the people she went to and went off to live somewhere else but that may be just gossip. Why are you asking?'

'I don't know. I don't care where she is as long as she isn't here.' I watched him fill the bottles from the kettle. 'Has that water main come through the village yet?' I asked.

'Aye. It came at the end o' the summer. It is right outside the front door there, but Tom and I thought we would wait till yourself came home before we did anything. You will know better than we do how to plan things.'

While he carried the bottles upstairs and Tom heaped more coal on the fire, I produced the whisky bottle and three glasses from the sideboard, a jug of water from the scullery.

'Are you hungry?' George asked when he returned. 'We are not much good at the cooking but we have a pot of broth ben there.'

'That will be fine. And don't worry about the cooking any more. I'll do it if you two will do the shopping. I'll need time to get used to walking up to my backside in snow again.'

'That's a bargain,' said Tom. 'We'll do the outside and you'll do the inside. And you'll have plenty to do. George and I have been fair beat to keep all this furniture clean.'

'I am not going to clean it,' I said. 'If you agree, I think we should sell most of it and use the money to help with the water supply. You can hardly move in here for furniture.'

'All the rooms are the same and some o' them worse,' Tom said. 'George and me are fair scundered with it but we weren't sure what to sell and what to keep.'

'Herself will know though,' George assured him, 'when she has had time to look at it all. And there's some of the old Reachfar stuff out in the garden shed. Jean said it was too old-fashioned for the Castle here.'

'Jean is a fool and always was,' I said. 'Well, let's all have a dram.'

'Where did you get that bottle?' Tom asked.

'In the sideboard. Jock brought it.'

'That fellow must think we are in the poorhouse,' George said. 'Put it bye for another time. Tom and I have a bottle of our own. It would be a poor thing if we hadn't a bottle for you coming home.' He fetched a bottle from a cupboard in the corner and began to pour from it. 'You are not to be worrying about the expense of bringing the water in and all the like o' that,' he said quietly. 'Tom and I both have the pension and a fair bit besides. Your father wouldn't take a penny o' the money we got for Reachfar. He gave it all to us although by rights the place was his.' He laughed. 'He said Jean would go fair past herself if she thought she was rich.'

'And so she would have done,' I agreed. 'But about the water supply, I think the three of us should go share and share alike in it. I've got some money.'

'You canna have very much with all the illness and trials you've had,' George said.

'And I have made some money in the last few months, not much, but some.'

'Were you working, then, while you were staying with Mr de Marnay?' Tom asked.

'In a way,' I said and burst forth desperately: 'Listen, you two, you'll hardly believe this at first but it is true. I have written three books and a publisher in London has given me a hundred pounds each for them.'

'Books?' They looked at me, then at each other, then

both raised their right hands and rubbed the backs of their necks, as they had always done when embarrassed or at a total loss for words.

'Written books?' Tom asked at last. 'Like Roddy you mean?'

'Yes, except that mine are nothing like Roddy's. And listen, I don't want anybody round about to know anything about this. When the books are in print will be time enough for them to know, if anybody notices them at all, that is. Maybe the books aren't worth a damn and nobody will want to read them.'

'I don't believe that,' George said. 'These clever men in London wouldn't have given you all that money for them if they weren't worth a damn. But what in the world gave you this notion to write books?'

'I don't know. I have had the notion as you call it for a long time, ever since I was at Cairnton Academy, I think. I told Dad about it once but I told him too not to tell anybody.'

'But why? It seems to me to be an odd sort of notion for you to have but there is nothing real disgraceful about it. Why were you so hidden about it?' George was frowning at me. 'It's not like you to be hidden.'

'I don't know why I kept it so secret either. Maybe it was because you two would say it was a queer thing to do, like you are saying now. Maybe it was because Jean was always calling me a fool who couldn't do anything. Anyway, you know about it now but just keep your mouths shut. It's nobody's business but ours. We'll just go easy and hope to make the odd bob out of the books.'

'And meantime we'll have another dram for luck,' Tom said.

And now all of us buried my strange new departure under the layers of day-to-day living.

* * *

20

The following morning, I came downstairs at eight o'clock to find George and Tom fully dressed, sitting at the scullery table, George with a sheet of paper in front of him and holding a stub of pencil while Tom had charge of a pot of tea and a tin of biscuits.

'I make it eleven,' said Tom.

'No, it's more than that,' George argued. 'Wait. Start again at the top at the west end.'

'The west end of what?' I enquired from the doorway.

'So it is yourself,' said Tom, contriving to imply that he would have been disappointed if the Queen instead of myself had entered the scullery. 'The oven is on. Open the door and sit in front of it and put your feet in and be warm. You will take a cup o' tea?'

'Thank you. Well, the west end of what?'

'We are counting electric bulbs,' George explained.

I opened the oven door as instructed and a considerable shower of sparks flew out, apparently from the hinges. 'God!' I said, jumping back.

'Ach, it often takes a bit of a spit to itself,' Tom told me. 'Never heed it.'

'And do all the lights play peek-a-boo and go in and out like the one in the room I was in?' I asked.

'No, only one or two o' them. Right, George, there's the west room at the top. That's one.'

'Listen, you two,' I said. 'You said young Murdo Dickson was an electric engineer. Could you ask him to come along here?'

'Can *you* not put bulbs in?' George asked, disappointed in me. 'Jock can. He showed us once but we never took to it.'

'It isn't a question of bulbs. This house was wired just after the war, wasn't it? This cooker and all the wiring are thirteen years old and after the war some of the stuff was second-hand anyway. It all needs to be examined by an electrician.'

'I see,' George said. 'Yourself knows best. Well, I'll go along for young Murdo as soon as it's nine o'clock and the shop opens.'

'Fine. I'll make some breakfast. You want your usual porridge, I suppose?'

While, warily, I switched on a plate of the antiquated cooker and made porridge and more tea, the faint grey dawn began to break over the firth about five hundred yards away and George and Tom lit the fire in the over-furnished sitting-room. I made up my mind that there was no point in telling them of the dangerous state of the cooker and the wiring, but over breakfast I did say, 'And you two will leave that cooker alone. Now that I am here, I will do the cooking.'

'And that will suit us just fine,' Tom said. 'It is a devil of a thing for boiling things over and burning the backsides of the pans forbye and besides.'

Shortly before nine o'clock, they went tramping away through the slushy seaside snow and returned with a short wiry young man who was the grandson of Mr Dickson, Ironmonger and Seed Merchant of the Achcraggan of my childhood.

'Herself will tell you what is wanted,' George said. 'Tom and I have to get some tatties out of the pit while we are clear of frost.'

'This is something like the thing,' their every gesture seemed to say as they shook the hated dust of the indoors off their feet and took to the outdoors.

'They don't seem to feel the cold at all,' young Murdo said.

'No, but I do,' I said, taking my overcoat from a peg in the front hall. 'I am just back from the West Indies. Well, let's start in the scullery. Take this cooker.' I pulled open the oven door and it took a bit of a spit to itself.

'No. You take it,' said young Murdo.

'How soon can you put in a new one?'

'As soon as you like. I am pretty slack just now. Things are always pretty slow in the winter.' He took a notebook from his pocket. 'What kind of cooker do you want?'

'I haven't a clue. I have been out of this country for ten years.'

We went over the house room by room and it was all as strange to me as it was to young Murdo, stranger indeed, for perhaps he had been in some of the rooms to change bulbs for Tom and George. Counting the ancient bathroom where none of the plumbing worked, there were five rooms on the upper floor and counting the scullery with the spitting cooker and useless chipped sink and washtub there were five rooms on the ground floor and every room was stuffed with furniture from wall to wall and every room had one twenty-five-watt bulb in a fancy shade hanging from the ceiling and no other power socket of any kind.

'This is going to add up to a fairish bit,' young Murdo warned me cannily, 'with the cooker and all the wiring and power sockets. It could easily come to about a hundred and seventy quid, counting my time.' We were in the parlour of the house when he spoke, the most furnished of all the rooms, where a hideously prosperous aspidistra in a pink china pot stood on the windowsill. This made me think of my friend Sashie de Marnay who had helped me through the breakdown I had suffered after my husband died and who, when I tried to be economical, used to say: 'A pox upon your scurvy faithless cheese-paring!' and adjure me to put my faith behind my pen.

'That will be all right,' I told young Murdo. 'The Reachfar name is still good, I suppose?'

He nodded. 'The Reachfar name is still good for any amount you say.'

'When can you start?'

'In an hour's time, if you like.'

'All right. Get going.'

In the course of that day, young Murdo recommended a

plumber from Fortavoch who arrived on the day following, and a day or two later the five large crates of crockery, cutlery, books and linen which I had shipped north by road from Liverpool arrived on an enormous lorry at the front door.

'Oh Lord,' I said. 'I had forgotten all about that lot. We can't get these crates in here.'

Young Murdo, the plumbers and Lewie the Joiner who was replacing floorboards in the scullery gathered round the lorry whose tarpaulin was crowned with several inches of frozen snow and scratched their heads.

'You two,' George said to the driver and his mate, 'will come in and take a drop of tea while we consider this,' and the consideration ended with his saying, 'If you two will be good enough to take me on your lorry the mile or so up to the smithy, John the Smith will keep these boxes for us till we are ready for them.'

The house was so busy, there were so many cups of tea to be made in addition to the regular meals that I had not time to notice the tremendous change in my way of life or even to feel the cold, but as it was growing dark on the day that the crates arrived, I said to George and Tom, 'Look here, you two, we've got to get rid of some of this clutter of furniture. It's like some Mad Hatter's tea-party, shifting it out of the craftsmen's way and shifting it back into somebody else's way. Anyway, who does it all belong to? Us or Jean?'

'Whose money bought it all?' Tom asked belligerently. 'When did Jean earn the money for all this?'

'I don't care a damn whose money bought it or who gets the money we sell it for,' said George, 'as long as I don't have to live with it any longer. The thing I like least in all the world is the taste of too much, whether it is drink or meat or money or sticks of furniture.'

'Young Murdo and the plumbers will get the money we sell it for,' I said.

'Where do we start?' George asked.

'Right here in this sitting-room. Look, go up the street before the shops shut and buy about fifty tie-on labels and we'll tie one on every stick we don't want.'

'Better bring a hundred or two,' said Tom.

At various times in the course of my life, I have felt that the concept of human free will is a great mistake. To a large extent, life is not at the control of the human will. By the middle of the next day, the house was hung as if with bunting with tie-on labels and Tom and George had blocked the upper landing by hauling out of a boxroom, which I forgot to mention when cataloguing the house, the most amazing collection of items, from broken umbrellas to a stuffed stag's head with enormous antlers and sad glass eyes.

'Where in the world did that come from?' I asked.

'Jean bought it for a shilling. She always bought anything that was what she called a bargain,' Tom told me.

'Even if it wouldn't be a bargain at half-nothing,' George added. 'It's a shame to waste a label on it.'

'Put one on it all the same,' I said. 'Let the auction-room men clear out all the junk even if they only throw it away. It's worth a label to get rid of it.'

In the local newspaper, I had seen the telephone number of the auction rooms but George and Tom, although fervent labellers of the unwanted, would have nothing to do with the telephone kiosk which stood at the end of the Shore Road.

'You know fine,' said George, 'that Tom and I have never taken to that bliddy unnatural telephone,' so there was nothing for it but to put on nearly all the clothes I possessed and go to the kiosk myself. My teeth chattering, my fingers numb as I pressed cold coins into the cold slot, I made the call and hurried back to the cottage where, from the road, I saw the aspidistra on the parlour windowsill in its pink china pot and once more I heard the voice of my friend

Sashie: 'A pox upon your scurvy faithless—' and I remembered that Mr Arden had hinted that I should have a telephone installed. I turned back to the kiosk and from the directory found the address of the Area Telephone Manager. This is what I mean by life being beyond the control of the human will. If Sashie had never spoken those words, if George and Tom had been more amenable about modern inventions, if the weather had been warm, even, the house would not, a week later, have been infested with two large tea-drinking telephone engineers, as well as with young Murdo, the plumbers and Lewie the Joiner. At intervals I would recall Sashie saying: 'Remember you are a *writer* now,' and wonder if other people who wrote fell through the foundations of their houses as they tried to make a pot of tea. I was sure that my brother-in-law Roddy did not, a thought which sent a cold chill down my spine. The avant-garde Roddy would probably be ashamed of his connection with me and my simple old-fashioned writings.

In the midst of it all, I had letters of one kind and another to write and my typewriter stood on a table at the sitting-room window, while my supplies of stationery were in a drawer in the scullery. One of the things I had to write was a short autobiographical note requested by my publishers for publicity purposes and this I composed in long-hand, then copied into type while George and Tom watched with fascination. All machines fascinated them although they gave them all a fairly wide berth.

'How did you learn to work it so fast?' Tom asked.

'Remember all those secretary's jobs I had before the war? I *had* to work it fast, especially for old Mr Carter.'

I thought no more of the matter until after supper that evening, when all the craftsmen had gone and we were sitting round the fire by candle-light. We were now at the transition stage between old and new wiring when nothing electrical was working.

'I have been thinking,' George said suddenly. 'You don't look at your hands when you are working that typewriting machine.'

'No. It is called touch-typing.'

'You were looking at the paper beside the machine with your neck all twisted.'

'I was copying.'

'Come on up the stairs. Bring your candles.'

When I said the house was over-furnished, this was an understatement. There were two rooms on the upper floor and two on the lower floor which were no better than store-rooms. They were crammed with Jean's acquisitions and while George and Tom struggled to bring some item out to a clear space on the landing, I discovered a strong resemblance between Jean and Madame Dulac, the mistress of the estate where my husband and I had lived in St Jago. The cellars of Madame's enormous house had been store-rooms for her acquisitions of the years and Jean had been another Madame on a smaller scale. Jean too, I remembered, was short and fat, with fat short-fingered hands like Madame and for a moment I seemed to be surrounded by ghosts in the flickering light of the candles.

'Maybe we shouldn't part with this thing after all,' George said, as he and Tom lifted a dressing-table out on to the landing. Like all Jean's purchases, it was a tasteless object, a bargain, no doubt, like the stag's head. It was made of mahogany, which seemed to me a butchering of good wood. It had two drawers on either side of a knee-space and two vertical columns on top which supported a looking-glass. 'Tomorrow,' George said, 'we could get Lewie the Joiner to take this looking-glass off and put a bittie wood along between these stands. Then when you are copying stuff on your typewriting machine, you could hang your writing in front of you with one of these metal clip things you have. I don't like to see you working with your neck all twisted, as if you were deformed.'

27

'George, that is a great idea,' I said. 'I have often had a stiff neck after copying for a long time, and I could keep paper and stuff in the drawers.'

'The very thing,' said Tom, opening his knife and cutting the label off the table leg.

I tell of this because it is illustrative of their ingenuity. I have often thought that the men who erected the Pyramids or the statues on Easter Island must have had something in common with George and Tom for, at Reachfar, they had contrived to move enormous boulders or huge trees that seemed to be beyond the strength of two men. And the reason for this piece of ingenuity was their dislike of deformity of any kind. They would never tolerate at Reachfar an animal that was not perfect of its kind; they always ignored with polite pity the crippled leg of Maggie the Tinker and if Jock or I made a clumsy or awkward movement of any kind, we would be told: 'Don't go at the thing all heels to Gowrie, as if you were deformed.'

When we had come back to the sitting-room fire, Tom asked, 'Now, before the auction-room lorry comes, are you certain sure that Mr de Marnay wants that ugly boogger o' an asperdester in the pink pot?'

'Yes,' I said. 'He mentioned it again in the letter I had yesterday.'

'But what does he want it *for*?' George asked.

'How do I know? It was Liz who offered it to him. If you knew Sashie as I know him, you wouldn't ask the why or the what of anything he does.'

'He must be a fine man,' George said, 'to take care of you the way he did and you could see it in the letters he wrote to Liz. It was just as if he knew the very kind of letter that a bairn like her would like. What is he like to look at?'

I had a photograph of Sashie, who had been a dancer, in his costume as the Prince in *Giselle* and I now fetched it from my bedroom.

'That was taken just before the war,' I said.

'My,' said Tom, 'what a fine-built fellow!'

'Sashie will arrive here sooner or later,' I told them now, 'and there is something about him that you ought to know. He lost both legs in the war. He walks on artificial legs but I don't want you to think of him as being deformed. There is nothing twisted or deformed about Sashie. He is small, like most dancers, but beautifully made as you can see, and one of the best people I have ever known.'

After a long hard look, George laid the photograph aside carefully. 'Up at Reachfar as we were,' he said, 'we had no idea how terrible that war was. When will he come to see us, do you think?'

'I have no idea. I have told him about this *buareadh* we are in and not to come until we are all settled,' I said.

George and Tom laughed before George said, 'We thought you would have forgotten your Gaelic after all this long time.'

'My Gaelic — about three words!' I scoffed but I was amazed at how readily the word for a muddle or a disturbance, pronounced '*boo*rach', had come to my tongue. As best I could remember, I had not used it or heard it used since my childhood. It was in small accidental ways like this that George, Tom and I were rediscovering our relationship.

*   *   *

As if from sheer spite, as if it knew that I had returned from the tropics and it had a grudge against me, the weather, according to Tom, was 'performing its very worst for about ten years'. My one visit to the telephone kiosk was followed by a heavy head cold which caused George and Tom to look upon me with something like disgust.

'What has come over you since you have been away foreign?' Tom asked and: 'You will stop in the house till the better weather,' George dictated, not in a sympathetic tone, but as if I were an idiot who allowed the weather to take advantage of her.

Achcraggan, seen from the air, lies on a promontory with the water of the firth on three sides and it is very unusual for snow to lie there. In my childhood, I frequently set off from Reachfar for school in a foot of snow which became less deep as I descended the hill, and when I reached the school playground there would be no snow at all. This year of my homecoming, however, the snow lay inches deep over Achcraggan until early March and it was impossible to keep the house warm or dry with the craftsmen tramping in and out. My temper, always inclined to be short, began to fray and a climax was reached on a Monday morning in January – I had been home for a little over two weeks – when Tom came down with a bundle under his arm.

'I am just going to take our washing along to Mrs Shaw,' he said. 'Have you anything that needs washing?'

Young Murdo was installing the new cooker, I was trying to make porridge on the newly kindled sitting-room fire while holding a handkerchief to my streaming nose and I was probably a little light-headed and running a temperature. Whatever the combination of causes, my temper flared up.

'Mrs Shaw? Washing? Since when does Reachfar need other people to do its washing?'

Tom looked dumbfounded and no wonder. 'Mrs Shaw has been doing George's and me's washing for the last three years,' he said placatingly, 'ever since Jean said her rheumatics was too bad to do it.'

'Jean isn't here now. *I* am here. Put that bundle in the back room there and get out of my road.' I had stood up and the porridge boiled over, reducing the fire to a damp smelly mess. 'Oh damn and blast it!'

'Mercy on us,' said George from the doorway to the front hall. 'It was myself that thought for a minute that Her Old Self was back among us.'

'Oh shut up,' I said, fetched another saucepan and began to make fresh porridge.

'You know, Tom,' George said when breakfast was over and having looked at me as he used to look at my grandmother to decide whether speech was to be risked, 'I was having a look at that electric book that young Murdo brought for Herself to pick out the cooker. There's washing machines in it.'

'Do you tell me that now?' said Tom.

'We can't afford a washing machine,' I said.

'Och, I don't know,' George said easily. 'If Tom and me has no money left when we die, if people will not bury us for love they will have to do it because of the stink. Young Murdo!' he called through to the scullery. 'Can you get Tom and me a washing machine?'

'Surely,' said Murdo and a few days later a neat white cabinet was carried into the scullery and Tom and George watched with fascination while Murdo demonstrated to me how to work it.

'Right,' I said. 'Go and get that heap of stuff out of the back room, Tom.'

'Just a minute now,' said George when Tom returned. 'This is Tom's and me's machine.'

'You mean—?' I stared at them. 'Nonsense! You don't like working machines.' I turned to Murdo. 'They won't even speak on the telephone. That is how I got this cold.'

'Telephones are different,' said George. 'We don't like speaking to people when you can't see their faces.'

'You can't see the faces of the news-men on the wireless,' I argued while Murdo, who had never heard a Reachfar argument before, looked from one of us to the other.

'That is different,' George said again. 'The men on the wireless are speaking to *us*.'

'And very nice civil-spoken gentlemen they are,' said Tom, confusing the issue further. 'But George and I have

31

been considering,' he pursued. 'George and I could work the threshing mill at Reachfar, that had a diesel engine that was equal to a good puckle horses and Murdo was telling us that you can make electric with diesel engines so electric is just the same as the threshing mill in the end of it. So this thing' – he knocked his knuckles against the side of the cabinet – 'is just a sort of threshing mill for dirty clothes and George and I will work it just fine. Now, Murdo, you said the white things first—'

'And not more than five pounds dry weight, mind,' Murdo cautioned.

'Tom, where is the old Bessemer from Reachfar?' George asked.

I sat down on a box in the corner to watch the performance, trusting that Murdo would not allow them to electrocute themselves. Bessemer. I had not heard the word since my childhood. It was the name given to the large brass saucer suspended from three chains, which were in turn suspended from a vertical spring balance with a hook at its top. It must have been invented, I thought now, by the Victorian Sir Henry Bessemer, for his surname was engraved on the brass of the balance. It must have been one of the earliest 'machines' to be used in the kitchens of the Highlands and it brought into the scullery an air of continuity as George suspended it by the hook from his fingers beside the new white cabinet.

'Have you some soap powder, Mistress?' young Murdo asked me.

'I don't know what we've got and what we haven't and I can't get at the cupboards. Will some shaved-down soap do?'

We had a further argument about the amount of shaved soap to put in. Tom and George, always generous, wanted to shave down the whole large bar.

'And you'll never get it rinsed out of the sheets,' I said. 'They'll be like dirty grey cloots like the washing Flora

Bedamned used to hang out and you won't put out that sort of washing while I am about the house.'

'Better do as Herself says, George,' Tom said hastily.

At last the various knobs were turned to their settings and Tom and George stood back regarding the machine benevolently. Nothing happened.

'Shouldn't there be a little noise o' some kind with that wheel thing you showed us going round?' Tom asked.

George took the lid off the tub. 'It's not going round at all!' he said indignantly. 'The bliddy thing's not working.'

'You have to plug it in here and switch it on,' Murdo told them and the machine began to hum.

'There we are,' said George with pride. 'But, man, Tom, we are a foolish kind of pair right enough. Fancy us expecting the poor craitur to work with no electric. It's not like us. It needs the electric to keep it going.'

They certainly did not need electricity to keep them going but they kept the washing machine going. They washed everything they could lay their hands on until I made a protest.

'Look here, you two, there's no use washing everything in sight and dumping it in the back room when it's dry. Is there an iron in the house?'

'Aye, but I wouldna touch it if I was you,' Tom said. 'We havena touched it since the day o' Davie the Plasterer's funeral when we tried to iron our collars. There's a dirl comes out of the handle of it that kind o' runs up your arm.'

'God knows how they haven't killed themselves,' I said to Murdo. 'Bring me a good iron next time you go back to the shop.'

While the work inside the house snowballed on, while the snow fell and froze and thawed and fell again out of doors, I began to feel a claustrophobic sense of frustration. During the later months of my stay with Sashie, I had come to regard my main function as that of a writer and now I became aware that payment for all this refurbishing of the cottage depended on my work as a writer while, at the same time, it was impossible to write in the midst of the chaos. I could do a little after I went to bed at night but that was all. Also, in the ten years I had spent in the West Indies, I had grown accustomed to large houses, large rooms with large windows that let in a great deal of light and I was finding the small rooms and the grey winter light from small windows a sore trial. The only room I did not find claustrophobic was the scullery, which had two windows that looked over the back garden and a strip of grass to the firth, but on most days the firth was invisible behind a curtain of snow, rain or mist. And the inside of the house was not helped by Jean's choice of wallpapers and carpets. Jean was a native of a grim little Lowland town whose industries were coal-mining and stone-quarrying and she was steeped in the housewifely tradition of that town that the greatest virtue in carpets, curtains and wallpapers was that they should not 'show the dirt'. Jean had always prided herself on her housewifely capabilities and in common with many Scottish housewives of her time, she was fanatically what she called 'clean' but her true although unrecognised attitude was that dirt did not matter as long as it did not show. Therefore all carpets were dark brown or grey, curtains were brown, wallpapers and woodwork a dark chocolate colour, shiny with varnish. After the strong light of the tropics, I found it all ineffably dreary, but most frustrating of all was the fact that I could not show what I felt. It was true that the cottage belonged to me, left to me by a great-aunt and I could do as I chose with it, but George and Tom had made it their home to which they had welcomed me and I did not want them to know of my dissatisfaction with it.

I vented my suppressed feeling and energies in an orgy of cleaning and re-arranging the rooms. As soon as Murdo had rewired my bedroom, had put in two power sockets and

Lewie had replaced floorboards and skirting-boards, I threw the rugs, the carpet, the linoleum and the layers of news-papers which had reduced the room's height by some five inches out on to the landing and scrubbed all the woodwork and the floor.

'It smells better,' George said when he came to call me down for an afternoon cup of tea, 'but you'll never make a Reachfar o' this place, Janet, so don't kill yourself at it.'

So was that what I was trying to achieve? Another Reach-far? Perhaps but, if so, it was in vain.

'The smell is from that carpet and all these rugs,' I said aloud. 'They are all alive with moth. What in the world are we going to do with them, George?'

'Take them down to the shore and burn them.' His eyes gleamed with anticipation. 'That carpet is older than myself and was never good stuff in the first of it. I am sure it was here before Aunt Betsy's time and Jean brought in all these rugs. Tom and me is fair scundered with carpets and rugs and curtains and cloots of all kinds. You canna find the ground under your feet or see out o' the windows for them. Come on down and get some tea.'

As I walked downstairs into the chaos of craftsmen, fallen plaster, wood shavings and dirt, I wished that it was possible to escape from the past and start all over again in some bare place all by myself but hearing George behind me on the stairs I knew also that I did not want to escape all alone. I wanted to do what was impossible, to be selective about life, to take Tom and George with me and leave behind what I did not want, but I had to bow to the knowledge that the rough had to be taken along with the smooth, that this was an essential condition of family relationship, that central relationship in living.

In the scullery, George announced with pleasure to Tom and the craftsmen: 'Janet has no more use for the carpets and cloots than us, Tom,' and to Murdo and Lewie: 'Next time you lift a carpet, don't put it back. Throw it out into the shed there.'

The following day, all three of us turned our attention to Tom's and George's rooms. There were two large and two smaller bedrooms on the upper floor and George and Tom used the two smaller ones.

'The big ones are visitors' rooms, Jean told us, when we came down from Reachfar,' Tom said.

'Visitors!' I exploded. 'Those two old sisters, you mean?'

'Och, they haven't been here since years,' George said. 'Jean had visitors' rooms but she didn't like visitors to come and dirty them. But she did Tom and me a favour without knowing it. The wee rooms look out to the firth instead of the Shore Road.' He gave the back of his neck a rub. 'You know, if I was you, I would move down into the closet. It would be a lot warmer than that room on the west gable.'

Also, I thought, it looks to the firth instead of the road.

'That's what I think too, forbye,' said Tom.

How much did these two know of what I was feeling and thinking?

'Well, we'd better get these rugs and carpets out to the shed, Tom,' said George. 'We've got to get this shanty cleaned up before that publisher man in London gives Janet the sack for not sending him any writing.'

I must have been home for about a month by now and this was the first direct mention of my writing. But just how much did they know about what I was thinking?

Very soon now we had the top floor to our liking, clean, clear of clutter and with our new bathroom in operation while Aunt Betsy's old bath – 'Now why, think you, did they put lion's feet on a bath?' Tom enquired – was relegated to a corner at the bottom of the garden. I would fain have retained the old lavatory which was a wooden box that held a porcelain bowl decorated in Willow Pattern, but the plug for the bottom of it was missing and the flush mechanism rusted and broken beyond repair, so it too was relegated to the bottom of the garden. George and Tom, I need hardly say, celebrated the new bathroom by setting about what they inelegantly called the 'shit-house', an outdoor chemical lavatory, with two of the heavy Reachfar fence-post hammers, reducing bucket and house to a shambles of bent metal and kindling wood in less time than it takes to tell.

'Those two are having the time of their lives,' Murdo said, watching them from the scullery window and I found this comforting, for none of the other old people I had known would have relished this sort of upheaval in their lives but George and Tom, it seemed, had never fallen into old age's trap of habit.

*   *   *

By the end of February, all the craftsmen were finished and the three of us set about the ground floor. We took everything out of the closet, the room off the sitting-room, and moved me and my belongings into it, then we set about the parlour. We had sold everything in it except the aspidistra in the pink pot and had a clear field to turn it into a bedroom for my brother and sister-in-law when they came up on holiday.

'And Liz can go into the closet off this room,' Tom said, 'and the boys into the big east room up the stair.'

'And we'll still have the big west room for Mr de Marnay when he comes,' said George. 'He can climb a stair all right?'

'You bet,' I said.

By the middle of March, with our house in order, the snow disappearing and the sky growing brighter, we all felt very pleased with ourselves. Beside my chair in the sitting-room, I had a small table which held my pen and the old atlas with my paper clipped to it which I held upon my knees as I wrote. At the window, was the converted dressing-table which held my typewriter and although, hitherto,

I had always written in a secretive way, shut in a room by myself, I found that I could write here with George and Tom going in and out about their business or sitting by the fire to smoke their pipes. They did not talk to me about my writing, did not ask what I was doing but quietly developed a habit of taking the letters from Rory the Postman and putting them on the typewriting table while, in the late afternoon, they would pick up the letters I had written and take them to the post office. They did not make spoken offers of help but contrived to convey that they were there to help in any way they could.

In the evenings, now that the weather was better and all the work in the house was over, they went out to the weekly village whist drive and on other evenings to visit three old cronies of approximately their own generation. One was Young Murdo's grandfather, another was old Mr Grant who had once been the village tailor and the third was Malcolm the Minister, so called because he had been handyman at the manse for most of his life and was now retired.

'You must ask them along here some nights now that we've got the place in order,' I said.

'Oh, we canna do that,' Tom told me. 'They are all too frail and old.'

I was about to say with some force that they were all a sight younger than he was but stopped myself in time.

'Murdo the Ironmonger fell and broke his thigh two years back,' George told me. 'And he was always weak in the chest the youngest day he ever was whatever. And Grantie is bed-ridden entirely, poor fellow, and Malcolm the Minister is more like a corkscrew than a man with the rheumatics that's in him. It is a poor kind of life that they have but they are all well looked after by their people and they have their televisions and all.'

I immediately found myself guilty of selfish thoughtlessness. We had a washing machine, a cooker, a refrigerator, all sorts of things for my convenience but I had not even thought of a television set for the amusement of Tom and George.

'We always go to see one o' them on a night when there's football or horse-jumping or the like,' Tom said, 'and on Saturday afternoons when the horse-racing is on but they know how busy we have been this last while and wouldn't be expecting us.'

'I am going to get you a television set of your own,' I said. 'We are doing better than I thought out of all the junk we sold. There was that third cheque yesterday.'

'Oh no!' George said hastily. 'You mustn't do that. If we had a television here, Murdo and Grantie and Malcolm wouldn't ask us any more. They would feel they were being an imposition. And we like to go to see them.'

'And *they* like to see *you*,' I thought, but did not say it aloud. Instead, I said: 'Well, please yourselves but you can have television any time you want it.'

'Surely,' said Tom. 'Likely we would have had it before now if it wasn't for Murdo and Grantie and Malcolm. People like to feel that they have something to *give* people, like.'

They employed their time as they had always done, doing the things they were in the mood to do and always something useful. The novelty of the washing machine wore off and they washed only on Monday mornings now, but they chopped wood, carried in coal, did the shopping and the dish-washing and soon now the spring gardening would be in full swing. We had a period similar to the inception of the washing machine when I acquired a vacuum cleaner. They called it the 'Suck-and-Blow', ran riot with it through the house, but after spending a tedious afternoon extracting from its innards a pair of my nylon stockings and incidentally ruining the stockings, they attained a sense of moderation and would only suck and blow when, for once, they could think of no other occupation.

We had a small world of our own inside the house and garden which, like all worlds, had its own importances and although I spent at least half my days in writing, I felt utterly detached from the world of publishing although letters from that world arrived almost daily.

About the middle of March, the day came when 'the weather took the turn' in the words of Tom. It had thawed during the night and when I came through to the scullery in the morning, the sun was shining, the dug earth of the vegetable plots in the garden was rich, black and shiny with the damp of melted snow and I could see the water of the firth and the hills on the other side clearly for the first time and the ruins of Jock Skinner's old croft on the grass near the beach.

'I wonder if Jock Skinner and Bella are still alive?' I asked over the breakfast table.

'Aye and living like,' said Tom. 'People will be seeing them in Inverness on market days. Jock is still at the dealing but he has a little sort of motor lorry now instead of the horsie.'

'What put you in mind of Jock?' George asked.

'The ruins of the old croft down there. What is that building a little to the west? I don't seem to remember it.'

'Andra Bull's old store,' Tom answered me. 'The Bull used to do a bit at the dealing as well as the unctioneering. He used to store tatties and oats and the like in there and wait for the prices to go up.'

I noticed that, when we were selling the furniture, Tom had spoken of the 'auction' rooms but when his mind went back to the past, he used the words of that time, so that auction became 'unction'.

'That building looks older than the other buildings on the Shore Road here,' I said.

'Aye, it is a good bittie older,' George agreed. 'I've heard tell that Poyntdale Estate put it up in the first of it, when the shore here was in crop before these houses were built. I believe it was old Sir Turk that sold off this land and the store went to Andra Bull when he bought the plot for the house.'

'The Miss Boyds' – they had been the daughters of Andra Bull – 'are all dead, aren't they?' I asked.

'Och, aye.'

'Who has the house now? Anybody I know?'

I was discovering that I knew very few people around Achcraggan now which was not surprising for I had been away from the district for nearly thirty years except for brief visits.

'None of us locally knows who the house belongs to now. It has been lying empty since old Daisy was taken away three years ago. Daisy died just last year. We saw a notice in the paper. People said the property would go to young Andra. You mind on him?'

'You bet I do.'

Andrew Boyd, the illegitimate son of Violet Boyd by Jock Skinner the Dealer and grandson of Andrew Boyd or 'Bull' the Auctioneer, had inherited the money-making although not scrupulously honest talents of his father and grandfather. At the end of the war, although only in his twenties, he had grown quite rich as one of the scavengers of post-war surplus stocks and when I had last seen him shortly after the war he was typical of the flashy over-tailored denizens of lounge bars who were known at that time as 'spivs'.

'Talk about blood running true,' I said. 'That fellow had his breed written all over him.'

'Whether that is a good thing or a bad,' George said, 'you shouldn't be scoffing about it. You are pretty true to your breed yourself. Besides, young Andra wasn't all bad although I'll grant you that he must have sailed gey near the wind to get as rich as he did and him so young.'

'He was very good to his old aunties until the day they died,' Tom said. 'They would have been in a poor way latterly but for what Andra did for them.'

'And when they all died off except old Daisy and she went funny in the head, he came and took her away to a home for such people in Aberdeenshire. We asked Jock about it and he said it cost a fortune to keep an old person in such a place with its own nurses and all.'

'Does Andrew Boyd ever come here now?' I asked.

'Have you a notion of him then?' George enquired blandly. 'All the ladies took to his father and grandfather when I think on it.' Then, probably because of the look I bent on him, he continued hastily: 'No. He has never been here since he took old Daisy away. A big van came from England somewhere and took away everything out of the house and it has been lying empty ever since.'

'It is my opinion,' Tom said, 'that young Andra sold that house to some foolish people from the south. He would have told them about all its rooms and its view o' the firth but he would forget to tell them that the water tank and all the pipes were bursted and the place full of dry rot. That is what the local people think whatever.'

The talk of Andrew Boyd and his aunts had sent my mind into the far past and I now said: 'On the way from Inverness when I came home, I noticed that Bedamned's Corner is a ruin. Where is Flora living now?'

'Nobody knows,' George said, 'or even if she is living at all.'

'You mean that she has left the district?'

'Bedamned' was another of those local byenames which had descended to Flora Smith from her black-browed surly father, the name having been given to him because it was a word that he used more frequently than any other. Flora had always seemed to be born to lose, for after having dragged up in poverty, after the death of her mother, her four brothers and her idiot sister, she had inherited the four children of her eldest brother after he and his wife were killed in an accident in the United States. It was true that this brother had left a considerable amount of money, so that Flora was no longer in poverty but nothing would ever make her anything but an under-sized drudge whose life would always be consumed by other people. The idea that

Flora had come out of her inertia of acceptance to pack up and leave the only place she had ever known astounded me.

'It is more that she was driven out of the district,' George said.

'Driven?'

'By people's tongues,' Tom explained. 'You mind on wee Jamie, young Jamie's eldest boy that you and Twice brought home from America along with the other three?'

'I'll never forget the young devil,' I said with venom. 'Breed again. He was the very reincarnation of his ugly old grandfather.'

'And the older he got, the more like him he got. He is in prison or one of these Borstal places as they call them.'

'What happened?'

'Ach, he was everlasting in trouble, even before he left the school at fourteen – drinking, thieving, stealing cars, fighting,' George said, 'but about a year just now he went past everything. He got into a fight with another fellow and stabbed him with a knife. The fellow nearly died and they put Jamie behind bars good and proper.'

'Poor Flora,' I said.

'Aye, she was aye a poor craitur,' Tom said, 'and never was fit to manage Jamie. He grew to be bigger than she was and used to abuse her terrible. Many a black eye he gave her. But you can imagine the speakylation round about when Jamie's trial was in the newspapers and all, and I think myself that it was the other three youngsters that got Flora to go away south or wherever she went. They were nice bairns but they hadn't the life o' dogs at Fortavoch Academy after Jamie did what he did.'

'Jock and Roddy will be arguing sometimes that the church and religion and all that is just superstition,' George said now. 'I don't know myself but if it is just superstition it does more good than harm. Wee Jamie's grandfather would have *liked* to put a knife in everybody he met but

43

the Reverend Roderick saw that he went to church and kept the fear o' God or the devil in him. There are some natures that have to be in fear o' something before they'll toe the line but there was nobody to put the fear into wee Jamie, the wicked devil.'

I turned away from Flora's blighted life and looked out at the garden, which was feeling the touch of spring.

'What is that bunch of green stuff coming up in the middle of that vegetable plot?' I asked.

'A puckle lilies,' George said. 'A bulb must have come in with a load of dung at some time and when it came up we just left it. There is quite a bunch now. A few lilies do no harm.'

And now I noticed that where the snow had been patches of colour were beginning to show, green, white, yellow, purple.

'There are snowdrops and crocuses and things out there!' I said with a burst of amazement as sudden as this sudden spring.

'Och, surely,' George said. 'There are bulbs and flowers all over the place. You know what your father was for flowers.'

And now I remembered how my brother had once described this garden to me and I opened the back door. Tom shut it again.

'Get your coat,' he commanded. 'We don't want you sniffling and sneezing and being ill-natured around the place again.'

Down the years I had spent away from my own district and particularly during my time in the tropics where there is little change of season, I had carried with me the memory of spring in the Highlands but it was worth all the years spent in other places to re-experience it in all its sharp chill beauty.

'Of course,' George said as we stood by a rockery where small crocuses had opened their petals to make stars looking up at the sun, 'Tom and I are not as good at the gardening as your father was. He wouldn't have buried a lily bulb in the vegetable plot by accident, like.'

'Things have a way of getting the upper hand of us,' Tom apologised further. 'It seems that we don't cut things back at the right time, then the bits we should have cut off come into flower and a body doesn't like to cut flowers off. Maybe you will keep us right now?'

'Not me,' I said. 'You are doing just fine. A garden can be too tidy.'

The garden was as my brother and sister-in-law had described it, the garden of a stately home in miniature but under the management of George and Tom it had features that a head gardener – or my father – would not have permitted. There was a certain lawlessness about it which I found lovable, as if nature in it were not a well disciplined adult but a wild free-running child.

At the bottom of the slope where a clipped hedge separated the sown of the garden from the desert of rough grass at the beach, there was a little orchard of some fifteen trees.

'Apples, pears, plums, greengages,' George said. 'And we have a lot of berries as well. Donaldson the Grocer takes it all in exchange for our tea and sugar and things.'

'We tried our hand at the strawberry jam once,' Tom said, 'but Jean was never good at explaining and you could have soled your boots with it.'

'And then she called you a pair of fools,' I said which made them laugh. 'Well, we'll try our hand at the jam again this year. I think I can still do it.'

Indeed, I was finding that a lot of old skills were coming back to me unbidden as the Gaelic word *buareadh* had come unbidden to my tongue. When, for instance, George and Tom were making up the grocery list for the first time in my hearing, one of them said: 'And a packet o' oatcakes.'

'You never used to like shop oatcakes,' I said.

45

'They are all we can get.'

'I'll make some.'

'What? There isn't a woman left in Achcraggan that can bake oatbread,' Tom protested.

'I think there is now,' I told him, and George scored his pencil through the item on the grocery list.

*   *   *

Although I did some writing every day now, the world of publishing was as far away as ever, and we did not talk of this side of my life. Sometimes, late at night, I would have qualms about the reckless fashion in which we had allowed our refurbishing of the house to get out of hand. When, towards the end of March, the bills came in, I was horrified, tried not to show it and said : 'We've spent a good bit more than we got for the junk, you two.'

'And we have saved a good bit too since you came home,' George told me. 'Donaldson the Grocer and Mackay the Butcher have only had about half what they used to get from Tom and me. We are doing just fine. You add these accounts together and tell us how much you need and we'll get the banker to shift the money from our books to yours and then you can settle the accounts with these cheques you write.'

'We'll split them three ways,' I said. 'Up to now, you two have been paying for everything, even the stamps for my letters.'

'Ach the pension keeps us going fairly well,' said Tom. 'If it doesna last the month we go to the bank but we never had to go at the end of February. In fact, we have a bittie over. You are about as good at skinning a louse as Her Old Self.'

On Good Friday, at the end of March, however, he said : 'There won't be any o' the pension left over this month, after a week o' the Generation.'

My brother had once referred to his children as the

46

Hungry Generation and the name had persisted.

'Do they still eat as much?' I asked.

'A goodish bit more,' George said. 'They are bigger and can hold more.'

'Listen you two,' I said now, feeling awkward, 'will you be extra careful about my writing while the Generation is here? I particularly don't want Roddy to know anything until the first book is actually published, so I don't want that little clip Liz to get the faintest hint that anything is going on. You know what a nosey and chatty little brat she is.'

'I have seen brats just as chatty and a sight nosier in my time,' George told me, 'but Tom and I will watch it, only I don't see why you have to be so hidden.'

'And I can't explain to you why. It is just how I am. I wish now that I hadn't written under my own name.'

'There is nothing wrong with your name,' Tom said, frowning.

'I know that and I don't want to disgrace it.'

'There's no fear o' that,' George said.

We moved the table that held the typewriter into my bedroom and the next afternoon the Generation was upon us. I had thought the house fairly chaotic when the crafts-men were with us but from the moment when the nearly twelve-year-old Liz took up her stance in the middle of the sitting-room floor and said: 'In the name of all our fore-fathers, what have you done with the brickety-brackety?' it was as if the house had been struck by a whirlwind.

'The brickety-brackety?' I questioned weakly as all four scattered in different directions through various doors and upstairs.

'Their name for that over-mantel mirror thing with all the little shelves and ornaments that used to stand over the fireplace there,' Shona, my sister-in-law, explained.

'You have fairly cleared the old dump up,' Jock compli-mented us.

'We've been in every single room,' Liz announced, returning, 'all the rooms that Granny Jean wouldn't let us go into and, Dad, there's a proper loo upstairs. George, what did you do with the old stinky?'

'Oh, hold your tongue, Liz,' said Shona.

'We hammered it to bits,' Tom said.

'Not fair,' commented my eldest nephew, Duncan. 'You should have waited till Gee and I came to help to hammer it.'

Unaccustomed to this rapid cross-fire of comment, I looked about me in a dazed way in search of the youngest member of the family, Alexander-Thomas, familiarly known as Sandy-Tom, who had been born about two and a half years ago while I was home on holiday. In the explosion of the arrival, I had seen a small fat figure in a scarlet sort of siren suit but he was no longer with us.

'The Professor is well away already,' my brother said, pointing to a corner where my second nephew George, known as Gee, sat on the floor with his back to us, a book open on his knees, but now the figure in the siren suit came in from the scullery, followed by a small, very hairy, very energetic dog. Sandy-Tom spread his arms wide as if embracing us all, then concentrated his gaze on me, pointed to the dog which was cavorting around my feet. 'Fie-dog,' he said with a genial smile, then went out again to the scullery, the dog following him. I suddenly became aware of my brother's eyes, very blue, looking at me hard and warily so that it was as if we were at either end of a bar of silence, lying between us and above the cross-fire of talk between Tom, George, Shona, Liz and Duncan before he looked away from me and said: 'Well, you lot, let's get the luggage out of the car.'

Gee remained in his corner with his book, the others all went out and I went to the scullery where Sandy-Tom was sitting on the floor, patting his dog and humming to himself. He looked up at me and smiled, then returned to his little humming noise. He looked like a gnome as illustrated in picture books, with the pointed hood of the red suit framing his chubby face while his blue eyes gazed up and out at the sky beyond the windows. I thought him beautiful but he was like no other child I had ever seen and certainly did not resemble any other member of the family. There was something a little uncanny in his separateness, his remote self-contained air that made me say: 'You are my very special fellow, aren't you, Sandy-Tom?' His head turned slowly and a slow smile irradiated his face before the head turned away again and the eyes looked away to the sky.

George came into the scullery and I looked up at him from where I was kneeling on the floor to find in his eyes that silent closed look that had been in the eyes of my brother. As plainly as if he were speaking the words, I caught his meaning: 'You know it and I know it but we do not *say* it by a look or an action or a word'. And now Tom came in, looked from one of us to the other and on to the child before he bent down and said: 'And how is your Fly-dog? Is he well?' The little boy nodded his head, then got up and followed by his dog set off in the direction of the loud voices of Liz and Duncan arguing upstairs.

This area of strangely communicative silence lay between Jock, George, Tom and myself and did not extend to Shona, who moved among her children in her placid way, equally unmoved, as she had always been, by their outbursts of quarrelling or their conspiracies of secrecy and as the spring days went past there was an atmosphere of happy ebullient family life, while I, very covertly, watched the quietly happy Sandy-Tom. The three older children obviously adored him, as if they knew by some instinct that he was to be the last child of their family, so that they must cherish him as the only one that all three could remember from the moment of his birth. They established roles for him in the games of pirates they played on the beach or of Robin Hood in the little orchard but there were occasions when Sandy-Tom did not want to take part and would stump off by himself in his red siren suit, followed always by his Fly-dog. It was if he deliberately withdrew from us all into a world of his own.

He spoke very seldom and never more than a word or two and it was in this connection only that Shona seemed to take particular notice of him, to see him as an individual in the four-fold ambience of her love and care. At table, when Sandy-Tom wanted more milk, he would point to the jug and then to his mug, whereupon Liz, Duncan or Gee would pour the milk for him. 'Don't do that,' Shona would say. 'Make him ask for it. You are always doing things for him and you are making him lazy.' The three children would try to remember but Sandy-Tom was very winning and cajoling, they liked to do things for him and it is difficult not to do pleasant things for someone one loves.

One afternoon, towards the end of the Easter holiday, I was alone in the house. Jock and Shona had gone to Inverness to shop and Tom, George and the children were playing cricket on the strip of grass between the garden and the beach. When I answered a knock on the front door, a very well-tailored woman of about forty, I thought, was standing there. She had very beautiful, luminous dark brown eyes.

'Good afternoon,' she said. 'This is Jemima Cottage? I am Doctor Hay. I have taken over Doctor Mackay's practice.'

'Good afternoon,' I said. 'Come in.'

When she was seated by the fire she said: 'I believe two senior citizens live here – Mr Forbes and Mr Sandison?'

'Senior—?' I was beginning, for this was the first time I had heard the term, when I realised that she was referring to Tom and George. 'Yes,' I said then, 'but they are out playing cricket at the moment.'

'Cricket?' She suspected me of being funny at her expense and drew some notes from her handbag. 'But—'

'I know,' I broke in. 'They are senior citizens as you call them but they still play cricket. I was going to make some tea. Will you have some?'

She accepted and while I made the tea, I explained my relationship to George and Tom, my recent return from the West Indies and she explained to me a little of the workings of the National Health Service.

'I like to call about once a month on the older people on my list,' she ended and then: '*You* should be registered with a doctor, you know. I don't mean me. Your doctor is your own choice but you ought to register.'

'Then you might as well take me on. The Achcraggan doctor has always been the Sandison doctor, only we don't do doctors much good. We are hardly ever ill.'

'All the better. We don't want you to be ill,' she said and laughed. She had beautiful teeth too. I found her very charming.

We were finishing our tea when the back door opened and the cricketers came streaming in from the scullery. 'This lady has called to see you two,' I told Tom and George.

'Us?'

Their tweed caps in their hands, they stood looking down at the doctor with polite interest while she looked up at them with open approval of their straight spare bodies and healthy ruddy skins.

'Doctor Hay is our new doctor,' I told them. 'She has to look after poor old craiturs like you.'

Liz stamped an angry foot. 'George and Tom are *not* old!'

'Are *not*!' said Duncan.

''*course* not!' said Gee.

'We won't have an argument,' said George, holding out his hand to the doctor. 'How d'ye do, Doctor Hay?'

Shona was meticulous about the children's manners and they were well trained in this respect. When Tom had shaken hands they held out their hands in order of age and when it came Sandy-Tom's turn, he moved close to the woman and did not move away.

'At home,' Gee said, 'we have Doctor Nancy.' Gee was

interested in information of all kinds, thought that every-body was equally interested in everything and was always more than willing to share his facts with anyone.

'And where is your home?' the doctor asked.

'Culdaviot in Aberdeenshire.'

'Oh, yes, so you know Doctor Nancy Huntly? You must give her my regards when you get home.'

'Huntly?' Gee questioned.

'Huntly?' Duncan repeated.

'Of course her name is Huntly, you stupid nits,' said Liz. 'Everybody knows that.'

Both boys rounded on her and it was Gee who spoke. 'Not fair!' he said. 'If you knew her name was Huntly you should have told us.'

'What are you fighting about?' George asked them. 'What does it matter if her name is Mulligatawny?'

'It is,' said Gee sternly, 'the principle of the thing.'

'Folk with principles are everlasting fighting about some-thing, Tom,' George said solemnly.

'And are just a danged nuisance, man,' Tom added.

Doctor Hay, trying not to laugh, watched the three children think this over before Liz said: 'Are you Aunt Janet's doctor?' I noticed that, although she had heard me say that Doctor Hay had called to see Tom and George, it was inconceivable to her that they might ever have need of medical attention and that in her eyes I was the only vul-nerable person in the house.

'I don't suppose she will need you very much,' Duncan said. 'She is pretty old but she stayed with us once for a long time and she never fell or got sick or anything.'

'Do you know about the Cobblers, Doctor Hay?' Gee now enquired, once more in his professorial role as imparter of information.

'Cobblers?' The doctor was perplexed momentarily before she said: 'The cliffs that guard the entrance to the firth, you mean?'

'They are a matter of folk-lore,' Gee informed her. 'They got their name in the days of the giants. There were two shoe-maker giants who mended all the other giants' shoes and one lived on the North Cobbler and one on the South Cobbler but they had only one hammer between them and they used to toss it across the deep channel between the cliffs, so the cliffs got known as the Cobblers. Do you find that interesting?'

'Very interesting.'

'Malcolm the Minister told me about it,' said Gee, then turned away and took the dictionary from the bookshelf, no doubt to glean further information to impart to the next person he met.

'Listen, Aunt Janet,' Liz said now, 'we are hungry.'

'I know. Go to the scullery and make tea for Tom and George and take what you want for yourselves. Call Tom and George when you are ready.' They went out and I turned to Sandy-Tom. 'Take your suit off, Sandy-Tom.'

He put a fat little hand to the zip under his chin but he did not pull on the catch. Instead, he bent his cajoling look on the doctor who undid the zip, helped him out of the suit, then pulled his sweater into place and pulled up his socks. He then smiled at her confidently, leaned against her knee and took on his faraway look as he gazed out of the window. Doctor Hay chatted to Tom and George until the cry of 'Hi, you two, tea!' came from the scullery. 'Come on, Sandy-Tom,' George said but the little boy, who seemed to be a natural master of mime, hunched one shoulder and turned his back, indicating very clearly that he did not want to go.

'Leave him,' I said and George and Tom went out, shutting the door behind them.

'You are a fine healthy fellow,' Doctor Hay said, taking Sandy-Tom by the chin and turning his face towards her.

I took a deep breath. 'Doctor Hay, that child is – is – *different*, isn't he?'

'What d'you mean different? They are all different and your brother has a fine healthy bunch.' She smiled at Sandy-Tom, then looked at me and the eyes which had been so luminous and expressive were as blank as ovals of cloudy brown glass.

'You know what I mean,' I said firmly, almost angrily.

She pushed Sandy-Tom gently away from her and began to rise from her chair. 'I am not the child's doctor,' she said.

'No but you are *my* doctor and this is my very special nephew. Doctor, *please* tell me.'

'But his parents—'

'I think my brother knows something. I think those two old rascals through there are on to something—'

'The mother? Your sister-in-law?'

I shook my head. 'Nothing.'

She stood up now, a commanding figure as tall as myself, robbing me of an advantage I had over many women. 'There is a reason for that,' she said in a final way. 'Now I have to go. Thank you for—'

'Look,' I said, 'I know already that there is something. I have known it for over a week and I have said nothing to anybody so far but if I don't have some sort of certainty, I might say, do something harmful.'

Abruptly, she sat down again, said: 'Sandy-Tom,' and when the child looked at her, to my amazement she stuck her tongue out at him. He was a natural mimic as I have said and he immediately stuck his tongue out at her in turn, then laughed uproariously. 'Hand?' she said then and he went to her, holding out a small chubby hand, palm upwards as she was holding her own. She took it gently, examined it closely, feeling the skin and each little fat finger.

'Good boy,' she said and stood up. 'Going to have tea now?'

He looked thoughtful, then decisive and went stumping through to the scullery. 'Come out to the gate with me,'

54

the doctor said now. There, standing by her car, she said: 'Sandy-Tom is Mongoloid – not a severe case but Mongoloid.'

'What is that?'

'So far, we know far too little about it. To put it simply, it is a handicap mental and physical, although Sandy-Tom is little affected physically and that is all I am going to tell you. I have no right to interfere in this at all but you are my patient now as you said. Only, if the mother does not know, she *must* not be told until her own doctor tells her. There is some reason why she has not been told so you must be extremely careful, do you understand?'

'Yes. I shall be very careful.'

'When do the children go home?'

'In another two days. I have managed so far,' I assured her, 'and I'll go on managing, believe me. And thank you for being so kind. You will come to see Tom and George soon again?'

'That will be a pleasure,' she said and drove away.

* * *

Jock, Shona and the children went home two days later and although I did not want to admit it even to myself, I was relieved to see them go. I felt physically exhausted which, at first, I scorned as ridiculous but I had to admit to myself that to be one of nine people crammed into a small house was not my way of life. Ever since my childhood I had spent a great deal of time alone and at the end of this period of tireless energy, constant rapid movement and the cross-fire of talk among the children, I felt that I had been trampled into the ground. In the three months since I had come home, George, Tom and I had established a busy but quiet and smooth way of life and on the evening that the family left I could see that Tom and George were tired too, saying little and glad to go to bed earlier than usual.

I waited till several evenings later before I said: 'Listen, you two, I had a word with Doctor Hay that day she called ... about Sandy-Tom.'

I was fearful, uncertain of their reaction and then amazed for the reaction was, somehow, the last that I had expected.

'And we had a word with Jock,' George said, 'that day we took the bairns up to Reachfar.'

Almost from the moment they had arrived, Liz, Duncan and Gee had set up a clamour to be taken to Reachfar, the old family home which was now part of a larger estate. It was four and three-quarter miles away, on top of a steep hill but Jock drove the car to Poyntdale and the remainder of the journey was made on foot from there. Sandy-Tom, however, could not have walked that last rough mile and a quarter, so he, Shona and I did not join the party. George and Tom were surprised, even hurt, when I said I would not go but with the children all around at a high pitch of excitement it was not the time to try to explain that I would never want to go to Reachfar again, that I wanted to remember it as it had been, full of the life of the people who had lived there. I did not want to see it as an abandoned semi-derelict house and steading that were now used as a store for animal food.

'What did the doctor say?' Tom asked.

'Sandy-Tom is what they call a Mongol.'

George nodded. 'That is what Jock said. They call these bairns by that name, it seems, because o' that slant in their eyes. There is not much of a slant in Sandy-Tom but it is there. It seems that he is' – he hesitated before bringing out the hateful word – 'deformed in his brain, poor wee fellow. Jock knows a lot about it but Tom and me couldn't follow the science of it, like. He was just born that way it seems and there is nothing the doctors can do about it.'

'This is the first time you have spoken to Jock about this?' I asked.

'Aye.' It was Tom who answered. 'Indeed this is the first

time George and me has spoken to each *other* about it. I think we were both hoping we were imagining the thing and that the wee fellow would be all right but then we saw that *you* were seeing the thing too.'

'Oh, God,' I said, 'do you think Shona noticed that I was—? Doctor Hay was terribly anxious that Shona shouldn't—'

George shook his head slowly from side to side. 'Shona didn't notice anything,' he said with certainty. 'That's just the bother. The doctors have known about Sandy-Tom since the minute he was born, Jock says. They usually tell the parents right away but Shona takes things awful hard. She just can *not* do with things going wrong, it seems. She had a bad time of it after her father died. She hardly spoke for months.'

'I didn't know about that. None of you told me.'

'What was the use of telling you and you away out there in St Jago with troubles enough o' your own?' George asked. 'Jock thinks that the doctors had the idea that Shona would come to suspect something about Sandy-Tom on her own and that she would come to *them* as Jock has done. They thought it would be better than telling her right away and then she had that food poisoning, if you remember, just after he was born. And she was very sick for a while that winter too. Anyway, what was done or not done was meant for the best.'

'And how long do we have to go on like this?' I asked.

'We are not going to go on like this. Jock is going to take Shona and Sandy-Tom to see the doctor in Aberdeen,' Tom told me. 'I think Jock himself feels that he canna go on this way much longer.'

'Myself,' George said, frowning at the fire, 'thinks that Shona knows quite plain about Sandy-Tom but she is not willing to *let* herself know it.' He suddenly turned his head and looked straight at me. 'Like you knowing that Reachfar is just an empty shell now but not wanting to see it that way.'

'You are right about me and Reachfar,' I admitted, 'but for me to see Reachfar would do nobody any good and it might harm my writing. But it is wrong to be as we are about Sandy-Tom. We all have to accept the truth about him and that includes Shona, especially Shona. I don't see anything we can do to help though.'

'Except be here if we are needed,' said Tom, putting into words for once part of his and George's simple philosophy, that they always be on hand if they were needed.

'Round about here,' George said, 'in the old times, it was always thought a disgrace if a family had a bairn that wasn't like the world but I don't feel disgraced about Sandy-Tom. He is a bonnie happy little fellow and none o' the devil in him as there is in the other three.'

The old-fashioned dialect phrase 'not like the world' struck me. It described Sandy-Tom exactly, with his strange faraway look and the intent tilt of his head sometimes, as if he were hearing sounds that were not of the world that the rest of us knew.

'When I came home here,' I said next, 'I think I thought that life would be plain sailing from now on with no more problems.'

'What problems?' George asked. 'Wee Sandy-Tom is no problem. He is just there and we must all do our best for him.'

'That's right,' Tom said. 'He canna manage in this world for himself. He is not weekied enough.'

'Weekied' was Tom's pronunciation of the word 'wicked' but by wicked he did not mean the watered-down sort of evil that the word connotes in most minds. Tom used the word to mean several things in human nature that he despised, such as the taking advantage of the weak by the strong, the aggressiveness or the destructiveness or the greed which are the guiding principles of many of us.

'We will just go on quiet-like in our own way,' George said, 'and everything will come all right.'

I could not but have faith in them for, since my infancy, George and Tom had always been able to make everything 'all right'.

'What with the noise and capers in the house this last while,' George said next, 'we forgot to wind the big clock. She has stopped. Turn on the wireless, Tom and get the time.'

We sat for what felt like an hour, but was probably five minutes, listening to a blare of raucous music until I said: 'Turn that off. I'll get the time from the telephone.'

George and Tom took little account of minutes, hours and days. They were not clock-watchers. George had owned only one watch in his life and that he had dropped into the midden drain at Reachfar long ago and if Tom had ever owned a watch, I had never seen it. I owned a wrist-watch which, since I had come home, had lain unwound in my jewel-box and the only clock in the house was an elegant 'grandmother' in a mahogany case which had been given to my father by a grateful employer. This clock was kept going by George and Tom, I had come to understand without spoken explanation, not to tell the time but because it had belonged to 'Himself' as they called my father and their weekly winding of it was one of their tributes to his memory, as was their care of the garden he had made.

I spun the dial on the telephone and announced: 'It is nine-fifteen and thirty seconds.'

'Now,' said Tom, 'that is very interesting. I didna know that thing could tell the time.'

They had both come to the windowsill where the telephone sat and were looking at it with interest more than dislike.

'How do you make it do it?' George asked.

I handed him the receiver, told him to listen and persuaded Tom to dial the letters TIM. After a second or two, George said: 'Thank you, miss. Goodnight,' and stood gazing at the receiver in his hand before he said: 'There is a young lady that tells one the time, Tom.' And now Tom had to have the receiver while George spun the dial and with one thing and another it was nearly ten o'clock before we had the clock going. It was vain for me to tell them that the voice they heard was a recording and they insisted, each time, on thanking the young lady at the other end. The immediate importance to me, while the dialling was going on, was that they were at last, in their own words, taking to the telephone for it would be a comfort to me, if I had to go away at any time, to know that I could contact them.

'Why don't we ring up Jock?' I suggested after the clock had been started. They drew back suspiciously. 'Come on, now. You know what Jock's face looks like and how his voice sounds. Surely if you can speak to a young lady you don't know, you can speak to Jock?'

For once, they had no argument that would hold water and I made the call. In 1959, calls of this distance had to be made through an operator and so after they had both spoken to him, George was persuaded to call the operator again, give Jock's number and our own number. When he heard Jock's voice this time, he still started with surprise and pleasure and said: 'Tom, it's Jock!'

I tell in detail of George's and Tom's taking to the telephone because it is a concrete instance of how they could demonstrate their sense of wonder, their gratitude for the miraculous, how sharply pleasant was their experience of the strange and new. In a century when there has been so much of the strange and new, I feel that too many of us have allowed our capability for experience to become blunted so that we accept passively much that should be looked upon and thought about with wonder and gratitude. If I could look upon the world and life with the freshness of sight that Tom and George still possessed at this time, I felt that I should be much enriched.

*　　　*　　　*

With every day now, as spring came over the hills, the garden became more beautiful and I could never go into it without being surprised by some new development that excited me as Jock's voice on the telephone had excited Tom and George. In the garden with them, I seemed to have returned to the self-contained world of my childhood where every plant and tree on Reachfar was individually known and cherished and the world beyond the garden gates was remote and unknown. The difference was that, in my childhood, I had looked forward to exploring the world beyond the boundaries of Reachfar but, now, I felt that I was glad that I had come in from that world to a secure place where everything that it contained was within my compass. Since my homecoming, I had never been further from the house than to the telephone kiosk or to the shore of the firth beyond the bottom of the garden. I did not want to go further and I did not want people to visit us. This world of George, Tom and me was enough.

But the world does come in and it came into Jemima Cottage in the middle of April in the form of a small parcel delivered by Rory the Postman. I looked at the label, saw upon it the name of Canterbury Arden & Company and felt a cold little shiver of something like fear.

'You open it, George,' I said and turned my attention to a letter which had also come. This was from Mr Arden and said : 'Dear Miss Sandison, We are mailing today an advance copy of your novel and hope very much that you will like its appearance. We think the dust jacket is very successful—'

The cold fear was still with me although I tried to tell myself that this was the logical progression of the writing, the typewriting, the proof-reading I had done but logic has no part in dreams and the realisation of a dream in the form of the volume which George was now holding between his hands was too much for quick acceptance.

'– a novel by Janet Sandison,' George was reading to Tom, who was carefully folding the wrapping paper and turning the string into a neat coil.

'Man, George,' he said, 'we are fairly in the writing business now and that's a fact.'

When I was a child, the three of us had done a great deal of reading together, our books had been precious and we always read every word they contained, including the name of the publisher and other contents which readers often ignore and George was still reading in this way. He had opened the book and was busy with the 'blurb' on the inner flap of the jacket and his eyes travelled down the print to the very bottom whereupon he read aloud: 'Fifteen shillings net.' He then looked wide-eyed at Tom. 'Godsake, Tom, will anybody be able to afford it, do you think?'

'Ach, surely,' said Tom. 'Look at the price o' tobacco now and you and me is still smoking it and books last better than tobacco.'

'That's true,' George agreed but he was still doubtful. 'It says this book is about a croft in the north here. Why did you make a book about that?'

'Because it is one of the things I know about. I think you have to write about things you know. I know about crofts and families like us who live on them.'

'But who is going to pay fifteen shillings to read about a croft?' he asked, outraged. 'Books have to be interesting if people are to pay good money for them.'

Curiously, his indignation was dispelling my fear and inducing confidence. 'Mr Arden thinks it is interesting. That is why he gave me a hundred pounds for it.'

George turned to Tom. 'Fancy a clever man like that thinking a croft was interesting. Do you tell in it about all the tedisomeness about lifting the tatties in the pouring rain and all the like o' that?' he asked me.

'Yes, I do.'

'Well, bless me,' said Tom, 'all that time at Reachfar I thought it was just fine but for things like rain at tattie time or frost in the midden when we were carting out the dung but I never thought of it being interesting to anybody else, like.'

'Well,' I said, my fear completely gone, 'the two of you had just better hope that life on a croft is interesting to other people for if it isn't the book won't sell and we'll make no more money and we'll all land in the poorhouse after all we spent on washing machines and the like.'

'You and Mr Arden knows better than Tom and me,' George capitulated, 'but we'll do the hoping. About the only thing we are any good at is hoping for the best.'

I returned my attention to Mr Arden's letter. 'Mr Arden suggests that I should go to London for a few days when the book comes out,' I said, 'but I don't think I'll bother.' I tried to speak in an off-hand way but the suggestion in the letter that the publicity manager should introduce me to a series of librarians and booksellers made my flesh crawl. I turned away to lay the letter aside and from behind me George said: 'It seems to me not right for you not to bother about what Mr Arden says.'

'He knows more than us about the right way to go about things,' Tom added.

A Reachfar battle was joined. I put forward every argument I could think of, that my job was to write, not gad about London, that the journey and the hotel would be a gross waste of money and ended: 'And what about you two? You can hardly boil an egg!'

'We are the first to admit that we are not as good at the cooking and the housekeeping as you are,' said George with dignity, 'but you are not going to make an excuse out of *us*.'

'No, that you are *not*!' Tom added with emphasis and then more gently: 'We will miss you for the few days you will be away for we have got used to a proper woman about the house but Mrs Henderson will give us our dinners and we will be all right.'

'And if you ring us on that telephone of an evening, we will answer it with you not here to answer it first,' George promised as if no man could offer a greater inducement, so, very unwillingly, about the middle of May, I went to London.

*   *   *

Mr Arden had booked a room for me in the residential hotel where his elderly sister stayed permanently and when I arrived there at about nine in the morning, after the night journey, I found a note which said: 'Dear Miss Sandison, Please come to my room for coffee at eleven. Aubrey will join us for luncheon. Rosemary Arden.' It had something of the ring of a royal command but it was comforting too, for Miss Arden contrived to convey to me, as she had done when, in January, I had met her for the first time, an off-hand near-scorn for her publisher brother and his entire world which struck such terror into myself. Miss Arden was a large lady physically and she was also large in self-assurance, a quality in which, in this new milieu in which I found myself, I was severely lacking. Perhaps, I hoped, as I bathed and put on fresh clothes, some of her self-certainty would rub off and stiffen my wilting spine.

When I had bathed and dressed, it was only a little after ten. I had finished on the train the only book I had brought with me and out of the need to escape into the printed word – any printed word – I sat down with the volumes of the London telephone directory. A. Had I ever known anyone whose initial was A? Anyone around London? There had been Rose Andrews but she would be dead by now. Her ex-husband's firm, Andrews, Dufroy and Andrews was still listed but the time when I had worked in its office seemed infinitely far away. I found Edward Dulac's name with an address in the Mayfair area, Lord Hallinzeil's with an address in Belgravia and Kathleen Malone's with a Hampstead address but I had no feeling of nostalgia and no desire to make contact with any of these people from the past. I was content to let my life narrow down to Achcraggan, with Canterbury Arden & Company as a distant market-place which would sell my books and provide me with enough money to pursue my contented way at Jemima Cottage.

'How nice to see you again,' Miss Arden greeted me at eleven o'clock. 'And your book comes out tomorrow. Aren't you thrilled?'

'Hardly. It strikes me as rather a minor event,' I said.

'My dear, you are so sensible and not in the least like most of Aubrey's people with their temperaments and nonsense.'

'I suppose you meet a great many writers?'

'No more than I can help,' she said brusquely. 'They expect one to have read every word they have ever written and of course one hasn't. One has better things to do than read the rubbish that many of them write.'

She spoke assuredly, as if she knew that I had, like herself, more sense than to write novels or spend my time among such peculiar people. She clearly did not see me as one of what she called 'Aubrey's bores' and the more she talked, which she did almost without pause, the more she cut my ground as a writer away from under my feet. Having dealt at some length with a female 'Aubrey's bore', she ended: 'The woman is a hysteric and to call her screams and writhings talent is utter nonsense. I can make no sense of any of her stuff.' She dismissed the hysteric by swallowing a large gulp of coffee and continued: 'I can make sense of *your* book though and I shall read every word that you write. You have written a charming novel, my dear, and Aubrey tells me the others are just as good. How many are there altogether?'

'Mr Arden has seven manuscripts all told now,' I said but the last shreds of my confidence had blown away on the wind of Miss Arden's rhetoric. I had written a novel that pleased this woman but how many women were there like her in the English-reading world? Very very few, I thought and the despised hysteric was the darling of the reviewers and an international bestseller.

Before I left the West Indies I had told Sashie de Marnay that I had a horror of meeting my publishers because they would talk about what I had written and here I was in the midst of the horror and even more embarrassed by it than I had ever thought I should be. I wished with all my heart that Miss Arden would leave the subject of writing and yet was surprised when she said: 'Let's not talk about your books any more. You don't like it. Tell me, how did you find your uncles when you reached home?'

This was better. I told her about Tom and George and our making over of the cottage. 'So with one thing and another,' I said then, 'I have hardly been beyond the house and garden. I haven't even been up the main street of the village. Of course, there is no point. All the people I once knew have either died or gone away.' I thought of my leafing through of the telephone directory an hour or so before and went on: 'And in any case I don't think I am much good at reviving old friendships and acquaintanceships. When I meet people again after a long time, there never seems to be much common ground.'

'I know. One has moved on and so have they but in a different direction.'

'I had a great friend once, during the war, when I was in the Air Force. Monica Daviot. I saw her name in the telephone book this morning but I hadn't the slightest urge to call the number. Is that disloyal or something?'

'No, merely honest,' said Miss Arden with conviction. 'I

once went to the most loathsome dinner. Away back about the time you were born, I was a member of the Suffragette Movement.' She gave me a sharp glance. 'I see that doesn't surprise you. For some unknown reason, some of the members decided to have a dinner and raked together all the relics they could trace of pre-1914. It was ghastly – the deaf, the blind and the halt telling one another how many grandchildren they had or how they had just retired from running women's prisons. That dinner taught me that the past is past and you can't re-create it. Of course, I was never a militant suffragette like some of the others. I got into the movement through medicine. Any woman in those days who was in what was still regarded as a male profession tended to sympathise with the suffragettes.'

'How did you come to study medicine?' I asked.

'Because I had more brains than looks,' she said with fearless frankness. 'I had enough brains to see that with my looks marriage was unlikely and I did not want marriage particularly in any case. And of course there was the attractive perversity of running counter to the family convention instead of being dragged round socially in the wake of my two elder sisters who were very pretty. My sisters did all the accepted things, like marrying friends of our brothers and so on. I felt the family could afford one renegade.'

'You are a large family?'

'Seven of us, three girls, four boys. Aubrey and I are the only two left. We have a welter of nephews and nieces, great-nephews and great-nieces. They are all very kind to us. Why are you so interested in all this for one can see that you *are* interested?' she asked me suddenly.

'I don't know. I always seem to be interested in anything anybody tells me. And I am not sure that the past can't be re-created. I agree that I wouldn't go to a dinner just to meet people like Monica Daviot that I knew during the war and try to re-create that time but I think personal pasts, like you running counter to your family's convention, are very interesting. George, Tom and I talk a lot about the past,' I added.

'Ah, that is different, my dear. Between your uncles and you there is obviously a strong family tie and you talk about your family past, don't you?' I did not correct her impression that Tom was my uncle for I had always regarded him as a member of my family. 'When you are as old as I am, I think you will come to believe as I do that love between people of a family is the strongest love of all, where it exists, that is, for all members of a family do not love one another. If one is honest, one has to admit that. I hadn't even liking for my eldest brother who was a pompous bombastic idiot in my opinion. But where love exists, backed up by the blood tie, it is the most enduring of all. Have you brothers and sisters, Janet? I may call you Janet?'

'Yes. I have only one brother and no sisters. My brother is ten years younger than myself.'

'Like Aubrey and me except that the difference with us is five years instead of ten. Is he married?'

I told her about my brother, Shona and the children. 'I find them a bit overpowering at times, the older three I mean,' I confessed. 'Little Sandy-Tom the Mongol is a nice peaceful person though.'

'Most Mongols are,' she said, 'and I know the overpowered feeling only too well. I get it every Christmas when all the greats are gathered together. The knots of family ties are firm but at times a good length of rope is desirable between oneself and the other family members. And I think too that life shows commendable understanding in the matter of children. If I had any, I could never have coped with them. This makes me think of those incredible triplets who were on the ship with you and turned up here. Have you heard any more of them?'

'No. I don't expect I shall and I shall certainly not arrange a re-union dinner but they were a splendid example of the blood tie, don't you think?'

'In their case,' Miss Arden was solemnly thoughtful before she became mischievous, 'I don't think the tie was primarily blood, more a sort of narcissism. It must be either very gratifying or very frightening to look out from yourself and see two of yourself reflected back to you all the time. Let us have a glass of sherry. Aubrey will soon be here.'

*   *   *

When Mr Arden arrived, he had a brisk air of being in-ordinately pleased with himself, his sister, me and the rest of the world and Miss Arden who was not given to beating about the bush said: 'You look like a dog with two tails. What has happened?'

I felt nervous again. The comfortable atmosphere of two women chatting was gone and the fact that Mr Arden who, hitherto, had been rather dry and distant was now so friendly and cheerful worried me for some reason that I could not identify, beyond feeling that I wished people who were normally dry and distant would stay that way. He beamed at me before turning to his sister to say: 'Wait until you see *The Times* tomorrow.'

'Good?' Miss Arden enquired.

Her brother beamed at me again. 'The word "enchanting" has been used.'

'*Enchanting*? From *The Times*?'

I gathered that they were talking some sort of pleasant publishing shop and was annoyed more than anything that they expected me to join in their pleasure when they were well aware that this whole world of theirs was a closed book to me. I was relieved when Miss Arden turned the conversa-tion to other matters.

After lunch was over, I went with Mr Arden to the offices of the firm and here too was this atmosphere of pleasure as if people had received a totally unexpected gift, but the visit was interesting too as I began to appreciate a few of the technicalities connected with the printing and presentation of books. When the publicity manager had given me a programme of the visits he and I would make on the following day to various bookshops and libraries, Mr Arden and I returned to the hotel where I went to my room, before having dinner with him and his sister.

I telephoned Jemima Cottage and it was George who answered. 'How are you getting on?'

'All right,' I said. 'Everybody seems quite happy. How are you two?'

'Fine but we are making a chocolate pudding for our supper and it is terrible thin-looking. It would run from here to Reachfar if we let it loose.'

'How much milk did you use? How much cornflour?'

Having corrected the quantities of the ingredients for their blancmange, I put the telephone down and had a schizophrenic feeling of being suspended between two totally different worlds, suspended from the cloud of an enchanted *Times* of London over a sea of chocolate blancmange. As a corrective to this, I employed myself until time for dinner by writing to Sashie de Marnay: 'I am here in London for the first book coming out tomorrow and it is all very odd but everybody seems pleased—' I began.

When I joined the Ardens for dinner, Miss Arden fired the first shot in what was to be, for me, a hard battle when she said: 'Well, my dear, you are news.' She handed me an evening newspaper and under the heading 'Book Bonanza' I read that I had made what was called a 'literary killing' by having seven novels accepted at once. 'Well?' Miss Arden enquired.

'It seems to me that Canterbury Arden are the news for having accepted them,' I said and was silently thankful that London evening newspapers did not reach Achcraggan, for I was not at all sure how George and Tom would feel about this sort of notoriety. I was not sure, indeed, how I felt about it myself for it had never occurred to me, when I was writing the novels, that this sort of thing could happen, and worse was to come.

When I arrived in the publicity manager's office the following morning as arranged, I was handed a telegram and a cablegram. The telegram said: 'Best of luck Reachfar' and had been sent by my brother and the cablegram said: 'Where there is no vision the people perish love Sashie' and I was very moved that the people I loved were with me in this enterprise which was so strange to me but here the pleasure ended. The programme drawn up for the day had been cancelled, the publicity manager told me, because the reception room downstairs was besieged with reporters and from that moment on I have only a fevered memory of people staring, asking questions and taking photographs and a more nightmarish memory of a televised interview on a news programme at the end of the long day.

Back at the hotel, I made a hurried call to Little John the Smith to meet me at Inverness the next morning, another call to George and Tom to tell them I was coming home two days early, said a hurried farewell to Miss Arden and caught the night train, feeling like a hunted beast. When I left the train at Inverness the next morning, George was at one side of the platform and Tom at the other and as George took my suitcase he said: 'What went wrong? Was Mr Arden not pleased?'

'Pleased?' I said. 'You bet he was pleased. They were all pleased except me.' I stopped and bought an Edinburgh and a Glasgow newspaper. 'Where is Little John?'

'Buying spares. What's your hurry? We'll go into the hotel and get some tea and a sandwich.'

I sat down in the hotel lounge and began to open a newspaper. 'Jock *said* she would be wild,' Tom told George.

'Jock? What *about* Jock?' I asked.

'You were that damn short on the telephone last night,' George told me, 'that we went through all that damn performance and spoke to him and asked him if he knew what was wrong.'

'And what did he say?'

'Ach, you know Jock,' said George disgustedly. 'You and him are as like as two peas and the one o' you will never tell on the other.'

A young waitress came to take our order, bent on me a long hard look and said: 'Weren't you on television last night, madam?'

'Yes I was, unfortunately,' I said.

'Now then,' said George sternly when she had gone, 'you can be as thrawn as you like with us that knows you but you had no right to take the face off that young lass.'

'So that's what young Liz was meaning when she was shouting about her aunt being a TV star,' said Tom.

'It was all awful,' I burst forth, then opened the newspaper and threw it before them on the table, photograph, headline and all. 'Look at that.'

'I never saw the photo yet that was the least bit like you,' said Tom.

'God bless me,' said George. 'This will keep Achcraggan gabbing for a month and stop them scandalising about the lighthouse keeper's French wife.'

'But I don't want people gabbing about me,' I protested.

'Och, a bit of speakylation o' the right kind does no harm,' Tom said, comfortably. 'It stops people scandalising as George said.'

'The author lives in a small Highland village with two uncles,' George read from the paper and then: 'You know, Tom, this is the first time you and I have been in the papers since we won the cup with Betsy the filly at the Inverness Show. How long ago was that now?'

'1912,' I said automatically, because I had always acted as what might be called Remembrancer of Dates to George and Tom. 'Or was it '13?'

'What's a year here or there?' Tom asked. 'The papers

must be hard-up when they have to write about us.'

My anger, which had been born out of mental bemusement and physical exhaustion, was abating under their influence and when Little John arrived and said: 'Saw you on TV last night,' I did not pounce on him as I had pounced on the waitress but Tom said: 'We will not be speaking about that. Sit down and take a cup o' tea.'

'No, thanks,' said Little John. 'If you are not in a hurry I have another message to do.'

'Why would we be in a hurry?' George asked. 'Be off with you and come back when you are ready.'

Never in my life had I seen George or Tom in a hurry and their calm was like a blessing after the noise and bustle of the previous day. 'I have never been more glad to be home,' I said when we were inside the cottage.

'There's a puckle letters and a parcel on your table there,' George said. 'There's one from Mr de Marnay among them and one from Japan. Who in the world do you know in Japan?'

I opened the letter and said: 'I haven't told you about this before because I was waiting to see if he would write. This letter is from Twice's son.'

It took a long time to explain to them how, on the ship that brought me home from the West Indies, I had met this son of my husband's first marriage, a young man now in his twenties.

'Now that his mother and his grandfather are dead,' I said, 'he is entirely on his own. I told him he could come here any time he wanted to. He is a fine young fellow, very like Twice in many ways.'

'I hope he does come,' George said, 'but what is he doing in Japan?'

'What were you doing in India when you were about his age, George?' Tom asked. 'He is seeing the world just like you did, likely.'

I laughed, amused as always when Tom and George kept

one another in order as they put it. 'Partly he is seeing the world,' I agreed, 'but he is an engineer and very interested in ship-building and the Japanese are coming up in the shipping world these days.' I laid the letter aside, took up Sashie's letter and said: 'Open that parcel, one of you.'

'My dear,' Sashie's letter began, 'My bones tell me that this letter is being opened by a full-blown novelist whose book is going to be read by thousands of people who do not know that she is so secretive that she does not want them to read it. Darling, now that it is out you must become accustomed to the outness and *when*, may I ask, do I receive a suitably inscribed complimentary copy?'

'This is our book,' Tom said, spreading the brown paper over his knees. 'Six o' them.'

'They are complimentary copies as they call them,' I explained. 'We get six for free, to give away if we like.'

'That is real kind of Mr Arden,' George said. 'Jock and Shona would like one.'

'And Sashie must have one,' I said.

'Surely,' said Tom, 'and Auntie Kate in America should get one and old Granny Murray—'

Their pleasure in arranging this distribution was indescribable, very moving to me and made up for much of the discomfort of the previous day, but this could not be put into words and I said instead: 'I am a bit sick of books for the moment. You can do up the parcels later on. Have you any grub in the house?'

'We bought some mutton chops in Inverness,' George told me. 'They are on the scullery table. Do you want me to bring in a young cabbage?'

'Yes,' I said and the exotic world of publishing and publicity faded away into the faraway background.

As soon as lunch was over, however, they could not wait to do up their parcels, so I signed the books for them, they parcelled them up and prepared to set out for the post office.

I gave them two pounds and said: 'Sashie's one has to go by airmail, remember.'

'But a *letter* costs sixpence!' George protested.

'I don't care a damn,' I said. 'Sashie's goes by air.' I could not explain to him or even to myself my feeling that this was not time for what Sashie would call scurvy cheese-paring.

*   *   *

The parcels posted, I felt that I had put the London world behind me and we could return to our normal routine of housekeeping, gardening and me going on with my writing when the spirit moved me. My attitude was curiously ambivalent and sometimes I would stand back, look at myself and tell myself that this activity of writing, which felt so private while I was doing it must inevitably result in the exposure to publicity which I had so much disliked. I had often accused life of extreme contrariness and in this writing activity the contrariness seemed to have reached its peak. The writing was acutely personal and private but its only logical end was extreme public exposure.

By the middle of June, it was obvious to me that my notion of living in two separate worlds, the world of London and the world of Jemima Cottage, had been very ill-conceived. This first became obvious through the mail. Hitherto, Rory the Postman had brought a few letters a week from friends, from my publishers and my agent but following the publication of the book there was a bundle of letters every day, from strangers.

'It is very civil of them to write,' George said.

'Very civil,' Tom agreed and I agreed too but I spent a considerable part of each day replying to the letters and was actually glad when, one day, a very rude letter arrived from a lady who lived in Sussex. 'That will put you two in your places,' I said, 'and stop you getting big-headed about everybody liking our book.'

The lady complained that the ploughmen in the book used a great deal of bad language to their horses which was extremely unkind to the horses and was of the opinion that I ought to be dealt with very severely by the Royal Society for the Prevention of Cruelty to Animals. There was also the matter of people having illegitimate children, she said, which was disgusting and such things ought not to be written about.

'The poor craitur canna be right in her head,' said Tom.

'If you didna give Dick at Reachfar a good cursing fairly regular,' said George, 'he would have yoked you to the plough instead of himself, the big devil.'

The writer of this letter was known ever afterwards as 'the Lady from Sussex' and for a long time every letter that bore the postmark of that county was regarded with deep suspicion until one day George said: 'Ourselves is as daft as the Lady from Sussex. We have given a whole county a bad name just because of one silly craitur.'

Because of the attitude of Tom and George, I became accustomed to what I had first regarded as an invasion of my privacy through the mail and began to look forward to the calls of Rory the Postman as much as they did. We were one of the last households on Rory's village round before he mounted his bicycle to go out to the farms, and he would come in to have a cup of tea to help him on his way. He was as interested in the letters as George and Tom, who would open them and read them aloud and each letter was discussed in detail. I came to feel that the replies I wrote to my correspondents gave no idea of the pleasure their letters gave or the interest they created and when, later, letters began to come from the countries of the Commonwealth and the United States, even the stamps they bore were studied, removed carefully from the envelopes and stored for our nephew Duncan who collected them. One day, we had a letter from the island of St Helena and George suddenly put his feelings into words: 'This one beats all, Tom. It makes one feel we have a big family scattered all over every corner of the world,' but no matter where the letters came from, no matter what the sex of the writers might be, Rory was always greeted with the words: 'Are there any Ladies from Sussex among them the-day, Rory?'

*   *   *

It was about the middle of June that the parish minister called and found all three of us at the bottom of the back garden. 'It's Gow the Minister,' George said as the soberly clad figure came round the gable of the house.

'If he is coming to be at us about going to church,' said Tom, 'he needna bother.'

Mr Gow was a middle-aged, insignificant-looking man, much in contrast to the Reverend Roderick Mackenzie, the Achcraggan minister of my childhood, but since then the entire church situation in Achcraggan had altered. The old church was used now on only one Sunday evening in the month, for the advent of the motor car had caused religion in the district to be centralised on another church further west. Tom and George had stopped attending church when the centralisation took place.

'It seemed the time to stop,' George explained, 'for we had come to think anyway that if all the church-going we did with Her Old Self and later on with Himself, your father, wouldn't get us into Heaven, going away west the country to church wouldn't help us now.'

The minister, however, had not called to request our attendance at church. With much circumlocution he explained that a bazaar in aid of church funds was to take place at the end of the month; with much flattery he requested a signed copy of our book to be auctioned at this affair and with terrible bogus humility he wondered if I would be good enough to declare the bazaar open.

As I have often remarked, I am extremely slow-witted and

77

I have this added foible of liking everything to be smooth and everybody to have what he wants so that, in a state of semi-consciousness I signed a copy of our book, handed it to Mr Gow and told him I would open his bazaar for him. It was only after he had gone away that I came to full realisation of what I had done.

'*I* am not a bazaar-opener!' I exploded at Tom and George.

'There is nothing much in it,' George said. 'Your father was quite good at meetings and speaking and all the like o' that.'

'And Jock can speak as good as a sermon,' said Tom.

'Don't be stupid,' I told them.

I had a very clear vision of what a bazaar-opener should look like, founded on my friend Monica's sister, the Lady Sybil, whom Monica was wont to describe as 'that bazaar-opener'. Lady Sybil, the few times I had encountered her, had been svelte and chic, with a model hat, a dress by Paul Caraday, several rows of pearls and an air of extreme authority. *That*, I told myself, was what bazaar-openers were like. They were not old women with rose scratches on their hands and arms, and blouses that had come out of their waist-bands at the back.

'And that book!' I said. 'The first bid will be half-a-crown and they'll have to knock it down for two-and-ninepence. Why didn't you two *say* something, *do* something?'

'God knows we always knew you were pretty thrawn,' George said, 'but since you've got older and took to the book-writing thrawn is hardly the word for it.'

'People should learn more sense as they get older,' Tom added smugly.

'Why can't people let one alone?' I grumbled.

'Now then,' said George, 'can you not see that people got the minister to ask you to show you that they are all kind o' pleased, like, about you and the book and all?'

'They feel that you have made the district and them as well kind o' famous,' Tom said. 'That's what Mrs Henderson and all them I have spoken to feel whatever.'

'Famous!' I exploded again. '*I'm* not famous and I don't want to be famous. I am just like everybody else round about.'

'You *are* just like everybody else round about,' George told me firmly, 'and more of round about here than a lot of people in the parish nowadays. And since you belong here, the least you can do is a little job like opening a bazaar when people ask you to.'

'And make it short,' Tom advised. 'The wifies at the bazaar just want to see you and speak about your dress later on. They don't want to listen to you droning on everlasting about the good cause the sale is for. They want to get at the jumble stall and the bargains.'

'I haven't *got* a dress.'

'Then you will go to Inverness and get one,' George told me.

'When Jock hears about this he'll die laughing,' I capitulated unwillingly.

'You are very useless at knowing when people will die laughing,' Tom said. 'You said that Roddy would die laughing at our book. He hasn't laughed at all and in my way of thinking he is hard put to it not to turn green in the face with envy.'

This was true. I had feared the scorn that I was sure Roddy Maclean would feel for my novel, for Roddy was one of the modern 'angry' school of writers, but Roddy had not been scornful. He had telephoned after my return from London, had been very complimentary about the book and had tried very hard to conceal his envy of the blaze of publicity.

In due course, therefore, I opened the bazaar and the autographed copy of my fifteen-shilling novel was finally knocked down for ten pounds to a wealthy farmer who bought it for his wife's birthday. This was my first general meeting with the local community and I had the impression that they were a little disappointed but at the same time relieved that I was so ordinary and like themselves. A few of the older people remembered my grandparents, many remembered my father and George and Tom, of course, were a passport into the good graces of the whole company. I actually enjoyed the function.

'I will make you a compliment,' Tom said when Little John had brought us back to the cottage. 'You are as good a hand at the speaking as your father. Us two stood right at the back o' the hall on purpose and we heard every word you said but not a word that that other fellow said.'

'Except that I thought he would never stop and everybody knowing already that you were Janet Reachfar,' said George.

As in my childhood, we enjoyed in detail every aspect of our outing and talked about it for days, about how Mrs Bain said that Mrs Dunn had won the rooster in the raffle only because her rich son from Edinburgh had bought a whole hundred tickets, about how Rory the Postman had spent a fortune at the bottle stall, trying to win the bottle of whisky and had come away with a bottle of vinegar, a bottle of hair oil which was useless, bald as he was, and a bottle of cascara sagrada which was also useless because, as he told us, his 'bowels were the other way and on the slack side'.

'We were right lucky to get that load o' firewood,' Tom said and asked me: 'How many tickets did you buy?'

'A pound's worth, half in your name and half in George's.'

'Mercy on us, you are as bad as the fellow from Edinburgh with the rooster.'

'The one thing I know about bazaar-opening,' I said, 'is that the opener is expected to spend a little money. It was difficult. We can bake our own scones and cakes, we can make our own jam and we have our own vegetables. The only things we could use were the firewood and those knitted sweaters I bought for the kids.'

'Well, that load o' silver birch will last us most o' the winter,' George said. 'It was the Poyntdale Hotel people that put it in, some o' the trees they took down when they built the chalets as they call them. I hope that hotel will pay after all the money they have put into it. What did you think o'

Mr and Mrs Rice, Tom?' Mr and Mrs Rice, whom we had met at the bazaar, were the people who were turning Poyntdale House into a hotel, a businesslike pair who tried not to speak with a Midlands of England accent.

'They put me in mind o' Jock and Bella Skinner,' Tom said, 'only better dressed and fancier spoken and maybe a little less honest.'

'Tom!' I protested, for Jock and Bella, during my childhood, had been regarded as the arch-criminals of Achcraggan.

'Well,' said Tom defiantly, 'George asked me and I am telling him. They will make their hotel pay all right.'

'They are opening on the first of July and have quite a lot of bookings already they told me,' I said, 'and by the way, they have asked the three of us to the opening cocktail party.'

'I have heard of such things but I have never been to one,' George said. 'Why do you think they want the three of *us* at it?'

'I think they regard us as what is called local colour,' I said. 'You had better shake out your kilts and give your sporrans a brush.'

The kilt was a long-standing joke among us as it is with most true Highlanders. It was regarded as a suitable hard-wearing dress for the young Liz, Duncan and Gee, of whom Liz the eldest was the only one ever to have a new kilt. Her first kilt had descended through Duncan and Gee and was now in storage awaiting Sandy-Tom. George had worn the kilt for seven years as a Seaforth Highlander, that is, as a uniform, but no grown-up Sandison would wear the kilt as a private citizen. It was worn mostly by landowners of English or even more foreign extraction or American tourists and a few exhibitionists who were possessed as a rule of physiques ill-suited to its exacting demands.

'Och, there will be no need for George and me to go to the party,' Tom said. 'It is yourself that they will be wanting and only asked us to be civil.'

'You will go, both of the two of you,' I told them. 'You got me into this bazaar-opening nonsense and you will take the consequences.'

*   *   *

I had, of course, no intention of forcing them to go to the party and they knew it. When I had first come home and we had embarked on our making over of the cottage, I found myself worrying when I saw them moving heavy pieces of furniture and exerting themselves in all sorts of ways, for I had spent five years in the avoidance of physical and mental strain for Twice. But I watched Tom and George in silence, for I could not say to them: 'You are too old and that is too much for you,' because, manifestly, they did not feel old and still did everything with the effortless ease that had always been characteristic of them. I had spoken to Jock on the subject during the Easter holidays when they were sawing and splitting a tree trunk that had been washed up on the beach, while we watched from the scullery window. George was swinging the heavy felling axe from Reachfar as if it were a willow wand and chatting to the children between strokes, while Tom was loading the split wood into the wheelbarrow.

'Look at him,' I said. 'He will be eighty in October and Heaven knows what age Tom is. Should we let them carry on like that?'

'I made up my mind long ago,' Jock said, 'never to tell them to do anything and never to stop them doing anything,' and this was the principle I now followed. George and Tom had always worked 'at their ease' as they expressed it. They were never in a hurry and, indeed, regarded hurry as a sign of inefficiency and rather bad form and they never gave the impression of having to meet a deadline, yet, at Reachfar, crops had been planted and harvested in due season, in spite of all the pauses they made to have a smoke, to watch the wild geese flying down into Poyntdale Bay or preach a sermon in mimicry of the Reverend Roderick Mackenzie. And even while Jock and I watched from the window, George laid his axe aside, he and Tom turned their caps round so that the peaks were over their left ears, joined arms and gave an imitation of the Miss Boyds, those ladies long dead, mincing down the main street of Achcraggan, causing the children to roll about among the sawdust in paroxysms of laughter.

It was certainly never necessary to ask them to do anything to contribute to the running of the household and the garden. More and more, they were aspiring to take over the entire running of both so that I might give all my time to writing, but when I explained to them that I could not write constantly, I was amazed at their understanding for, after all, they were very old dogs to be learning new tricks.

Like most writers, I am subject to 'off' spells when I cannot find the right words for what I want to say and I have learned that at such times the only thing to do is to have patience, put down the pen, do something else and wait for the words to come. The first time this happened at the cottage and I did not pick up my pen for three days, George said: 'Shouldn't you be at the writing instead of darning socks?'

'We each have a whole drawer full o' socks,' said Tom. 'Granny Murray gives us socks every Christmas.'

'The way I write,' I explained, 'is a bit like growing a turnip crop. You sow the seed and you have to wait for the plants to be big enough to hoe. I get started on a bit of writing but sometimes I have to wait for the next bit to show itself.'

'I see,' said Tom.

'That is reasonable,' said George.

The understanding was there but the writing was still strange to them, at the utmost edge of their comprehension, and I did not want it to drive a wedge between us especially as, daily, I was becoming more and more certain that any talent I might have had been nurtured largely by themselves. They were natural tellers of stories, natural dramatists and actors with their mimicry of the people around them, natural selectors of the foibles of humanity and natural observers of life in all its facets. It was the pen, the paper, the typewriter, the printed page and the bound book that made them stand back in awe for, in their own words, they had never 'taken to the schooling and the education' and all this paraphernalia reeked to them of the academic.

Nor did I want a social wedge to be driven between Tom and George on the one hand and myself on the other and the experience of the bazaar had indicated to me that this could happen. I had received a number of cocktail and dinner invitations from people who knew me only from the newspapers and which I had turned aside as politely as I could. At this time of my life I had had all the experience I wanted of cocktail and dinner society and this apart I did not want a false persona thrust upon me. There was much change in this district and its people since my childhood but one thing, it was now clear to me, had never changed. In spite of forty years of full living in many places, in spite of exposure to many influences from many people. I was still essentially Janet Reachfar and Tom and George were part of me and nothing was to be allowed to threaten that bond.

A day or two after our visit to the bazaar, George and Tom were giving me some anxiety. Near the bottom of the garden, there was an old elm tree which had died and they had decided that this was the day the tree had to come down. It was over three feet in diameter and they were sitting on the garden seat, filing the teeth of the cross-cut saw preparatory to starting work. I was very glad to answer the front door to find a man of about twenty-five there while, at the gate, there stood a tractor hitched to a trailer that held a mountain of firewood. This, I thought, would distract Tom and George from the elm.

'Good morning, Mistress,' the man said. 'Is Tom and George in?'

'Good morning. I'll fetch them.'

84

I called them away from the elm and brought them round to the front of the house.

'So it is yourself, Hamish,' said Tom. 'Janet, this is Mrs Henderson's Hamish. My, but that is a bonnie load you brought.'

The tractor was now taken down the lane to the side gate of the garden, the wood unloaded and Hamish came in for a cup of tea. 'You needn't bother about that elm tree now,' I said as I poured tea. 'The shed won't hold any more wood.'

'The elm will have to come down whatever,' George told me. 'It is dead rotten and the branches may soon come down any day and hurt somebody walking down the lane.'

'I think it's too big for the cross-cut,' I argued.

'Is it that one on the west side?' Hamish asked. 'I have the power saw on the tractor.'

'Can you spare the time, Hamish?' I asked quickly. 'What about Mr Rice—?'

'Ach, what he doesna know will never hurt him,' said Hamish, voicing the familiar philosophy of my childhood. 'He'll think I am in the walled garden or somewhere.'

This immediately made the project attractive to George and Tom, that our tree should come down by the illicit use of Mr Rice's power saw in Hamish's time which theoretically belonged to Mr Rice, for they subscribed to the Highland belief that the rich were there to help the poor, whether they were aware of their philanthropy or not, so we all repaired to the elm which Hamish brought down in very short order.

As time went on, I discovered that Hamish had picked out of the air my anxiety about Tom and George and with no word spoken we would find on a November morning that the load of heavy farmyard manure, delivered the day before to the bottom of the garden, had been distributed in neat manageable heaps at the edges of the vegetable plots. Hamish was a big man but he moved with a 'poacher's step' and we never caught him at any of his helpful ploys.

Mrs Henderson, I discovered, was an Englishwoman who had married a shepherd of our district some forty-five years ago. She had had six children but, like most of young Achcraggan, five of them had left the district and only Hamish, the youngest, remained with his widowed mother. I was out at the front of the house one day when Hamish came past and naturally I asked after his mother who had been so kind to Tom and George and he said: 'Ach, it's Monday and she is at the washing again. She is not fit for it but you can't stop her.'

'Just like my two,' I said, hoping that he would understand my gratitude for all he did for us and I think he did understand but, over lunch, I had speech with Tom and George.

'First thing next Monday,' I said, 'do you think you could persuade Mrs Henderson to give you her washing to put in your machine? It would pay Hamish something back for all he does for us.'

'Man, Tom,' said George, 'it takes brains to hit on an idea like that.'

'And us fair beat to think on a turn to do for Hamish.'

From that point forward, the machine washed for Mrs Henderson on Mondays and for us on Tuesdays and this led to my being invited to take a cup of tea with Mrs Henderson, which was the kind of invitation I wanted, as opposed to those proffered at the bazaar.

It turned out to be a disappointing experience from my point of view. Mrs Henderson had invited me to thank me for our help with her weekly wash but she followed her thanks with: 'How does somebody like you—' she hesitated and lowered her voice before she went on '—that writes books and everything—' her voice returned to its normal pitch '—know about washing blankets?' and it seemed to me that there was something of resentment in her attitude, as if I had no right to invade the province of 'ordinary' women, and this barrier persisted throughout our conversation.

The next morning, while we opened the mail, I said to George and Tom: 'I don't understand the effects this book-writing business has on people. It brings in all these friendly letters from Ladies from Sussex but it seems to stand between me and people like Mrs Henderson.'

'Mrs Henderson doesn't read books,' Tom said. 'She just takes a look at the *Ross-shire Journal* once a week maybe. She thinks people who write books are a bittie queer maybe. Although George and I have done a fair bit at the reading with you and Jock when you were little, we never thought of imagining the people who wrote the books and most o' them were dead whatever. Am I not right, George?'

'Aye, partly,' George frowned, searching for words. 'Our Ladies writing is different from seeing you face to face. Besides, you don't look as if you could write books.'

'What does a writer look like then?' I asked, reasonably enough.

'Well, like Roddy. You know at the first look at him that there is something different about him.'

It was true that Roddy was very dramatic in appearance and he was also given to indulging in extremes of self-expression which might be loosely called fits of temperament.

'And Mr de Marnay,' George continued. 'From his photos I would say that he could write a book if he took the notion. But if anybody had asked me about you and Jock in such a way, I would have said that Jock would be the one to write books. Jock *looks* clever, with that high forehead of his. I'll give you that you were fairly clever at the school but you never looked it and the older you got the dafter you seemed to get.' He frowned at me while I thought that if I had little self-knowledge it was not his fault. 'You and the books is not *reasonable*, you might say,' he concluded.

'I wouldn't worry about it though,' Tom comforted me. 'People will get used to the books, the people round here I mean, and forget to notice them, with you not looking clever and all.'

'What you don't seem to understand is that I am *not* clever,' I said. 'Cleverness is nothing to do with it. Jock *is* the clever one of us, the one who uses his mind. The writing is an accident, a gift, if you like, something that was given to me and that I have done nothing to earn, like being born beautiful.'

'Then stop complaining and get on with it,' George told me.

I took his advice and got on with my writing, but it was now that I reached a little landmark in self-discovery. I came to recognise factually what I had known instinctively during all my years of secret writing, the fact that any artist, however minor, is a solitary and is confirmed in his isolation by the attitude of society at large. I might have been acceptable as a one-day wonder by the news media but my acceptance by people in general was limited.

*   *   *

With the coming of the finer weather, I began to go about the village a little and found that it was much changed, no longer the busy local metropolis of forty years ago. The little houses and narrow alleys of the Fisher Town, where my friend Bella Beagle used to live, were deserted and derelict. Miss Tulloch's shop was boarded up, for Miss Tulloch had died long ago and a similar fate had overtaken Mrs Gilchrist's Drapery Warehouse which used to be grand with its bolts of fine cottons with such exotic names such as 'Madapollam' and 'Tarantulle' and its cards of 'Chan-*till*ie' lace all the way from the looms of Lancashire. Many properties in the village were willed to descendants in Canada, New Zealand or other parts of the world who did not trouble to claim them, because property had little value in a dying outpost on the edge of the North Sea and in many cases property was not willed at all. The aged owners died and were buried, if not by relatives, by the remaining neighbours, the sparse contents of the houses were sold to pay the funeral expenses, after which the house itself was shut up and abandoned. The only part of the village which was fully inhabited and cheerful with the noise of children was the new council housing scheme which bureaucracy had jerry-built instead of modernising and refurbishing the solid well-proportioned cottages and houses which had been built in the late eighteenth century when the village had been at its most prosperous. The narrow streets of the old village were depressing and having made a tour of them I retreated into our more cheerful cottage and garden on the Shore Road.

'What is that big new place across the firth and just west of the North Cobbler?' I asked George.

'The new distillery. It gives work to the men in the housing scheme. A boat takes them across every day. But for that and the Forestry Commission, the whole of Achcraggan that are not old-age pensioners would be on the dole.'

'It is all very different from what I remember,' I said regretfully

'Och, things come and they go. When I was going to the school, Achcraggan was even poorer than it is now. That is the way of the world. Things go up and they go down.'

It seemed to me that the only places in the village that were not stagnant were our own house, for stagnation and Tom and George were natural enemies, Mrs Henderson's cottage, for Hamish was of the same kidney as George and Tom, and the hotel at Poyntdale, which seemed to me to be a considerable and courageous gamble in the midst of a dying community.

*   *   *

As things fell out George and Tom accompanied me to the opening cocktail party at the hotel because, a few days before it took place, I had a letter from Sir Ian Dulac, the owner of the sugar plantation in St Jago where I had spent most of the ten years of my married life. Sir Ian was not a fluent writer and the letter opened with some stilted congratulation on the success of my book but went on to tell me that he would be staying at Poyntdale Hotel for the months of July and August. It was not a cheerful letter, it conveyed nothing of the bluff hearty Sir Ian I had known and it was not only the stilted language that rendered it so spiritless. It was the letter of a disappointed, disheartened lonely old man and I found its impact almost unbearable.

When I told George and Tom that Sir Ian was coming to Poyntdale, they needed no persuasion to attend the party, for the Dulac family had been very kind to Twice and me during our time with them and Tom and George welcomed the opportunity to render the thanks they felt were due to Sir Ian.

'But what brings him to Achcraggan when he is rich enough to go anywhere in the world?' George asked.

'I used to tell him about Reachfar and the district some-times,' I said, 'and he says in his letter that he saw an advertisement about the new hotel and took a notion to come up.'

I found Poyntdale much changed, like the rest of the district, but in a different way. The house had been built sometime between 1800 and 1850, a solid rectangular block, undistinguished in architecture. I had been in the house a number of times after the war, after Monica had married Torquil Daviot, its owner, but my clearest memory of it was of an evening in 1918 when the Harvest Home was to be held in the big barn of Poyntdale Home Farm. The hotel guests were assembled in the hall and it was here that some of the guests had been assembled in 1918. Through the tinkle of the glasses I seemed now to hear faintly on the air the tinkle of the musical box which had been produced to amuse me as a child of eight, until the ladies and gentlemen were ready to leave for the barn and the Harvest Home.

The ladies on this summer evening were less formally

dressed and less elegant than the ladies of autumn 1918 and
the men seemed to me to be less handsome, with their too-
large stomachs developed behind money-making city desks,
but the jewels of the ladies were, if anything, bigger and
brighter and the cigar fumes were everywhere and not confined to the smokeroom as in 1918. Mr and Mrs Rice had
studied their market carefully and were providing exactly
what their patrons required, the atmosphere of the country
house-party which, strangely enough, one of the patrons told
me in the course of the evening, had been 'snobbish affairs
that died out because they couldn't afford them any longer'.
It was interesting to listen to the 'them' of today criticising
the 'them' of yesterday in a precisely similar setting.

George and Tom were taken in hand by Hamish who, in
his navy-blue suit and with his lively hair slicked down, was
acting as a sort of general factotum on this evening, while I
was dragged round the room by Mrs Rice. When I had been
told by about twenty women that it was 'very nice' that I had
written a book and feeling that I had done what was required
of me, I said: 'Has Sir Ian Dulac arrived as yet?' Mrs Rice
was not quite clever enough to conceal her surprise. 'Yes.
This afternoon. Do you know him?'

'Yes, I do. He wrote me that he was coming but he didn't
leave me enough time to reply before he left London.'

'He hasn't come down yet. He said he'd be down for
dinner.'

'Perhaps you could let him know that I am here.'

Hamish was despatched upstairs and I stood beside Tom and
George, looking round the room.

'As Hamish says,' George said under the brouhaha of
chatter, 'they fairly have the gift o' the gab.'

I was not surprised that Sir Ian had excused himself from
this party for the male guests were what he, who had his
own form of snobbery, would call 'box-wallahs', a term
which he applied to financiers, stockbrokers and money men
of all kinds.

When he came into the room beside big Hamish, he seemed smaller than I remembered him only a year ago, diminished in every way, his skin paler from the loss of the St Jagoan tan and even his step seemed to be less firm. He was shakily emotional and pathetic as he shook hands with me.

'George Sandison, Sir Ian,' I said, 'and Tom Forbes.'

'I am right glad to meet you, sir,' George said and everything seemed to change, as if this were the first occasion in a long time when Sir Ian was convinced that somebody was glad to meet him.

'Are you here alone, Sir Ian?' I asked.

'Got Smith – big Maxie the sugar-boiler's youngest, ye know – with me. Drives the car an' cleans me shoes an' that. All the young St Jagoans want to come to this side now.'

I had been asking if his son Edward and his daughter-in-law Anna were with him and Sir Ian knew it and his reply indicated to me, if to nobody else present, that he had been abandoned by them, more or less, but when Hamish put a glass of whisky into his hand, he brightened to something of his former self.

'I am delighted with this success you've had with your book, me dear, delighted. Always knew you'd set the heather on fire before you were done.' He turned to Tom and George. 'She dam' nearly set the sugar-cane on fire a time or two.' Sir Ian had always been prone to dwell on some of my less well-thought-out escapades and I did not consider that this was the place or time for this sort of reminiscence but there was little I could do.

'Remember the night o' the play when you and Sashie had the shootin' in the drawin'-room?' he asked.

'The drawing-room at Paradise,' I informed George and Tom firmly, 'was about four times the size of this room we are in now,' and as plainly as if he had spoken the thought, I heard George say: 'Shooting? Just wait till we get home, my lady,' but he took the social hint and said: 'Janet has told us that your Paradise Estate went to thirty thousand acres, Sir Ian?'

'Give or take a thousand. Glad to be rid o' the dam' place at last. Missis Janet told me you got rid o' your place too. Pity. Fine farmin' country round about here.'

'Reachfar isn't like Poyntdale here,' Tom said. 'Our best crops up there were boulders and heather.'

When it was time for us to leave, Sir Ian seemed to grow smaller and took on a wistful look and although I felt he would find our cottage very small and cramped and our way of life very strange, I was impelled to say: 'Would you like to come down to us at any time, Sir Ian? We have only a small house but the garden is rather nice.'

'Delighted, me dear, delighted. Tomorrow? After lunch?'

'Any time,' I said.

'The poor old gentleman,' said Tom when Little John had deposited us and we were inside the cottage and as I looked round the small warm sitting-room I thought that poverty took many forms. Sir Ian, since the sale of Paradise, must be a millionaire several times over but on this evening he had seemed to be a great deal poorer than Tom or George.

'What,' George asked, as I had expected, 'was that about you and Mr de Marnay shooting one another at Sir Ian's place?'

'We weren't shooting one another,' I said and went on to explain the episode before saying: 'And you don't want to believe everything Sir Ian says. He exaggerates things and mixes them up.'

'You must have been among the crows before you got shot at,' George told me uncompromisingly. 'Well, Sir Ian is a fine old fellow and it canna be much of a life for him up there at that place all on his own. All these men with the bellies and these women with the red nails are no company for him.'

Apparently Sir Ian took a similar view and very soon he

was at the hotel only to have dinner, sleep and have break-fast. Sometimes I would find myself at the scullery window doing a double-take as I looked at him sitting on the garden seat between Tom and George, smoking his cheroot while they smoked their pipes and at the same time remembering how he used to stride around Paradise in his white drill riding kit and highly polished boots. He was of a background very different from that of George and Tom but he had in common with them the powerful factor of having witnessed great social change. He had seen the feudal estate of Paradise pass to a huge, faceless commercial combine and they had seen the hospitable laird's house of Poyntdale turned into a profitable commercial enterprise. Then, when he discovered that George had served with the Seaforths in Egypt and India and that Tom seemed to know as much of this experience as George did, an entire new territory of common ground was opened up.

*   *   *

In the first days of July came the school holidays and the Hungry Generation was upon us again. Once more my writing equipment was moved into my bedroom, not for secrecy this time but simply to make more room.

'What was it like being on television?' Liz greeted me from the car, cheekily and before anybody else could speak. 'You looked terrible, just like an old witch.'

'Liz, hold your tongue,' said Shona, then thrust Sandy-Tom at me from her lap and burst into tears.

'Come into the house, you lot,' George said to the older children. 'We have a new gentleman for you to meet.'

Shona now sprang from the car, dashed into the house and straight up to the bathroom.

'The doctor told her last week,' Jock said to me from the driving seat, 'and she is taking it very badly.'

' 'Lo,' said Sandy-Tom, rubbing his face against mine and

94

I said: 'Hello yourself,' and then to Jock: 'But why, I mean it is an accident and not a very bad one surely?'

He shook his head. 'She blames herself, thinks it is somehow her fault.'

'Tea?' Sandy-Tom questioned, using his word for food of all kinds.

'Yes, you will get tea,' I told him, set him down and led him into the house.

I was glad when, shortly, Sir Ian went back to the hotel. Tension was criss-crossed between us all like unyielding but invisible steel wires while Shona sat silent in a little cell of suffering and the older children, feeling the strain but unable to identify it, released their frustration in one shrill quarrel after another. I understood now that Liz telling me I had looked like an old witch on television arose out of the need to be noticed, even if she might be punished for what she said. The sudden plunge from the even tenor of our lives into this maelstrom was too much for George and Tom who lapsed into a closed silence.

After the children had gone to bed on that first evening, I thought it best to try to draw Shona out of her silence. By this time, I had had many talks with Doctor Hay on the subject of Mongolism, for she seemed to like to visit us and was very kind and patient in answering my questions.

'Shona,' I began, 'you must try not to take this so hard.'

She ignored what I had said but she spoke the thoughts that haunted her mind, more as if she were speaking to herself than to Jock or me.

'I did everything they told me to do when I was carrying him, just as I did with all the others,' she said, weeping, looking at the floor.

'But Shona—' I began and as if Jock and I were not even present, she went on: 'What is going to happen to him later on? People laugh at people like him. My baby is an idiot. And everybody knew about him from the moment he was born, everybody knew except me.' Her drowned eyes focused on me momentarily as she said accusingly: 'My mother knew, Sheila knew and all of you knew and none of you said a word—' Her voice was rising towards hysteria and I broke in loudly: 'You are being quite unreasonable, Shona. We were all obeying the doctors. We had to do what they thought best.' But she merely withdrew into her alienation again instead of growing angry with me as I had hoped and took up in her toneless voice that coil of thought in her mind: 'I did everything they told me to do when I was carrying him—'

For the five weeks of the holiday, she hardly spoke during the day-time and in the evenings would only repeat the words of her sad litany. During the days, she stood alone at windows looking out at the sky or in corners of the garden looking out at the sea. She was totally withdrawn from all of us, even from the older children, taking no interest in what they said or did and attending to the needs of Sandy-Tom in an impersonal distant way, as if he were an inanimate doll to which she owed some sort of duty. This was the most frightening thing of all, arguing as it did a total change of personality, for Shona had been, formerly, a mother first and all else in a secondary way.

Liz, Duncan and Gee were all academically bright – what Tom and George called 'clever at the school' – and the fact that Shona was ignoring them urged them towards a strident striving for attention to which their sharp minds brought a devilish ingenuity. They indulged in all sorts of destructive mischief and behaviour close to the savage, and my brother, his nerves taut with worry about Shona, dealt with them more harshly than he would normally have done, so that the tense days were punctuated by the howls of three punished children shut up in separate rooms. And there was no rest during the nights either. Shona ate very little and seemed to sleep hardly at all but prowled about the house all night, unable to keep still. She tried to move quietly but, of course, we were all aware of the constant stealthy movement and gathered for breakfast each morning in a jaded state to face another day of Shona's silence and the obstreperous behaviour of Liz, Duncan and Gee, who seemed to be monsters in comparison with the reasonable creatures they had been formerly.

The only member of the family who was utterly himself and totally lovable in my eyes was Sandy-Tom, who lived and moved for most of the time inside his own happy world and came out of it occasionally with a seraphic smile to make some loving gesture towards one of us.

On the morning after the family had gone back to Aberdeenshire, George said: 'Well, Tom and I had better bring your writing things back into the sitting-room.'

I stood with my back to them, looking out of the scullery window.

'At this moment,' I said, 'I feel that I shall never write another word ever again.' I turned to face them. 'I feel as Liz did the day she said she was going to run away, when she told us she was fed up with the lot of us and didn't want to be part of a family any more.'

'But as Tom told her,' George said, 'it would not matter if we all ran to separate ends of the earth, we would still be part of the family whether we liked it or not.'

'I do not understand Shona at all, at all,' Tom said now. 'Wee Sandy-Tom is as he is and a fine little fellow at that and we all have to be doing with things as they are.'

Tom and George, I thought, would never understand that all of us were not endowed with their capability for doing with things as they were, or that some of us were even incapable of seeing things as they were because we did not wish to see them. The greatest difficulty with Shona was that she would not or could not listen to or absorb anything one tried to say, as if by refusing to discuss Sandy-Tom she would cause his handicap to disappear.

'I used to think it was very hard on Jock and you that your mother died when you were so young,' George said with seeming irrelevance, 'harder for you than for Jock, maybe, for he never knew what it was to have a mother but now I am not so sure. Maybe things have gone too easy for Shona for too long. She has had very little practice at putting up with hard things. I saw it in her when her father died, a sort of sulking at life, you could call it. And it's no use you worrying yourself to bits as you have been doing,' he told me. 'Shona has to find her own way through this and nobody can help her and to my mind all these pills the doctors are giving her are only making her way longer and harder. She will have to be doing with things as they are in the last of it and the sooner she comes to it the better.'

'Wee Sandy-Tom will bring her to herself in the end,' Tom said. 'She won't be able to help herself for he is a very taking little craitur.'

'Come on, Tom and we'll shift that table,' George said next and to me: 'and I wish you would give Sir Ian a call on the telephone and ask him to come down for a cup o' tea or a dram. He has been keeping away lately and I don't blame him.'

The cottage returned to normal but the strains of the last five weeks had still to manifest themselves fully. After the death of my husband, I had suffered a general breakdown, mental and physical and one of its manifestations, I realised later, was an almost intolerable itch on the palms of my hands and the soles of my feet. After some three days of this, the skin rose in dry blisters and then began to peel off in long ragged strips. It was a disability which disgusted me and probably the disgust was one more stress which merely made the condition worse. I had had a mild attack of it after the blaze of publicity in London but now, after the family left, I had a second attack that was much more virulent. It made me very ill-natured, partly because I had to sit by and instruct Tom and George in the preparation of the food, partly because I had been told that the condition was nervous in cause and I had no patience with these nerves that were part of me yet over which I had no control.

George and Tom, who had more sense than to let themselves get into a mental state such as mine, did not believe me when I told them that my skin trouble was of mental origin and even when Doctor Hay confirmed that this was so, they insisted that it should be medically curable, 'like ringworm', the only skin disease they knew and which they had seen only in cattle. They were disapproving more than sympathetic, as they had been about my head cold in January, which irritated me and consequently my disease and when, one morning, George said : 'The hands are no better ?' and added : 'I am sure I don't know what is wrong with you and Shona, the way you let things get on top of you,' I wanted to burst into tears and escaped into rage instead.

'Shut up !' I shouted. 'I wouldn't have my hands like this if I could help it.'

'Don't you shout at me, you young limmer,' he said loudly.

'Now, now, both of the two of you,' Tom intervened, 'shouting is going to do none of us any good. We have all been too much on top of one another in this wee housie this last while. None of us would be without Jock and Shona and the bairns for anything in the world but people have to be on their own now and again too. That is the way families are. So now, George, you will come out and help me to clean up that flower border, if you please and' – he turned to me – 'you should go for a walk along the shore, the way Her Old Self used to take to the moor and forget about the whole lot of us for a while.'

I watched them go down to the flower border and then I did as Tom had suggested and went for a long walk westwards along the stony beach towards Poyntdale Bay. 'That is the way families are,' Tom had said and it was true and it was also true that I would not be without Jock, Shona and the children for all the world but why was life so full of contradictions and paradoxes ? Why, simply because one

99

loved people enough to be concerned about them should one be subjected to this disgusting thing that Doctor Hay glorified with the name 'Stress Dermatitis'? On a different level, why should the Ladies from Sussex who had now started to call at the house in person during the holidays, meaning to be complimentary, have been turned into a further irritation by the family circumstances of Shona sobbing in one room while three children howled in the other rooms? I remembered a phrase from one of the Psalms of David: 'God setteth the solitary in families', something regarded as a blessing, but on this morning I felt that the blessing was rather mixed.

*   *   *

At the end of August, Sir Ian decided to retain his rooms at the hotel and spend the winter there. I think his liking for Tom and George was a large factor in this decision but he also liked the countryside and in his genial way had made friends with all the shopkeepers and many of the village people. Sam Smith, his negro chauffeur, was something new under Achcraggan's sun at first. The village had seen the occasional East Indian peddler of carpets and drapery goods but never a negro until now, and Sam was a well-built coal-black specimen but his magnificent smile and permanent good nature ensured his acceptance in friendship when the first strangeness had abated. Sam and Hamish became close friends and kept Mrs Henderson's and our table supplied in season with game poached from Dinchory Moor and salmon poached from round the Cobblers and Sam became the first negro to play for the Achcraggan football team. When Sam and Hamish came together into the sitting-room or the scullery, I felt as Gahta, Sashie's old cook, felt about Caleb, Sashie's headman, when she would say: 'Take yo'self outa ma way wid yo' great big feets!' There seemed to be so much of them that the small rooms felt as if their walls might fall outwards and their ceilings rise into the air.

In October, I had to visit London again for the publication of my second novel but the publicity was much less this time and I enjoyed the few days spent largely in the company of Miss Arden. When I had first met her, she had seemed to be rather over-powering but now that I knew her better, her sound common sense appealed to me and I was grateful to her for reducing her brother to more human terms. She had no compunction about stressing the fact that she was his senior, if she deemed it necessary, and even went so far on one occasion, during this visit, to say to him in my hearing: 'Don't be more of a fool than you can help, Aubrey.' He was a dry distant man who was more at home in the world of the written word than in the world of actual human relations which he seemed to look upon from an Olympian height when, that is, he was aware of it all. I had realised now that, when I first came to London on my return from abroad, he had taken me to dinner with his sister because he was even more scared of meeting me than I was of meeting him. He usually, I had gathered, avoided contact with all writers as far as he could and his chosen environments were the solitude of his own office and his own flat or hidden behind a newspaper at his club or in the company of his sister.

I was a little surprised, therefore, when, on the last afternoon of this visit, he asked me to come to his private office, a book-lined room with heavy mahogany furniture and a thick carpet on the parquet floor.

'I understand that the sales people have asked you to undertake a tour of the Midlands?' he asked, as if the 'sales people' were some foreign breed who had peculiar customs of which he preferred to know nothing.

'Yes, Birmingham and Leicester next month,' I said. 'Bookshops and libraries.'

In one sense I felt rather foolish telling him of an arrangement which his firm had made and the expenses of which it would pay and in another sense I felt that he would not know the details of the arrangement unless I told him but, yet, now that I had told him, he was not in the least interested. I was aware now that he had brought me in here to talk of something quite different and that he was finding the matter difficult but after a long awkward pause, he got up from his desk, looked out at the rain beyond the window and spoke with his back to me.

'It is our custom,' he said, 'to pay a small advance on a book and then to pay the royalties that have accrued to the author – royalties in excess of the advance, that is – early in April of each year. Your first book was published in May and I understand that considerable royalties have accrued already. If your financial position is in any way difficult, arrangements could be made for you to draw on these monies, Miss Sandison.'

My life-long failing, if that is what it is, of 'There's naething here but Heilan' pride, Heilan' scab and hunger' rose in me and I said: 'That will not be necessary, Mr Arden, thank you. I should like you to deal with my affairs in the normal way.' He turned to face me and I went on: 'It is nearly four o'clock. I must get back. I am having tea with Miss Arden.'

His relief that the terrible moment was over was palpable and his haste to telephone the commissionaire to tell him to order a cab for me confirmed his joy at being rid of me and my threatening mundane affairs.

Over tea, Miss Arden asked: 'Did Aubrey have a few private words with you?' and I answered: 'Yes, he did,' and then added the words 'Thank you' as I recognised the spur that had driven Mr Arden to that moment which he had found so painfully intimate. She then said: 'I do enjoy your visits to London, my dear, and hearing about this family of yours. You all seem to be so very close to one another.'

'I am beginning to think,' I said, 'that we are a little too close – not Tom and George, I mean – but all the others and now there is Sir Ian as well. Sometimes I feel like the atom being bombarded inside the atomic pile what with the family and the Ladies from Sussex and mankind in general. It is not that I hate them all and I don't want to sound precocious and temperamental, but I do wish sometimes that the world would just go by and leave me just to do my writing.'

'It is not precocious or temperamental,' Miss Arden said, 'for you to require conditions suitable for your work. As a doctor, I had a right to demand the accommodation and the equipment I needed. Virginia Woolf once wrote a little book called *A Room of One's Own*. Somehow, you have to convince people that you need a room of your own in a mental sense as well as a physical one but you are a contradiction in terms really, Janet. You obviously like people and you attract them towards you. I can understand why all these people called on you in the summer. Your books are more like letters to friends than novels, so people call on you and get in your way. You are your own enemy.' She was smiling at me but I looked back at her solemnly as I recognised the truth of what she had said. 'Indeed,' she was saying now, 'we are all our own enemies. Perhaps that is why we need friends.' She laughed and went on more lightly: 'I had thought of proposing myself for a visit to your countryside next spring but now that I see myself as something of an enemy I relish the idea less.'

'Oh, you must come. George and Tom would love to meet you.'

'There you go.'

'I know but I really would like you to come,' I said. 'I shall find a way to sort myself out. After all, I have always managed to write before and when I look back over the masses of people I have known I wonder how I ever wrote a single word. Doesn't one encounter a fantastic number of people in a lifetime?'

'Yes, one does encounter a lot but I don't think we all pay as much attention to them as you do. If I had met those terrible triplets of yours on a ship, I would have been so abominable to them that they would never have dared speak to me again.'

*   *   *

It is always difficult to trace the elements that come together into an idea and a plan for action but all the frustrations and strains of the summer seemed to come together constructively on the night train to Inverness while I drowsed rather than slept. My mind drifted from Miss Arden's high-ceilinged sitting-room in the Victorian hotel to the small rooms of Jemima Cottage and back to Guinea Corner, the house in St Jago where I had spent almost ten years, much of the time alone in one or another of its large rooms. To think of Guinea Corner was to think of Twice and now the memory came to me of one of our frequent arguments when he had said to me: 'You always think in terms of infinity. I think it must have been because of being born on that hill at Reachfar and seeing the four corners of the earth from the first moment you could see anything at all.' I slept for a short time, then was awakened by the voice of Tom telling me to go for a walk on the beach as my grandmother used to take to the moor and after more fitful sleep I seemed to hear Mr Arden say: 'Considerable royalties have accrued' while the wheels of the train seemed to repeat over and over: 'A room of one's own. A room of one's own.'

When George and Tom met me at Inverness, we followed our usual procedure of having tea and sandwiches while Little John went about his errands and as I took off my gloves, George asked: 'How are your hands?'

'All right, thanks. I am getting used to things and there was very little fuss this time. I spent a lot of time with Miss Arden. She is thinking of coming north for a holiday in the spring.'

'It will be fine to see her when she has been so good to you,' Tom said. But George's enquiry about my hands had sent my mind back to my shameful fit of temper on that morning in August after the family left the cottage when I had gone walking along the beach as Tom had told me to do, past the old storage building which had once belonged to Andrew Boyd the auctioneer. I had walked round the building, looking at it in detail. It was a rectangular block of whinstone masonry with no windows except a boarded-up opening high in one gable above which hung the rusted remains of a block and tackle which had been used to hoist items to the upper floor. On ground level, there was a heavy wooden door, large enough for a horse and cart to pass through, so that the building had something of the look of a fortress, silent behind a portcullis. It lay within four yards of the high tide mark, on a north-east south-west axis and as I walked round to the south-west gable, I discovered that the skyline from this angle was the hill of Reachfar, which I had not been able to see from any other part of the village.

It was probably only a few seconds since Tom had spoken but in their passing all the thoughts and memories of my fitful night had coalesced into four words: 'I want that building.' With a sense of achievement, with a feeling of having come to the end of months of frustration, I laid the thought carefully away in my mind and said: 'I have to go south again next month,' and told Tom and George of the projected visit to the Midlands, then added: 'It is a nuisance but once it is over we should have peace for a bit.'

'I don't think it is right,' George said, 'that you should call anything Mr Arden asks you to do a nuisance.'

I felt rebuked and said: 'You are quite right. I shouldn't, especially since he told me that my first book had made quite a bit of money.' I told them of how Mr Arden had said I might draw on this money and of the reply I had made.

'And I should just think so too,' said George.

'As if we couldna keep going until the right time comes for paying the money,' said Tom and I felt comforted that I had no monopoly in Highland pride, scab and hunger.

'He told me I should have a chartered accountant to look after the money because of income tax and all that,' I said next.

'What is a chartered accountant?' George asked and I tried to explain, then asked: 'Is there one in Dingwall, do you know?'

'Not us,' Tom told me. 'We never had enough money to need anybody to look after it,' but in the car on the way home I was inspired to ask Little John: 'Do you have a chartered accountant to look after your garage affairs?'

'Lord, aye,' he replied. 'The days when my grandfather shod a horse and got paid with half-a-boll of oatmeal are long bye.'

'Then you had better take me to see this man next week,' I said.

'If you make it Thursday,' Tom said, 'George and I could go to the cattle sale while you see the man. It is a good while since we were at the sale ring.'

George and Tom had this way of bringing things that were strange into Reachfar terms so that we were no longer going to Dingwall to engage an accountant but to attend a cattle sale and in the event we did not go with Little John but in Sir Ian's Rolls, driven by Sam. When this was first suggested, I protested that I had already engaged John but George said: 'You are away behind the fashion. Little John will be glad if you put him off. He would rather be in the garage mending tractors than looking at cattle.'

'Indeed,' Tom said, 'I am not sure that Little John knows the difference between a cow and a horse.'

Sir Ian, as always, was interested in 'somethin' doin' about the place' as he called it, whether it was a cattle sale or the making of a potato clamp in the garden and as I sat in the front of the car with the three of them in the back, I felt like an elderly governess taking three young charges on an outing. When they dropped me at the address Little John had given me, however, I found myself thinking that the only thing

I liked about being a writer was the writing itself and I quailed at the thought of presenting myself to this Mr Linton. However, a girl showed me into an office where a man rose from behind a desk and said: 'Good morning, Miss Sandison. Weren't you at Cairnton Academy once?' Astonished, I agreed that this was so. 'I thought so the moment I saw you on television. I was in the fifth year when you were in about the third.'

Linton, I thought, and a memory rose out of the grey mist of Cairnton.

'You were captain of the football team,' I said.

'That's right.'

'But how did you make your way up here?'

'When I qualified I got the idea that there might be an opening for an accountant in a place smaller than Glasgow or Edinburgh. I came up here, opened an office and it paid off.'

'Goodness, I am glad you did. I have got myself into this writing thing and I have no idea how to cope with the business end of it. Will you take me on?'

'Delighted. We are more at home with farm and commercial business of course but accounts are just accounts after all.'

'So they are,' I said, as if I were making a discovery, for this was how I felt. There was no doubt that the public side of my writing had induced some sort of psychological block, for I had done quite a lot of book-keeping and accountancy work in my time. 'What sort of records do you want me to keep?'

He gave me a few instructions, then the girl brought a tray with coffee and I felt that I had found not only an accountant but a friend as he said: 'So you intend to settle in the north here?'

'Yes.' I thought of Jemima Cottage, then of the old building on the beach and said: 'Mr Linton, is there any way I can find out who owns an old building in Achcraggan?'

'Simple enough,' he said. 'You want to buy some place?'

I told him about the old barn. 'The thing is that I think it is only part of a property. An awful Victorian villa goes with it and I don't want the villa.'

'We can find out who the owner is and what *he* wants,' Mr Linton said. 'Are you on the telephone?'

I gave him our number and he promised to ring me the following day.

'Well,' George asked when we were back at the cottage, 'how did you get on with the accounts man?'

'I had the most incredible luck,' I said and told them about Mr Linton. 'I never thought that any luck would come out of Cairnton.'

'It seems to me,' said Tom, 'that if you fell off the Cobbler into the firth you would come up with a fish in your mouth.'

'Aye,' George agreed with him. 'You may have had some hard times but things are fairly going your way now,' which reminded me, temporarily, to be grateful for my good fortune.

I did not tell them about my interest in the old barn on the beach. I wanted to feel my way a little, to try to find out how fond they were of the cottage or even how merely accustomed to it they were and whether they would dislike the idea of moving to a new place. They were fond of the garden, I knew, but the barn was only a few yards from the bottom of it and they could still spend their time there. They were both in the garden the next day when Mr Linton telephoned. 'The owner,' he said, 'is a Mr Andrew Boyd,' and he gave me an address and a telephone number in Birmingham.

Immediately, I sat down at my typewriter, then I thought the better of writing a letter as I visualised Andrew Boyd as I had last seen him. I could do better with that individual face-to-face, I decided, and I was already committed to going to Birmingham on the bookshop tour. Instead of writing to Andrew Boyd, I wrote to the sales manager at Canterbury

Arden and asked him to arrange for me to stay in Birmingham for an extra day after the tour was over.

*   *   *

We had now made a habit of telephoning my brother each Sunday evening but there was little genuine communication in these calls. 'We are all as usual,' he would say and then pass on to speak of trivial matters and make no mention of Shona's condition.

'There is nothing you can do,' George would tell me. 'Jock always goes inside himself when things are not going well. You just have to wait.'

But I was not very proficient at waiting, either for Shona to return to normal or to visit Andrew Boyd in Birmingham. Like my grandmother, I had to be 'at' something and I went at my writing like a fury. At Guinea Corner in St Jago, I had stacked manuscripts in the linen cupboard and now I was stacking them in a cupboard in my bedroom. The cupboard was a dark hole under the staircase where we also stored the Suck-and-Blow and a day came when George said : 'We'll soon have to find another place for the Suck-and-Blow with that heap you have in there. What you should have is a proper study, as they call it, with a desk and all, like Roddy has.'

'I wish you would stop comparing me with Roddy Maclean,' I said. 'I'd feel a fool sitting in a study and besides I wouldn't hear the vegetables coming to the boil.'

'I have little knowledge about writers,' Tom said, 'except that I am learning they can be damnable contrary but I don't think many of them write books and cook a dinner at the same time.'

'And I don't think many people would grow sweet peas in Aunt Betsy's old lavatory bowl and Brussels sprouts in her old bath,' I countered. 'You two have no right to make out that I am queer in the head.'

'We weren't calling you queer in the head exactly, only different,' George said.

'You sound like old Jean,' I told him, 'always wanting people to be like ither folk as she called it,' and this silenced them whereupon I continued: 'I wonder where Jean is, by the way?'

'There is no profit in wondering about that,' Tom said but no happening, however trivial, is without its reverberations, and since Sir Ian had come to the hotel, I had had one or two uneasy moments about Jean, for it is in this way that the strands of life are interwoven. Sir Ian had the air of having been abandoned by his son and daughter-in-law and although he had made a new place for himself with us and the people round about, he still seemed to feel that he did not quite belong, that he had no people who were truly his own. And Sir Ian, more than most people, needed people, people in whose lives he could take a benevolent interest, such as he had taken in the lives of the thousands who had depended on his sugar plantation for a living. Watching Sir Ian, I would find myself thinking about Jean and thinking that she too needed people, as we all need them and the fact that Jean needed them to quarrel with, to exercise her malice upon, made her no less deprived than Sir Ian was. The thought of Jean was a nagging in the mind and something a little shameful for, although I did not like to think of her as an old woman among strangers, I still shuddered at the thought of her returning among us to disrupt our peace, as she undoubtedly would do.

*   *   *

Early in November, when the wild geese were flying down from the north in long skeins to settle in Poyntdale Bay, I left for Birmingham. I would have been very reluctant to go but for the piece of paper that bore Andrew Boyd's address which lay in my handbag. My tour over, I parted from the man who had bear-led me from place to place, went to bed and arose the next morning feeling that the day of battle was here at last. In the parlance of Achcraggan, Andrew Boyd's father had been 'fit to steal the sugar out of your tea' and another Achcraggan adage was 'Like father, like son'. I very much wanted the barn on the beach but I did not want to pay an inflated price for it.

I had not telephoned to make an appointment but pre-ferred to spend the whole day, and longer if necessary, in try-ing to see Andrew Boyd with as little warning as possible. Birmingham was a city I barely knew and when I gave the address to the cab-driver, I expected to be taken to some seedy back street where I would enter a dark office like some hole in a wall where a weasel might live so that, when the cabman deposited me at the wide glass door of an office block in a street of such blocks, I felt that Andrew Boyd, after all, had won the first round. Having studied the large board in the hall, which told me that the offices of Boyd Enterprises Limited were on the third floor, I went up in the lift feeling that I was making even a greater fool of myself than usual. An executive of a firm with offices of this kind, I told myself, might be anywhere on earth between China and Peru and would certainly not be waiting here for me to call on him about an old barn that he had probably forgotten he pos-sessed. I think I would have turned tail and pressed the down button of the lift but for an echo of my grandmother's voice in my memory saying: 'You started this, my lady. You finish it'. I opened the glass door ahead of me and found myself in a reception office where a young woman wished me good morning.

'Good morning,' I replied. 'Would it be possible for me to see Mr Andrew Boyd any time today?'

She ran a forefinger down the page of a large diary. 'He won't be in until eleven,' she said, 'and he has an appoint-ment at eleven-thirty. Today is rather difficult.'

I looked up at a clock which showed the time as ten twenty-five. 'May I wait?'

'Very well. May I have your name?'

'Mrs Alexander,' I said and she indicated a corner of the room where there were some chairs and a low table which held some brochures advertising hotels and a heavy glass ashtray.

As the hand of the clock moved towards eleven, the door opened and Andrew Boyd came in. He was of about my own height, slight of build, but he was well-dressed and not at all of the 'spiv' flashy appearance that I remembered. I could remember the time when he was born and although he was only about forty, his dark hair was turning grey at the temples. His eyes were as sharp and alert as ever and as he glanced at the corner where I sat, they seemed to concentrate, his quick step seemed to check for a split second but he disappeared so quickly into another office that I thought I must have imagined that glance and check.

'Mr Boyd will see you now,' the young woman told me to my surprise after a moment or two, and I rose and followed her into a large office, one side of which was glass and which was furnished in up-to-the-minute style with a desk of laminated wood whose top was roughly S-shaped, and a chromium and plate glass stand with shelves full of evergreen plants that might have been made from green plastic, so uniform were they, stood in a corner.

'Good morning, Mrs Alexander,' Andrew Boyd said. 'What can I do for you? Please sit down.'

I thought of the corny joke: 'What can I do you for?' with which Mr Cervi the ice-cream and sweet-shop man at Cairnton used to greet some of his clients, while the sharp eyes looked me over from head to foot as the eyes of his father might look over an animal at the Inverness Horse Fair.

I sat down and said: 'Perhaps I ought to have made an appointment. It is kind of you to see me.'

He waved a hand airily. 'I have plenty of time.'

The texture of life is very dense and everything is connected to everything else so that there is no such thing as an isolated incident of Janet Alexander meeting Andrew Boyd in an office in Birmingham. Nothing takes place in a vacuum and now words that Twice had spoken long ago of George and Tom came to my mind. 'They would make first-class business executives. All the best ones have plenty of time and are never in a hurry.' The large desk held a blotting pad, a pen in a stand and a cigarette box and ash-tray. There was no clutter of papers, no indication of what went on in this room.

'I come from Achcraggan in Ross-shire,' I began and paused to take a deep breath before telling him why I had come but in the pause he said: 'I know. You are Janet Sandison, Janet Reachfar.'

I laughed and said: 'That's right.'

'You made quite a how-d'ye-do with your novels back in the spring. Congratulations. I only read detective stories as a rule but I liked your book.'

'Thank you.'

'So you have come home to Achcraggan?'

'Yes. I was abroad for ten years. Then my husband died and I came home to my uncles at Jemima Cottage, just next to your place on the Shore Road.'

'George and Tom,' he said, 'they are still alive?'

'Very much so.'

'Aye. Achcraggan always said that the Sandisons lived so long they nearly had to be shot.'

'I didn't know that.'

'*You* wouldn't,' he pointed out to me.

'Jemima Cottage,' he said next on a thoughtful note. 'That's where that old bitch Betsy used to live. She caught me pinching her plums once and tanned my backside with a garden cane.'

'She was my great-aunt,' I said, 'but you are right. She *was* an old bitch. You never come up to Achcraggan now?'

'I was up in Dingwall something over a year ago,' he said, 'but I didn't drive out to Achcraggan. There was no point. I have no people there now. In fact, I have no relations anywhere that I know of. It seems that I am the last of the breed.' He grinned at me. 'Some would say that is just as well.'

He had a disconcerting trick, I was to discover, of showing that he was well aware of his status in the eyes of Achcraggan and he seemed to know of and be enjoying in a mischievous way my struggle against this traditional image of his.

'I was looking at some brochures in your reception office,' I said. 'Are you in the hotel business?'

He gave me the sort of cunning leer that his father used to bend on his mother and his aunts when he was selling them inflated-priced coal. 'Oh, a bit of this and a bit of that,' he said airily and cagily while I wondered if he knew who his father had been and if he realised how strongly he resembled him.

'But I mustn't waste any more of your time—' I began and he interrupted me with: 'Plenty of time' and he must have pressed an invisible button for a middle-aged fat woman, who reminded me of Lily Slim with whom I had worked in a London office long ago, came in and said: 'Yes, Mr Boyd?'

'Cancel Winterton at eleven-thirty,' he told her, 'and tell Hall I'll lunch with him tomorrow.' She went out and he said: 'You will have lunch with me?'

'Thank you,' I said, trying not to sound surprised.

I felt that he had taken a liking to me and I found that I was liking him, although unwillingly, for the prejudice against his ancestry, that prejudice bred in me in my childhood was still strong as were all the tenets of Reachfar in my character. Reachfar believed that people lived only by hard work, that the acquisition of wealth was a long slow process of economical living and the storing of surplus shillings in the bank and sudden wealth was always suspect. In the eyes of Reachfar, such wealth could not be acquired honestly and I was remembering the time when this man's father committed the crime which forced him to flee the district. The police had failed to bring him to justice and I had a suspicion that the man across the desk from me was capable of evasion of the law on a grander and more knowledgeable scale but, looking back to that time forty years ago, I remembered something else and remembered too how, as a child, it had puzzled me. When the police had failed to lay Jock Skinner by the heels, my upright honest family – even my stern grandmother – had begun to laugh. This attitude, following on all the disapproval of Jock's crime, had puzzled me and I had had speech with Tom on the subject and he had said : 'You canna but laugh when you think on that wee craitur making a fool of half the police force and them such fine big fellows with their uniforms and all'. There had been something like admiration, unwilling admiration, in Tom's voice with an undertone of the age-old Highland dislike of faceless government as represented by the uniformed police.

It was a similar admiration that was growing in me now for the man across the desk and I began to feel a kinship with him for was I myself not on the way to growing rich by Reachfar standards if my publisher's forecasts about my novels were true? I had not worked hard for this money. As I had told George and Tom, my ability to write was a gift with which I had been mysteriously endowed, a gift born probably out of my ancestry and the influences to which I had been subjected. It seemed logical that Andrew Boyd had been endowed with a different gift arising out of a different ancestry, the gift of financial foresight and for making shrewd investments, not the sort of talent that I admired particularly but still a talent.

'You have certainly put Achcraggan on the map,' he said now. I looked round the plush office again. 'You have made quite a map of your own,' I said, 'but without the vulgar publicity that came to me. It wasn't my idea of fun but, as my publishers tell me, it does sell books so I have to put up with it to some extent. But there is a limit. Jemima Cottage is bang on the roadside and I had far too many people calling on me last summer. It is kind of people to do it but it does disrupt family life a bit.'

'I know what you mean. I am not fond of the public eye myself,' and he contrived to imply that in his case and in the words of Tom and George, 'what the public did not see would not hurt them'. In a curiously sensitive way, he could show understanding of what I felt and at the same time mark the differences between us.

'And this is why I came to see you,' I continued. 'I understand that you still own your aunt's property in Achcraggan?'

'Seaview?' he asked, raising his eyebrows. 'But it is as close to the road as your own cottage.'

'I don't mean the house. I mean that old barn on the beach. If you are willing to sell it, I would like to buy it,' and I did not say in words: 'And don't try any of your financial tricks on *me*,' but something must have shown in my face, for he looked at me hard and said: 'You are the image of Mrs Reachfar, your granny.'

'So I have been told. I have no idea of the value of that barn but you name a price and if I can't afford it, that is that.'

He leaned back in his imposing chair and laughed uproariously, then said: 'You don't beat about the bush, do you?'

'No. I don't see the point. How much do you want for it?'

He looked at me straight and levelly, with no hint of a cunning smirk or leer. 'I value it at two hundred and fifty pounds,' he said. I was utterly taken aback. 'That is ridiculous,' I protested. 'It must be worth more than that.'

He ignored me. 'You intend to turn it into a house?'

'Yes.'

'Right. You go back north and get an architect to look it over. I haven't been inside it for about twenty years. The roof may be falling in or it may be riddled with dry rot like Seaview. After an architect has seen it, it is yours for two-fifty if you still want it. If the walls and the roof are sound, you are on to a good investment. It will cost you a bit to convert it but it will still be worthwhile.'

I felt embarrassed. 'This is terribly kind of you, Mr Boyd.'

'No. I am offering it at its present market value as a derelict building at the back of beyond but a year or two from now it will be worth a lot more. Property up there is going to rise.' He rose from his desk, undid some sort of catch and a window opened and suddenly the room was filled with the roar of the traffic from the street below. Until that moment, I had not realised how peaceful the office had been. He closed the window and sat down again. 'People are getting to the point where they can't stand the racket much longer. Quiet places are going to be at a premium. Let's go and have some lunch.'

Over a good meal in a hotel where he was not only well known but obviously well liked, he said : 'You have a brother, haven't you?'

'Yes, John.'

'I remember him coming into the First Year at Fortavoch Academy shortly before I left – a big chap for his age with red hair.'

'That's Jock. He is married now with four children.'

'Have you any children?'

'No.'

'But you were happily married?' he asked with a curious air of anxiety, as if it were important to him that I had been happy. There was something strangely sympathetic about him.

'I was very happy,' I said.

'I am sorry he died.'

117

I shook my head. 'I am grateful for the time I had and another door has opened now with this writing thing. You have never married?'

'Why do you sound so sure I never have?' he asked, looking at me narrowly with those sharp eyes.

'You have that self-contained look that bachelors have,' I told him.

'You are quite right. I am not the marrying kind.'

'You seem to do very well as you are and you have done very well by me today. Thank you again for the barn.'

His glance changed, his eyes suddenly widened. 'I am going to be dead honest with *you*,' he said with a slight emphasis on the pronoun, which seemed to indicate that he was admitting that it was unusual for him to be 'dead' honest. 'I am doing well by myself in selling you that building for I'll like to see it turned into something decent and brought into use. I am going to tell you something, Janet Reachfar, but it is strictly between ourselves. I want to see a lot of Achcraggan restored and preserved. That is why I bought Poyntdale when it came on the market.' If he noticed that he had taken my breath away, he did not show that he had noticed. 'Poyntdale itself is nothing much,' he continued, 'but as the kind of hotel it is now, it will bring people with money into the district, the kind of people who are going to want a quiet bolt-hole, people with the kind of money to buy and restore old houses. That is why I am buying everything in Achcraggan I can lay my hands on, but it isn't easy to trace the owners.'

I was utterly bemused, uncertain whether I approved of my childhood metropolis being turned into a refuge for retired stockbrokers, uncertain if it was even moral for Andrew Boyd to make another fortune out of his birth-place, until he continued: 'I like that village. I was born there. I don't want to see those old houses demolished and more jerry-built stuff stuck up on a shoestring but I don't want the folk up there to look on me as the local millionaire. I just want them to see me as young Andra Bull as they always saw me.'

I liked him for this and said eagerly: 'And will you come back to live in Achcraggan for part of the time?'

'Not to live at Seaview. I'll put a bulldozer through that bleeder when I get around to it but I might keep one of the older houses and do it up. Anyway, if you hear of anything coming on the market, give me a ring and reverse the charges.'

I laughed. 'I'll ring you but I approve enough to pay for the calls.'

I felt that my mind had had a considerable and probably much-needed shake-up. 'Only, you won't turn the place into a precious sort of artists' colony like some of the Cornish villages, will you?'

'No chance. I don't like precious people. I like people who have their feet on the ground and I won't sell a stone to anybody I don't like,' he said, contriving to inform me that if he had not liked me he would not have agreed to sell me the barn. 'Now about that barn,' he went on, 'get Orr and Paterson to survey it for you. They are quite good. They did the work at Poyntdale. And if their report is bad, don't touch it. We'll find something else for you. If it passes the survey, tell your solicitor to write to me.'

As he left me at the door of my hotel, I thanked him again and he said: 'The whole thing has been a pleasure. Goodbye.' From the doorway, I watched him walk away along the busy pavement, a neat slim figure that seemed to melt into the crowd and yet have no contact with any member of it; like a weasel, the thought came to me, disappearing into a stone wall of its own brownish colour but without its slippery sides touching the stones.

*   *   *

When I returned to Inverness, George, Tom, Sir Ian and Sam

were at the station with Sir Ian's car. Tom and George always came to meet me, I noticed now, but much as they enjoyed the drive to Inverness, they did not ever come to see me go away. When I had left for the Midlands, they had gone out into the garden before the car came for me and when I called from the back door: 'Hi, you two, I'm off,' their only response was a casual 'Aye, aye' from behind the hedge.

That evening, after Sir Ian had gone back to the hotel and we had had supper, I said: 'Do you know who I saw in Birmingham? Andrew Boyd.'

'The Miss Boyds' Andra?'

'Young Andra Bull?'

'How in the world did you come across *him*?'

I did not answer them directly but asked instead: 'Listen, you two, what do you really think of this house, Jemima Cottage?'

'Think about it?' George frowned at me. 'I have never what you call thought about it. Your father asked us to come here when we sold Reachfar so we never thought about it. We just came.'

'If you were going to build a house, would you build one like this?'

George and Tom looked around them, from the small fireplace, to the small window and up to the low ceiling. 'Maybe not,' George said. 'I would have made it bigger – not bigger all over, like, but less rooms but bigger ones.'

'And I wouldn't have put that dirty angle in the stairs that the bairns are always falling on and I would have made it look to the firth instead of the road,' Tom said, 'but why were you asking?'

'Because I don't like this house either and I am thinking of building a better one.'

'Building a *house*?' George frowned at me again. 'Janet, it takes a lot to build a house these days and we have spent a lot on this one.'

'Jock and Shona can have this one for the holidays. I have

enough money for another one. That is why I went to see Andrew Boyd. He is willing to sell me Andra Bull's old store.'

'That rascal! You must be out o' your head—' George began.

'Wait a minute,' I interrupted. 'He may be a rascal in some ways but he was very decent to *me*.' I told them what had passed between Andrew and myself and how he had even given me the name of an architect who would survey the building for me. 'And if the architect says it's not worth two hundred and fifty, he pretty well told me that he wouldn't sell it to me,' I ended.

'Two hundred and fifty? The walls o' that building alone are worth more than that,' George said. 'They are a yard thick if they are an inch and sitting on that gravel rise it is as dry as bone.'

'And the roof is solid Ballachulish slate,' Tom said, 'not that thin stuff you can spit peas through.'

Once more, George was frowning at me but in a puzzled way this time. 'What kind o' spell did you put on Andra Boyd to get a bargain like that?'

'I'd like to see anybody put a spell on Andrew Boyd. I just asked him what he wanted for it and he said two hundred and fifty.'

'Then you see that Mr Graham the lawyer has a good look at the title deed before you part with a penny,' Tom advised me.

'Andrew Boyd told me to get a solicitor to deal with him about it,' I told them.

'Well, this beats all,' said George. 'She is up with another fish in her mouth, Tom. Dang it, I can't get over this. Andra Boyd!'

'It is very queer,' I agreed with him. 'Looking at him, I wouldn't trust him as far as I'd kick him and yet I trusted him in his dealings with *me*.' I thought for a moment and went on: 'Maybe he makes everybody feel they can trust him in relation to *them*. No, that's not right either. He *was* honest and decent with me. He went out of his way to give me a fair deal.'

'Mind you,' Tom said to George, 'he may be as twisted as a grassy rope but at the same time he was very good to his old aunties. He must have taken a notion to you, Janet.'

'Notion my behind. Rich young men don't take notions to old women of fifty.'

'Well there it is,' George said, 'and I can hardly wait for the morning to go down there and have a look at the old store.'

'Oh, Lord,' I said, 'I haven't got a key. We can't get in.'

'Key? You don't need a key. It's been lost long ago likely. Tom and I have often gone in there for a smoke on a wet day when Jean was on her high horse.'

The next morning, as soon as it was light, we made our way through the November sleet to the barn. The light from the big doorway showed inside walls of rough masonry like the outside and a fixed ladder led up to a rectangular hole in the wooden ceiling. George gave the ladder a thump with his fist and a kick with his boot and then began to climb, Tom following him, so I followed Tom. When we reached the upper floor, we discovered that, round the walls, it was several feet deep in bird droppings.

'These danged pigeons,' George said. 'They come in and out through there,' and he pointed to a hole at the east end where the beam that held the block and tackle went through.

'That's good stuff,' Tom said. 'You must put a spell on Andra to give you a good bittie ground for a garden, Janet. You have the dung for it ready made.'

We were all in high spirits which led to a certain coarseness. 'Maybe I haven't a spell strong enough to get the dung,' I said. 'It is pretty powerful-smelling stuff.'

George gave one of the rafters a bang. 'Sound as a bell. As for the dung, when you take the ship, you take the cargo, as Willie Beagle said when he married Katie Boatie and her seven months gone.'

I telephoned the architect when we went back to the house and he agreed to visit us two days later. On the morning of his visit I had a letter from Sashie. George and Tom were behaving as if we could move our beds down to the barn without further ado. There was no doubt that the old place appealed to them as much as it did to me but now that the dream was threatening to turn into reality, I was a little uneasy about how much the conversion was going to cost.

Sashie's letter was opportune. 'You can't be as disappointed as I am that I haven't been over to see you and the aspidistra,' he began, 'but who would have imagined that that Adonis, Don, should fetch up with two broken legs and a broken arm? Even if it wasn't his fault and that Argentinian who crashed into the car was so drunk that they had to *pour* him into the police cell, I have been spiteful enough at times to wish that Don's too-handsome face was permanently scarred. It is not, of course. It is, if anything, rendered handsomer than ever by all his plaster and bandages and I did not really wish him to be scarred, not *really*, as Liz says, although having to do his job for him is the most frightful bore. You are being even more than usually stupid and bloody-minded about continuing to live in that old house that you so much dislike. You are nearly fifty years old, have spent much of your life in places you did not like and your life expectancy according to the bible is only another twenty years. You must have made enough money by now to be able to rent if not buy a place where you can spend your final years with pleasure, instead of making do with a place that sounds even worse than the top floor of Paradise Great House. As soon as I can get over there—'

Even at a distance of four thousand miles, Sashie could give me courage and when the architect had pronounced the barn fundamentally sound, I said: 'How much would it take to make it habitable?'

'Depends on what you call habitable,' was his reply and in

the end I asked him to draw a plan for the interior as I had outlined it to him and estimate what it would cost to carry the work through.

*   *   *

Winter was now upon us, a very severe winter that year, so that we did not see the family at Christmas because some of the worst roads in Scotland, blocked with snow, lay between them and us. We still made our Sunday evening telephone call but this was a communication of words only and much of the deeper communication in our family, especially between my brother and myself, was more by look and gesture than by spoken word.

'Time will put things right,' George said.

'Time and the world,' said Tom and I believed them but, as ever, I found it more difficult to wait with patience than they did.

Our Christmas present was the old yellowed title deed, laced with faded pink tape, of the barn and attached to it was a newly drawn plan which granted to us the land between the garden wall of Seaview and the beach. This meant that we could have a garden, not as large as that of Jemima Cottage but large enough, and our northern boundary was 'the foreshore at the line of the spring tides'.

Between Christmas and the New Year, when the earth was spongy with melted snow, the three of us accompanied by Sir Ian went down and paced off our new territory, Sir Ian more enthusiastic than any of us for this was indeed 'somethin' doin' about the place'. 'Come February,' said George, 'we'll dig this west plot over and put a crop of tatties in it in the spring.'

'And the builders and plumbers and people will tramp all over it and dig it all up,' I said. 'You will have to wait until the work on the barn is finished.'

I think this was the first time I ever saw them display real impatience but when the weather cleared about the end of February and the masons, plumbers and joiners moved in, their enthusiasm was re-born.

The architect's plan for a large living-room, small kitchen and fuel store on the ground floor with four bedrooms and a bathroom above, had meant little to them.

'Never was a damn o' good at paper-work,' Sir Ian said. 'Never could make head or tail o' all these drawin's Twice used to show me when he was doin' things at the factory. What's that?'

'The fireplace and the line of the chimney.'

'But the damn' thing is right in the middle o' the place,' George protested.

'The old Rosecroft housie,' Tom contributed, 'not the one that's falling down now but the one before that had the fire in the middle of the floor and the smoke going out through a hole in the roof. The wrinkles in old Mary Fraser's face was full o' years and years o' smoke. Like a kipper she was, indeed.'

'I am going back to the old style of fire in the middle of the floor,' I explained, 'but putting a chimney right up through the building and through the roof.'

'Well, yourself and Mr Orr knows best,' said George, 'and maybe the old people of long ago were not without sense after all.'

At the New Year, all three of them had gone out first-footing in the village, a half-bottle of whisky in each of their pockets and they returned with an extraordinary story told to them by Malcolm the Minister.

'According to Malcolm,' George began over breakfast the following morning, 'Andra Bull's first wife – you will mind that he was twice married? – went wrong in the head before she died and she took to hiding things the way old Jamie Bedamned did. Andra used to get terrible drunk and all her life the poor craitur was afraid that he would drink her and the bairns out of house and home, so she got into the way of emptying all the money out of his pockets while he was sleeping off the drink, and hiding it, so when her mind gave way she went on hiding things.'

'Malcolm says,' Tom continued while George ate his porridge, 'that his old father till the day he died told the tale of how, when he was a wee boy, he saw Mrs Bull running down the garden to the old store with a spade and burying something near the west gable. Then the daughters came running down after her and she threw the spade into the bushes and went running off along the shore and old Malcolm was frightened and ran off home.'

'Are you telling me,' I asked, 'that as well as the cargo of pigeon dung we have bought a cargo of buried treasure? What a hope! Why did old Malcolm not dig the thing up?'

'He was only a little bairn at the time,' George protested, 'and forgot all about the thing but it came back to him later on, only by then he wasn't sure of the place. He did dig a bit on the quiet, Malcolm said, but he never found anything.'

'And neither will we,' I said.

'You never know,' George said.

'Who can tell?' Tom asked.

* * *

When, about mid-April, the family came up for the Easter holidays, George and Tom told the children about the buried treasure. By this time, work on the conversion of the old barn was in full swing, Tom, George and Sir Ian were spending all their time down there watching progress and now the children spent all their time there too, digging for treasure. George provided Sandy-Tom with a small spade and he dug too, imitating the other three but only for part of the time. At intervals, he would straighten up, lean on his spade and gaze out over the firth to the hills, looking strange and other-worldly, yet at the same time looking like a miniature of George or Tom, who used to pause in their work in this way and look out from Reachfar over the wide expanse of land and sea.

Shona was still pale, silent and withdrawn, never speaking unless a question was asked of her, still going away by herself to some corner of the house or garden while Jock, for the sake of the children, tried to appear normal but could not entirely conceal the strain he was feeling. Only the interest in the buried treasure, which kept the children out of the house except at meal-times, made the ten days bearable and I marvelled at the in-built knack of Tom and George for turning to good account every little quirk that life could throw up.

I also marvelled at their stability. I knew that they were as disappointed as I was that Shona was no better, showing no sign of a return to her former personality, but during the days after the family left, when my hands and feet began to itch and shed their skin, I looked upon them with sheer envy. I knew that my worrying about Shona was useless and would make no contribution to her betterment but I could not stop the worrying and its disgusting physical manifestation and as I observed Tom and George, I began to feel that I had not the grip on my own personality and on life itself that they had. They seemed to be endowed with some inner strength which armed them to face with equanimity everything that life could bring, until I began to see that their endowment was not an armour with which to face life and fight it but the strength to absorb what life brought, assimilate it, go along with it and even be grateful for it. They accepted life as they accepted summer heat and winter cold and turned everything it brought to what Ecclesiastes called 'a purpose under Heaven'.

*   *   *

In May, I went to London again for the publication of my

third novel and while I was there I had lunch one day with Monica Daviot. The meeting was not of my seeking for, as I had told Miss Arden, most of the attempts I had made at reviving old friendships had been unsuccessful, but one of the people who had written to me after the publication of my first book had been Monica. She had asked me to get in touch with her next time I came to London and I had shirked the meeting in October but arranged it this time because, as ever, Monica had been persistent.

I had last seen her nine years before, but she was as beautiful as ever and, if anything, more elegant, although she had two step-children and five children of her own, including twins who were now three years old. She must have been about forty when those twins were born but now she looked a svelte thirty-five in a pale green suit and an impudent little pill-box hat.

'You look a lot older,' she told me, 'but it suits you. Fancy you turning into a writer but that suits you too. You do it very well.'

'Thank you,' I said. 'You look a lot younger than you should but it suits you. I was so sorry about Torquil, Monica.' Torquil had been her husband who had died some two years before.

'We were happy. So were you and Twice.'

'We were lucky. It was good while it lasted.'

After that, we talked of her children and the children of my own family and then, inevitably, the talk went back to the past, to the Do-you-remember? I think that this is what I dislike about meetings after long separations, this recalling of past situations which, brought to the present, so often seem to me to be embarrassing. One laughs, but the laughter on my part is always a little strained and shamed. To recall my childhood with Tom and George, by contrast, is pure pleasure and the only reason that I can find that this should be so is that the child is too instinctively wise to play the fool. It is when the wise instinct is put in abeyance by the thrust of the ego that leads to the taking of stances and poses that situations develop which, recalled at a later time, become ludicrous and shaming.

'And what are your plans?' Monica asked towards the end of lunch.

'None. I am no more of a planner than I ever was. At the moment, I am writing. I like doing it and I'd like to go on doing it if things work out that way. What about you?'

Her tone was casual. 'I shall marry again. I am what they call the marrying kind.'

Like the quick movement of a weasel, the memory of Andrew Boyd crossed my mind as he said: 'I am not the marrying kind either' but I made no comment on what Monica had said. Her attitude, put suddenly into words, was so different from my own that I needed time to grow accustomed to it. In Air Force slang, marriage in my mind was something I had 'had', an experience that I could not imagine repeating with a new partner but even while Monica paid the bill and I pulled on my gloves, I remembered that her marriage to Torquil Daviot had been a cool, reasoned affair, quite unlike the stormy bonnets-over-the-windmill union of Twice and myself. Monica was wealthy in her own right, was probably wealthier now as Torquil's widow and she came of a family with a long tradition of marriage as a political institution for the conservation and increase of wealth.

'I shall probably come north later in the summer. It will be fun to see Poyntdale as a pub,' she said as we left the restaurant for the street.

Here was another gulf between us. The last thing I wanted to see was Reachfar in its new guise. 'Pub is not quite the apt word,' I said. 'It is still very much the dignified country house.'

'Dignified? Poyntdale?'

'Not on the scale of Beechwood, perhaps,' I said. Beechwood, an enormous historic mansion, was her family home.

'Still, Poyntdale is a pleasant hospitable house. You don't miss the life you had there?'

'Beechwood is no longer what it was,' she said. 'It is full of people who pay half-a-crown to see the spare bedroom. And the way of life I had at Poyntdale is finished too. I enjoyed working with the old people and the Women's Institute and all that but with the coming of the Welfare State and television, I got the feeling I was no longer required.' She hailed a passing taxi. 'Well, goodbye, Janet. I hope to see you in the north before too long.'

The taxi seemed to disappear not into the crowding traffic but into the tunnel of the past. I thought it unlikely that Monica would come north later in the year. That had been a sop she had thrown to the pretence that something still existed between us. She had declared her real intent for her future when she had said she would marry again and there was no suitable *parti*, as far as I knew, in the Achcraggan district. Whoever Monica married would have to be rich and he was more likely to be found in London, Paris or any of the other capitals around which her numerous relations were scattered than among the hills and moors of Ross-shire.

*   *   *

When on my return, George and Tom met the train, all thought of Monica was swept out of my mind for almost the first words George spoke were: 'Jean has been seen here in Inverness.'

'She will have heard about you and the books,' Tom said, 'and is on her way back to see what is in it for herself, the old devil, as well as having nowhere else to go by this time likely.'

To an onlooker, the degree of my shock at this news would have been incomprehensible for no one other than myself had any intimate knowledge of my relationship with Jean.

Even as a child, I had seen in her everything that I most disliked. She was stupid and at the same time cunning, she was physically coarse and fat as she grew older but at the same time vain, she was avaricious but at the same time ostentatious and she was capable of acute mental cruelty yet endowed with the ability to forget that she had ever been cruel. Jean did not deny, merely, things that she had said. She could forget literally and at will, it seemed, that she had ever said them. This intimate knowledge of her was peculiar to myself, this was Jean through my eyes only, but Tom, George and Jock had a similar though less intimate knowledge and in Achcraggan at large her malicious tongue and her vicious temper were a by-word.

I knew Jean better than did anyone else because I had first met her when I was ten years old and had lived in her shadow for six impressionable and, I think, observant years, but more important than this by way of gaining knowledge of her was the fact that she hated me. Jean had little capacity for liking and loving. Indeed I think that the only person she ever had any liking for was my father, who had given her the things that she most valued in life, which were the marriage title and a home that was financially secure. Hatred can be as potent as love in the revelation of a personality and Jean's hatred for me was great enough to expose her fairly fully to my observation.

Down the years, I had not gone to the trouble of hating Jean in return. I simply avoided all contact with her, forgot her for most of the time and laughed about her when she came to my mental notice. But deep in my mind my knowledge of her had hardened into an almost physical thing, I discovered now, a thing from which I recoiled in horror as I would from a rodent or a reptile.

'Now then,' George said in the lounge of the hotel when I let my teaspoon clatter into my saucer, 'you are not going to worry about this, Janet.'

'But do you think she *will* come to the cottage?'

'Quite likely but there is no need for you to lose the skin off your hands over her.'

'She will be grudging every penny she has to pay in boarding-houses and places,' Tom said. 'She never thought o' that when she ran away. Jean could never see an inch in front of her face.'

'But what are we going to do?' I asked. 'I can't see an inch in front of my face either. I simply know that life with Jean in the house will be pure hell.'

'She is not *in* the house yet,' George said, 'and she won't get in if I can help it at all, not before the old store is ready for us anyway.'

But I felt that if Jean arrived at the door of the cottage, we would all let her enter for my father's sake and I went on feeling this, tried not to show what I was feeling, and spoke of Jean not at all although haunted by her for five long weeks until, late in June, the doorbell rang the change in the entire situation. I opened the door to find a police car at the gate and a young policeman on the mat who wished me good morning and then asked: 'You are Miss Sandison?' I nodded. 'It is not a very common name, Sandison,' he said. 'Are you by any chance related to an elderly Mrs Sandison who has been living in a boarding-house in Inverness?'

George and Tom, as if they had scented trouble from the barn down on the beach, appeared in the doorway behind me. 'Is her name Jean Sandison?' I asked. 'If so, she could be my – my – stepmother.'

'I am sorry to tell you that she is critically ill in the Infirmary. She was taken there from the boarding-house. The people knew nothing of her except her name. Will you contact the hospital?'

'Yes,' I said, confused between guilt, relief, new un-wanted responsibility and the desire to be free of any con-tact of any kind with Jean.

The policeman gave me a few particulars and then, seem-ing to exude satisfaction from every seam of his neat blue uniform that one small chore on his day's list had been completed, he walked down the short path to his car and drove away while I stood staring at Tom and George. 'Critically ill,' I repeated. They were silent, as dumbfounded as I was by this turn of events, but I felt they had a sense of relief similar to my own that it was a policeman and not Jean who had rung the doorbell.

'I'll telephone the hospital,' I said, feeling that I was trapped in some macabre web.

They stood close to me and they heard as clearly as I did the words of the ward sister after I had identified myself. 'I am sorry to tell you that Mrs Sandison passed away half-an-hour ago.' Then there was a pause, for I could think of no response to make. 'Are you calling from Jemima Cottage, Achcraggan?' the sister asked now.

'Yes.'

'Then you seem to be the party concerned. We have found a bank book with that address and the name Mrs Duncan Sandison.'

'Yes. That is my stepmother.'

'Somebody will come to make the formal identification?'

'Yes.' I could feel that the woman was worried by my short unmoved responses and she now attempted to humanise me.

'I am very glad that you have been traced, Miss Sandison. We worry about people who are all alone. You will arrange matters?'

'Yes, we shall attend to everything and I'm very grateful, Sister, for all you have done.'

I was not sorry that Jean was dead but I felt sadness as I replaced the receiver, for the sister with the kind voice was not to know that Jean had always been all alone, that by her very nature she had set herself against the rest of the world.

'Well, there it is,' I said to George and Tom.

'Aye,' said George, 'and for the best in the end of it.'

'This is a very queer thing,' Tom said. 'But for your writing and you putting your writing name o' Sandison in the telephone book, the hospital might have had to bury Jean that hated you for all she was fit as if she was some tramp that they found at the roadside.'

'Oh, don't, Tom, for heaven's sake!' I protested.

'What Tom says is true enough,' George insisted. 'Jean always got more from people than she ever gave and was never thankful for any of it and she went on getting to the last. Well, we'll see to the funeral. We'll wait till dinnertime and give Jock a call on the telephone. He will see to identifying her and the whole thing.'

'Jock has enough on his plate,' I said. 'I can see to everything if you two will do the identification bit.'

'No.' He was adamant. 'Maybe this will make Shona see that there are harder things than wee Sandy-Tom. You will call Jock when he will be in from school for his dinner. Come, Tom, it is time we went back down below,' and both of them, their backs very erect, marched out of the house.

'Harder things in life'. I repeated the phrase to myself and it came to me that, once again, they were trying to turn the events of life to the ongoing of life, hoping that the shock of Jean's death might, if only temporarily, release Jock and Shona from the cage of tension in which they lived.

*   *   *

The attendance at the funeral a day or two later was larger than I had expected but there was pathos in the fact that it was not Jean who was mourned but my father all over again, for the people of the district made this very clear. Jean's name was not mentioned as they gathered around the house and garden but many people whom I did not know spoke to me of my father. I did not go to the churchyard but stood at the door of the house watching the cars drive along the road and then up the hill and I was still there in the June sunshine when Sir Ian's car came back to unload himself, Tom and George, followed by Jock's car carrying himself, Roddy and Hamish.

'Well, quite a good turn-out,' Sir Ian said. He always enjoyed any occasion which gathered a few people together. 'Fine old churchyard that. Splendid view from it, for those that can still see, that is.' I wished that I could say as his mother would have done: 'Be silent, Ian,' but George was equally effective with his: 'Get out the bottle, Janet. We could all do with a dram.'

Jock looked thinner, I thought, but when I said: 'Well, tell me how they all are,' he assumed an air of false cheerfulness and said: 'They are all fine but Liz says that Mr de Marnay is a rotten fickler for not coming to see her and she is not going to write to him any more,' so that there was nothing to do but conceal my concern and chat on the level he dictated for the few hours he was with us. I was sorry now, though, that I had allowed him to be burdened with the arrangements for the funeral.

Roddy, in a few snatched moments in the garden, could bring me no comfort either. 'Shona seems to get more like an automaton every day,' he said. 'Sheila and Granny have tried their best but none of us can get through to her. She doesn't listen, doesn't want to listen. It is getting difficult to visit the schoolhouse because of the way she looks at young Rob with those big sad eyes of hers.' Robert was Roddy's and Sheila's two-year-old son. 'She makes you feel that you are torturing her. Jock is a better man than I am. I couldn't stand up to it.'

'Not necessarily better,' I said, 'but different. Jock was brought up largely by George and Tom and he plays things quietly and patiently as they do.'

'I am not sure about all this quietness and patience. At times I think a good-going hair-tearing row would do more good.'

'Shona is not Sheila,' I reminded him. 'I can't imagine

135

anyone achieving a hair-tearing with Shona.'

That evening, when George, Tom and I were alone again, we talked a little about Jean. We talked about her as we had always done, recalling her fits of temper, laughing about them, as if she were still alive but with gratitude that the menace to our peace which she had been during the last few weeks was no longer there.

'We are simply awful about her,' I said after a fit of laughter at some absurdity.

'Maybe the best thing she ever did is to leave us laughing over her going instead of crying,' George said.

'Anyway, there is no use in being hypocrites,' said Tom.

'According to Roddy,' I told them now, 'Shona is no better.'

'I thought Jean's going might make her think twice,' George said, 'and maybe it will yet.'

'You know,' I said, 'I think things like the Old Testament and the law and all that took too much of a grip on Shona.'

'I don't follow,' Tom said.

'I think she thinks things like Sandy-Tom being as he is are a punishment for sin and she can't think how she has sinned so she thinks the punishment is unfair. I remember going on a bit at Sashie once about things not being fair and he told me not to be a fool, talking about life as if it were a game of hockey. I think Shona is still thinking in the game-of-hockey way.'

'If she is, how do you make her stop?' Tom asked.

'Roddy said that if Jock started a good hair-tearing row with her it might help.'

'Jock and Shona *don't* make rows,' George said. 'They are not like Roddy and you, for ever ready to blow the roof off the house if the wind doesn't please them.' He paused before continuing: 'Besides, I doubt if people get into a state like Shona is in – I would call it an unreasonable state myself – whether they can be helped out of it by anybody else. They have to come out of it in their own way.'

'Sashie helped *me* out of a lot of rubbish I was thinking at one time,' I argued.

'You wouldn't have come out of it unless you were willing to come. You are far more thrawn than Shona too. You came out of your rubbish because your time had come to come out of it.'

'All right, I take your point. People have to be willing to change before they can change so how does one make them willing?'

'They have to come to it on their own.'

'So we are just back where we started?'

'Just that,' George agreed. 'But sooner or later Shona will come to see that Sandy-Tom is not the worst thing that can happen.'

'Then I hope it is sooner,' I said.

The turning-point came sooner than I had expected and in the most unexpected and alarming way. On the last evening in June I picked up the telephone to hear the voice of Liz: 'Aunt Janet, it's me, Liz, and the boys.' The child sounded scared, worried, as she backed herself up with her brothers. 'Aunt Janet, I rang up because we – well – we are all in a muddle.'

'What sort of a muddle, Liz?' I asked as calmly as I could but George and Tom rose from their chairs and came to join me at the window.

'Daddy and Mum and Roddy have all gone away to the hospital.'

'Is Mum sick?' I asked.

'She hasn't been very well for a long time but it was *Daddy* –' the sobs of fear came jerking along the line – 'that the men carried downstairs on a stretcher and put him in the ambulance.'

My impulse was to repeat the word 'Daddy' with even more emphasis than Liz had given to it but I managed to say instead: 'Liz, we must all try to be very sensible. The men have taken Daddy to the hospital to make him better, you know. Now, have you and the boys had supper?'

'Yes. We had bacon and sausages and beans.'

'That's fine. And have you put Sandy-Tom to bed?'

'Yes but he isn't sleeping yet. Fat-Mary is here and he likes her and she is not usually here at bedtime and he is having fun.'

'Is Fat-Mary staying till Mum comes home?'

'Yes.'

'You must give her coffee and biscuits or something around nine o'clock if Mum isn't home by then.'

'All right.' Liz's voice was calmer now.

'And do you think you and the boys can stay up till Mum gets back and ask her to ring George and Tom and me?'

'Oh yes!' There was relief in the permission to stay up late on this frightening evening.

'Tell me, Liz, when did Daddy first get sick?'

'It was yesterday. He didn't get up in the morning. But, Aunt Janet, he wasn't proper throwing-up sick!' There was a loud note of protest that this illness that had attacked her father was beyond the ken of Liz and her brothers who knew only of 'throwing-up sick' due to over-eating at parties or at berry-picking time. 'He only had a sore back,' she added.

I felt relieved. Unlike Liz, I was glad that Jock was not throwing-up sick, which can be one of the symptoms of heart failure. 'Listen, Liz, women often get throwing-up sick especially when they are going to have babies but men very seldom do. It is good that Daddy isn't throwing-up sick.'

'Is it *really*?'

'Yes, Liz. It is *really*. I think Daddy must have strained his back somehow but the hospital will put it right.'

'Will they give him X-rays?'

'Probably.'

'Will they hurt?'

'No. The hospital won't hurt him at all in any way.'

'Aunt Janet,' came the voice of Duncan, 'we didn't like them carrying him on a stretcher.'

'I know but that was so that he wouldn't feel his sore back.'

'Oh.' The voice sounded relieved.

'Aunt Janet,' came the voice of Gee, 'we've got the holidays but we don't want to come up till Dad is better. Is that all right?'

'Of course,' I said. 'We are going to look forward to Dad being better and we'll go for a sail up the firth in the mail-boat.'

'It will soon be the pips again,' Liz said now, 'so we'll stop but we'll give Mum the money for the call. It will cost quite a lot.'

'Never mind that. Tell Mum I said you were to call George, Tom and me any time you like and we will pay for the calls. What are you going to do now?'

'We'll play cards, I suppose, till Mum comes home.'

'I'll give a shilling to the one who wins most games, six-pence to the next and threepence to the next. Tell Fat-Mary that I am asking her to keep your scores.'

'All right,' and there came the three goodnights one after the other.

George and Tom looked stunned. 'What in the world can have come over Jock?' George asked.

'We'll have to wait until we hear from Shona,' was all I could say. But when Shona telephoned about two hours later, there was little she could tell us. 'We both thought it was 'flu,' she said. 'He was full of aches and pains and his temperature was high but the doctor hasn't told me what he thinks. They are going to do some tests and we'll know the day after tomorrow. He said he was feeling better before I left the hospital. They gave him something to ease his pains.'

We lived with this scant knowledge until the third evening when she telephoned again. 'He has got brucellosis,' she said.

'What in God's name is that?' I asked.

'It is a disease people catch from cattle. There is a lot of it among the cattle in this part of the country it seems. Doctor Turner admits now that he suspected it right away. That is why he took him to hospital.'

'How serious is it, as a disease, I mean?'

'They can treat it. The doctor says not to worry but sometimes it takes a long time to clear up. He may be in hospital for weeks.' There was a long pause and then: 'Janet, I hate to bother you with this but could you take Liz and the boys for a bit? Sheila would take them but they hate the city and would be sure to get into trouble and they hate going to the hospital and I can't leave them here on their own and Fat-Mary can't be here all the time and—'

'Of course they must come here,' I broke in on her worried near-hysterical harangue. 'Put them on a train and I'll meet them at Inverness. The three will take good care of Sandy-Tom, or would you like me to come down for them by car?'

'Oh I don't want to send Sandy-Tom up!' she said in a pleading protesting voice. 'He is such a happy fellow and no trouble and if I have him with me I won't miss the others so much. He can stay with me can't he? He loves the car and going to the hospital and everything.' She sounded as if half of her secure world had fallen about her ears and as if I were trying to rob her of the other half.

'I don't think I *can* part with Sandy-Tom just now,' she was saying.

'You don't *have* to part with him,' I said. 'I was only trying to be helpful in my clumsy way. You keep Sandy-Tom and send the other three.'

'He has a way of making me feel that things are not so bad,' she said, as if asking me to excuse a weakness and I led her away into the arrangements for the despatch of Liz, Duncan and Gee.

'You heard?' I said to George and Tom. 'Sandy-Tom is winning. Worried as she is, she sounded more like herself than she has done all this long time.'

'It is very strange,' Tom said, 'how it sometimes needs another bad thing to make a bad thing better.'

* * *

Jock remained in hospital for six weeks in all because of the recurrent fever which would raise all our hopes by disappearing for two days, then flaring up again for no apparent reason, a symptom, Doctor Hay told us, that was characteristic of the disease.

Liz, Duncan and Gee, when I met them at Inverness two days after Shona's telephone call, were entirely different from the young fiends they had been during their last visit.

'It is queer,' Liz said. 'Since Daddy got sick, Mum has got better.'

'It would never do for everybody to be sick at once,' George told her.

During the two days since Jock's illness was diagnosed, it seemed, they had sensed the change in their mother and with their young resilience had already returned to their normal selves. They were worried, of course, about their father and not yet accustomed to the idea that he was a mortal who could fall sick, but there was so much to engage their attention that their anxiety showed only at the time of the evening telephone call and became less acute as the weeks went by.

Early in July, Monica arrived, much to my surprise, to stay at the Poyntdale hotel.

'Just fancy!' said Liz in an affected voice when I told her who had telephoned. '*Lady* Monica and *Sir* Ian! Our family gets stylisher and stylisher all the time.'

'Not with you talking like that,' said Gee the Professor. 'There's no such word as stylisher.'

'Stylish phooey,' said Duncan, 'and they're not family anyway.'

'And just as well,' I said. 'With the complications this family can make and the arguments it can get into it is quite big enough already.'

Such arguments died away, however, before the greater interest of invitations from Hamish and Sam to go fishing.

'Keep a firm hand on them,' Shona would adjure me over the telephone but I found the children very reasonable and easy to manage.

Monica was having tea with George, Tom, Sir Ian and me next day when the doorbell rang and I said : 'Hang it, it will be a Lady from Sussex. Can you get rid of her, George?'

'Lady from Sussex?' Monica asked.

'Our name for the people who read our books.'

But the caller was not a Lady from Sussex. It was Andrew Boyd and Monica, as ever, was the first to make the social response.

'Good afternoon, Andrew,' she said.

'Hello, Monica. I didn't know you were up here.'

'I arrived last night. When did you come up?'

'I've just arrived.'

'You two know each other?' I asked in the unnecessary way one does. 'Tea, Andrew?'

Suddenly I knew why Monica was in Achcraggan and suddenly I knew too whom Monica intended to marry. Unbelievable, at first thought, as such a union might be, my six years of wartime intimacy with Monica, during which I had observed many pursuits of males on her part, made my very bones aware of *that* tone of voice, *that* sidelong smile, *that* glance of her green eyes as she looked up at Andrew.

George and Tom were attacked by an uneasiness with which they seemed to affect Sir Ian and after exchanging a few words with Andrew, all three took themselves off down to the barn, and Monica and Andrew did not stay very long either.

The children were out on a fishing picnic with Sam and, alone in the house, I recognised in myself a rising indignation and ill-temper, the reasons for which I began to identify. I disliked, I found, the Vénus-toute-entière attitude of Monica, the determination of her pursuit. She was much older than she had been during the war and a much more finished and deadly femme fatale. But more than by Monica, I found, my indignation and ill-temper were being aroused by the attitude of Andrew Boyd. He seemed to be dazzled by Monica, to be taken in, as I found myself describing it, and proving me to be utterly wrong about his nature, for the one thing about him of which I had been certain was that he was incapable of being taken in by anyone in any way. We are all egotists and in the final analysis I was furious that Monica, by making Andrew behave like a fascinated rabbit, was proving my estimate of him to be wrong.

Later that evening, when the children were in bed, George said : 'I didna know Monica knew Andra Boyd.'

'Nor me either,' said Tom. 'All the time she was at Poyntdale, he was only here for a day or two here and there and was hardly seen about the village. He mostly stayed in the house with his aunties.'

Their uneasiness of the afternoon persisted. I do not think they had recognised as clearly as I had the signals of Monica in pursuit, but some adumbration had reached their acute minds. George and Tom had never had any use for fairy tales or romances about Cinderellas and princes and peasant boys and princesses and the very thought of anything in common between Monica and Andrew Boyd was an absurdity in their eyes.

Because Andrew had told me that he did not want Achcraggan to know of his enterprises in the district, I had not even told Tom and George of his ownership of Poyntdale but now, quite illogically and unfairly, I felt that he had let me down by being such a fool about Monica that I had no compunction about letting *him* down by not keeping his secret. Besides, I told myself, telling George and Tom was like telling the secret to Ben Wyvis. They would never tell any more than the Ben would.

'They would have met when he bought Poyntdale,' I said.

'Andra Boyd buy Poyntdale?' George scoffed. 'You are out o' your head.'

'No I'm not,' I said and told them of Andrew's plans for Achcraggan.

'He is a clever young devil,' George then said unwillingly. 'He can't have got as rich as that just by ordinary thieving. There must be brains in him too.'

'He has certainly got brains.'

'Ye know, George,' Tom said thoughtfully, 'Duncan always held that he was a dog that had been given a bad name.' He turned to me. 'Himself, your father, always held that it wasn't Andra that stole the money out of the butcher's shop. In fact, I have always suspicioned that your father helped him to get away when the police came after him. Your father aye held that Andra was too clever to shit on his own doorstep like that.'

'Now that I mind on it, these were his very words – too clever,' George agreed. 'Himself always said it was Curly Sandy that took the money and goodness knows Sandy was drunk for a month after the money went until he fell into the harbour and drowned with his pockets full o' pound notes, only him being dead, nobody ever spoke about the money that was on him. Of course, Andra was a devilish cunning mischievious lad when he was at school. No wonder he got a bad name. He pinched all the apples and plums out of all the gardens and used to sell them to the other bairns over at the Academy and he was running a gambling game for his own profit in a corner of the football field and him but twelve years old. And he would poach the sea-lice off a salmon's back. He used to sell the salmon in Inverness, right under the noses o' the police and the water bailies.' There was enthusiasm in George's voice as he recounted the poaching misdeeds but the enthusiasm gave way to puzzlement as he added: 'Still, it was queer to see him and Monica blethering away at their ease. I would have said he had a notion of her if it wasn't so outlandish.'

'Outlandish or not,' I said, '*she* has a notion of *him*.'

'Ach away with you,' said Tom. 'Monica will stick among her own kind.'

'Kinds of people are not so distinct as they used to be,' I argued. 'You wait and see. And Monica's family isn't as rich as it used to be and Monica is not the kind for genteel poverty.'

'She is after his money, you mean?' George asked.

'Yes, but when she marries him she will be a good wife as they say – play the game and all that.'

'You talk about *her* marrying *him* as if he had no say in the thing. Andra may not be willing.'

'As I see it, he won't have much say. The only man I have ever known who didn't fall to Monica on the hunt was Twice.'

'Twice?' Both stared at me as if I had said something blasphemous.

'You needn't look so scandalised,' I said, 'and it's an old story now, anyway, but you remember that time Monica arrived at Reachfar and had the nervous breakdown? You all thought she was a poor little thing that Twice and I had mistreated, but before she ended up at Reachfar she had been chasing Twice round hotel bedrooms in Birmingham in a pink satin nightdress.'

I had thought sincerely that this episode between Monica and myself had been forgotten and forgiven long ago and I was genuinely amazed that I remembered even the detail of the pink satin nightdress. It seemed to indicate that I had forgotten nothing and this made me question whether I had genuinely forgiven anything. While George and Tom stared at me in only half-belief, I went on: 'Her carry-on with Twice was explained at the time as part of the breakdown but it seems to me that when people break down mentally they stop being what they pretended to be and turn into what they really are for a bit. When I was ill out there in St Jago, I turned into a drunk who didn't know who she was. Well, I have always liked drink and I have never been too sure who I am. You read about people murdering in a fit of madness. I don't think they are mad at all. They are just born killers who turn into their real selves for a time. And I think Monica is a born man-hunter, only she puts it more politely and calls herself the marrying kind.'

'You speak as if marrying was some sort of sin,' George said.

'No, I don't think it a sin. I just don't like Monica's way of doing it.'

We let the subject drop, but an area of irritation remained in my mind that Andrew Boyd was deserting the image I had formed of him by responding to Monica's lure in such a banal way. The last I had expected of him was the banal.

At the end of two weeks, Andrew and Monica went south, driving their two separate cars but virtually together, and Liz said: 'I suppose they'll get married in London now. I hoped they would do it up here and I could have been a bridesmaid again.'

'You'd best be careful o' the bridesmaid business,' Tom told her. 'Three times a bridesmaid, never a bride, they say.'

'Just fancy!' said Liz, her eyes round. 'That just goes to show they don't teach you anything at school. Sir Ian, we learn all our most real things from the family, mostly Tom and George.'

'Never learned anythin' at school meself that mattered a damn either,' Sir Ian agreed with her.

'If you get married again like Lady Monica, Aunt Janet, don't ask *me* to be your bridesmaid. I have finished with that. I want to be a bride some day.'

'Ha-ha-ha-hee-hee-hee, elephants' eggs in a rhubarb tree!' her brothers chorused. 'Who would want to marry *you*?'

'Actually,' said Liz, 'I *could* be your bridesmaid, Aunt Janet. That would be only twice I've been it. I'll save my second time for you.'

'Don't bother,' I told her. 'I am not going to need a bridesmaid.'

*　　*　　*

What with the children, the work on the barn, the Ladies from Sussex at the door, time flew past while Jock made his slow dreary fight against his infection. He was no longer seriously ill or even confined to bed but the infection was still present and the battle was now more against boredom than anything else. We had two red-letter evenings in the week when the children spoke to him on the telephone. On these days one or another of them would say: 'I wish it was telephone time,' but otherwise they were very contented, co-operative and busy around the barn with the craftsmen or doing various things on the beach.

By midsummer, when Miss Arden arrived at Poyntdale for her promised visit, the world of writing and London had come to seem very far away, while I cooked, made jam and ran the house. I was a little nervous of this, feeling that it was one thing for me, as an adjunct of her brother's firm, to chat to her in her sitting-room and quite another for her to see me at home with my entourage of children and elderly men. No other of Canterbury Arden's writers, I felt sure, lived as I did in a welter of cooking and jam-making, wearing an apron and wielding a rolling-pin rather than a pen for most of the day.

Her visit, however, was a success from the start. I told Sir Ian of her impending arrival; on the following day she drove down to the cottage with him and it was already obvious that they were going to be friends. George and Tom, because she was connected with that other-world of publishing, were inclined to stand a little in awe of her at first but when Tom and the children were busy with the newspaper during her second visit, she asked suddenly: 'Don't you wear glasses even for reading, Mr Forbes? I have to wear them and I am sure I am younger than you,' the awe died away.

'You will call me Tom, if you please,' said Tom. 'No, I have not taken to the spectacles as yet.'

'I have specs all the time,' Gee said.

'So I notice,' said Miss Arden.

'Except for football and cricket. It is because of being long-sighted.'

'That is very interesting.'

'He was born like that,' Liz informed her, 'like Dunk being born with red hair. I am the only one that's normal.'

'Except that you're a girl,' said Gee. 'The rest of us are boys. Boys are normal in our family.'

The lips of Liz tightened, her shoulders began to square and I was feeling that Miss Arden was going to experience a Generation battle when she said: 'I prefer girls. After all, I was a girl myself once.' At this, the three pairs of eyes widened as they looked back over the long years and then Liz spoke for all three. 'We are going down to the beach, Aunt Janet. Will you ring the bell for tea-time?'

Like Sir Ian, Miss Arden began to spend most of her time at the cottage. When it was fine, they walked about the village and the beach or sat in the garden; when it rained, they played cards or board games with Tom, George and the children.

It was all very pleasant, this feeling of lying in a summer backwater where there were no currents or winds and everybody was happy, but I began to long for the winter days, when the house would be quiet and I could absorb myself in the conflict of my writing.

'It is not that I don't like the kids and Miss Arden and Sir Ian but—' I tried to explain to George and Tom.

'You are just in need of the fir trees above the well,'

George told me, admitting for the first time that he had always known of this 'Thinking Place' of my childhood.

'You pay far too much heed to people whatever,' Tom said, 'and all Liz's gabbing about Monica and Andrew Boyd getting married. What does it matter if Monica marries him? He can look after himself.'

It annoyed me that Tom had noticed my caring about this matter.

'It *doesn't* matter to me,' I said loudly and angrily because the statement was a lie. It did matter to me that Monica should beguile Andrew into marriage but I did not know how or why it mattered and this made me angrier still.

'When you were little,' Tom continued, 'you were everlasting asking about this one and that one. If it wasn't the Miss Boyds, it was old Granny Fraser and when one told you what you were asking, you said that people were driving you out of your head. You just weren't reasonable and you are not reasonable yet. If you didna want Sir Ian and Miss Arden to come here, why did you go speaking to them about Achcraggan in the first of it?'

'I have told you already that people have to talk about *some*thing,' I defended myself. 'And it's not that I don't want them to be here—'

'The barn down there will be ready before too long,' George said, 'and then you can take to the beach when you get tired of people. Now that you are the half-hundred, you are more like Her Old Self than ever.'

This expression of theirs, 'the half-hundred' for the age of fifty had always made me laugh and my complaints about people impinging on me died away.

The conversation had taken place in the morning when the children had gone out and George and Tom were having their after-breakfast smoke by the fire. As they tapped out their pipes, the telephone rang and I picked it up to hear the words: 'Is this Miss Janet Sandison the writer person?'

'Sashie!' I said. 'Where are you?'

'At a tiny airport near Inverness, darling. May I come to call?'

'Oh yes, come right away.' I put the receiver down and said: 'It's Sashie. He will be here in an hour.'

Tom and George looked at one another. 'After all that speaking we just did,' said George, 'about wanting people and not wanting them, and being driven out of your head by them, did you hear her on that telephone, Tom?'

'But Sashie is different,' I said. 'Get out of here, you two and let me get the house tidied up.'

*   *   *

Sashie certainly was different but nearly two years of separation from him had made me forget precisely how different. In St Jago, once, looking at his brilliantly coloured clothes, I had told him that he would be a riot in Achcraggan, but when he stepped out of the car, he contrived to appear very small and almost colourless in tweeds of an indeterminate greenish-grey. I had spoken of him a great deal to Tom and George and I think that, expecting someone flamboyant, they were disappointed or perhaps relieved at first to meet this small man who moved slowly and quietly. Sashie's resources with his artificial legs seemed to be endless and he had adopted this slow gait for Scotland instead of the mincing dancing gait he used in St Jago as he had adopted the tweed suit as opposed to the vivid shirts and slacks he had affected in the tropics.

He shook hands quietly with myself, George and Tom but when I brought the children forward, he looked at Liz and his black eyes sparkled. 'Ma Princesse Lointaine,' he said. It will be obvious by this time that my niece Liz is not easy to overawe but she was silenced and spellbound by Sashie, her large blue eyes fixed on him, her mouth a little open as if she were short of breath and her brothers, who always unconsciously followed her lead in situations strange to

150

them, also stood silent until with one accord all three ran out into the back garden.

The hired car was sent away, George carried Sashie's bag into what had been the parlour where the aspidistra still adorned the windowsill in its pink china pot.

'There it is,' I told Sashie.

'Darling, it is too *too* magnificent. It is really mine?'

'You are sure you want the ugly b—' said George and stopped short.

'More than most things in the world. It will be just the thing for my new flat in London.'

'You have taken a flat?' I asked.

'Yes. It is quite awful and I loathe it but it will do for the moment. I am in a hurry this trip. I am going back round Montreal and Toronto.'

'I told you you would never retire from that hotel,' I said. 'How long can you stay with us?'

'Only till Monday.'

'Monday?' George said frowning. 'But this is Friday already.'

'It wasn't worth your while coming away up here for a couple of days,' Tom protested.

'Oh, but it was. Janet, I long to see the rest of your domain.'

'There isn't much to see but we are extending it as I told you. Come down and see the barn.'

From what I had told them of Sashie, I think that George and Tom had preferred to think of him at a safe distance and had been a little alarmed at his sudden descent upon us, but by the time we sat down to have lunch, they were treating him as an older member of the family like myself and the children had decided that he was not so strange after all.

'What's for dinner?' Liz enquired.

'Broth, boiled beef and apple tart,' I replied. 'Go and wash your hands.'

'With Sashie here it should be caviar,' she told me and to Sashie: 'Do you have caviar at your hotel? Is it nice?'

'Yes at the hotel but no it isn't nice. It is quite revolting. British soldiers who were in Russia once called it fish jam and that describes it exactly. I much prefer broth and apple tart.'

'Fish jam. Yuckers!'

'It is sturgeon's roe really,' Gee contributed.

'Sturgeon yourself,' said Duncan scornfully. 'Tripe.'

'It isn't tripe. Tripe is cows' stomachs. I read about caviar in a book.'

'You and your reading.'

'If you lot don't go and get cleaned up,' I threatened, 'you'll get no dinner at all.'

While George, Tom and the children washed up after the meal, I baked some scones and put a cake in the oven while Sashie chatted to us all, then Sir Ian and Miss Arden, who had been in Inverness that morning, arrived in time for tea.

'Good God,' Sir Ian greeted Sashie, 'how did *you* get here?'

'In a tiny aeroplane,' said Sashie while the children giggled, 'and the same to you. What are *you* doing here?'

'Nice part o' the country, nice people too. Rosemary, this fellah is called Sashie de Marnay, knew him in St Jago. This is Miss Arden.'

'How d'you do, Miss Arden?' said Sashie and then to Sir Ian: 'That's all lies. Nobody has *ever* known me in St Jago or anywhere else,' which made the children giggle more loudly than ever, for Sashie's subversive attitude towards an 'elder and better' like Sir Ian was new and delightful to them.

Sir Ian ignored him and turned again to Miss Arden. 'He's the fellah,' he informed her, 'that had the shootin' with Missis Janet in the drawin'-room. Damnedest carry-on I ever saw.'

'Shooting?' said the children one after the other but the

tale missed being told for perhaps the hundredth time because Hamish arrived with a brace of pheasants and stayed to tea. Then, in the middle of tea, a touring bus stopped at the gate and through the open window we heard the voice of the courier as he began his spiel over his address system: 'Ladies and gentlemen, this is the home of Janet Sandison—'

'Bless me liver and lights,' said Sashie.

'Aunt Janet, a whole bus-load of Ladies from Sussex,' said Liz. 'Come on, you two. Let's go out and look.'

'Sit down,' I bellowed at the children and the bus drove away along the road.

'Does this happen often?' Sashie asked.

'Too often and it is largely your fault,' I told him.

'Sashie's fault?' Sir Ian barked at me. 'What's *he* got to do with that bunch o' women?'

'He was the one who practically forced me into this writing business.'

Sashie turned to the children to say provocatively: 'I don't know why your aunt is such a contumacious woman. The rest of you Sandisons seem to be very even-tempered.'

'What's contumacious?' Liz asked, giggling again.

'It's what Fat-Mary calls coontermashus,' Gee explained.

'And means backside against all waters,' said George.

'Be quiet for pity's sake,' I said. 'Does anybody want more tea?'

When Liz was going to bed that night, she said: 'Aunt Janet, did you hear what Sashie said to me when he came today?'

'Yes.'

'It was French, wasn't it? I don't know much French yet and he speaks so fast. What did he say? What did it mean?'

'Ma princesse lointaine,' I said slowly. 'It is difficult to translate into English and it doesn't sound so pretty. It means my faraway princess but lointaine is such a musical word compared with the English word, don't you think?'

She nodded and then said thoughtfully: 'He is sort of lointaine himself. Even although he is right here, he is still lointaine.'

'Except that, being masculine, he is lointain without the "e".'

'You are a proper old coontermashus pernickety about anything to do with words,' she said, getting into bed while I wondered if my brother and Shona would approve of Sashie's influence on the children which made them criticise their elders and betters.

* * *

The two following days of Sashie's visit passed in a similar way, in the usual welter of people, meals, washing up and arguments between the children but Sashie and I sat up late on the Sunday night after all the others had gone to bed.

'People are too extraordinary,' he said. 'Think of Sir Ian going in for a twilight romance. But there is one blessing. He can never refer to his Rosemary as a nice little woman. She is quite enormous and makes you look utterly shrimpish.'

'Sashie, do you really think—?'

'I should not be at all surprised. After all, think of what his Cousin Emmie went and did. Where, by the way, are Edward and his bit of Chinese torture?'

'Your guess is as good as mine. Sir Ian never mentions them and I don't ask. Actually, I'll be quite glad if Sir Ian and Miss Arden do something.'

'How delicately you put something which is really rather indelicate but, there, people will be people.'

'Won't they just? Remember I told you Monica was here? She is on the hunt too, hard after a man called Andrew Boyd—' and I went on to tell him of Andrew.

'And why,' he asked when I had finished, 'don't you want Monica to have Andrew Boyd?'

'Don't be silly. I don't give a damn whether she has him or not.'

'Don't you? Then it must be that *I* don't want her to have him.'

'What can you mean?'

'I simply have a feeling that Monica shouldn't have Andrew and I thought the feeling was coming from you but it is probably my own feeling because I have never wanted Monica to have anything she wanted.'

'Why?'

'Because she has always wanted too much and has always got too much. She is a rapacious little beast. I never *took* to Monica, as Tom and George have it.'

'I didn't know that. You were always very civil about her in St Jago.'

'She was four thousand miles away then,' he reminded me.

'I had never thought of her as rapacious,' I said, 'but, yes, she does rather go for what she wants, always has done. Dear me, I am fifty years old and losing all my illusions.'

'And at fifty it is high time you did. I should like to meet this Andrew Boyd.'

'Why?'

'You made him sound rather like my kind, darling.'

'I couldn't have done. No two people could be more different.' I then added almost against my will and rather waspishly: 'But call Monica when you are in London – I can give you her number – and no doubt she will arrange a meeting.'

'No, I shan't do that. I don't want to meet him in the company of Monica or any other illusion. Now, tell me, do you live all the time as you have lived since I have been here?'

'Live?'

'All the cooking and barn-building and Ladies from Sussex and Sir Ian and his large Herb booming around the place?'

'Oh, I see. Yes, this is how it seems to go on but we don't have the children here all the time of course.'

'And do you write at all?'

'Of course. Three novels are out but we still have six in hand. I have written two since I came home. You didn't think I had stopped because I didn't say anything in letters? You know I don't like talking about writing.'

He made no direct answer but said instead: 'You know, darling, that barn down there is not going to do you one damn of good. You would contrive to get yourself mixed up with a gaggle of people even if you went and sat right on the very top of the North Pole.'

'You are quite wrong,' I argued. '*I* didn't ask Sir Ian or his large Herb as you call her to come here. Monica came chasing Andrew Boyd who came because he has property here. I didn't invite all the Ladies from Sussex and the children are here because of Jock—'

'Like myself,' he interrupted me, 'they are all here fundamentally because you are here.'

'That is rubbish. I don't specially want them to be here. I often complain to Tom and George about what pests people can be, even the family.'

'I know. They told me.'

I was flabbergasted. 'Then they had no business.'

'Yes they had. They know that I love you nearly as much as they do and they wanted advice. They asked if it wouldn't be better if they stayed on in the cottage here when you moved into the barn.' I was horrified that anything I had said had made George and Tom think in these terms and amazed that Sashie, in such a short time, had gained their confidence to the extent that they had talked to him in a way in which, I believed, they would not have talked even to Jock. 'But that's awful,' I spluttered at last.

'Yes, I told them that,' said Sashie calmly. 'I told them you would not like that at all.' He now seemed to go off at a tangent. 'Do you remember staying with me at Silver Beach?'

'What a stupid question.'

'Do you remember what you did there, after you were well, I mean?'

'Yes, of course. I wrote all day and talked to you in the evenings.'

'You did *not* write all day. You copied into type work that you had already written. Where did you do all that writing?'

'What is all this about?' I asked. 'I did it at Guinea Corner before Twice got ill. You know that.'

'Yes I do but you seem to have forgotten. You did all that writing, seven novels, with the house full of excursions and alarms, people shouting about cricket, arguments about the sugar factory, Sir Ian booming around, not to mention Madame's calls on your time and me darting in and out. Then, when I offered you the quiet seclusion of my gentleman's residence, you did not write one creative word but copy-typed from morning till night.'

'You were the one who egged me on,' I expostulated. 'You couldn't wait to airmail those typescripts.'

'If Silver Beach had been a place where you could write,' he said, 'I could have egged you on until I and the eggs were addled and you would not have typed a word.'

'Oh rubbish! Anyway, what are we talking about?'

'You. You hate to be called an artist but I don't object to the word and I used to be something of an artist. All artists are not alike but I think I have discovered that you and I have a similarity. I could always work better when things were not going smoothly or were even actively annoying me. When you saw me in *Giselle*, I was probably, in my private self, in a blind fury. All through that season, Mama and I were having a series of rows about an admirer of hers. Mama didn't want admirers but she was always collecting them and I hated most of them. I suppose I was jealous but

I never thought any of them good enough for her. Anyhow, I was livid half the time but this sort of tension paid off for me as a dancer. I am drooling on in this egotistical way to try to make you see that you, although you may not know it, create your own tensions. I could scream at Mama in my self-important way that I had to *dance* tonight while she played the fool with this disgusting man and you – although you are too well-behaved to scream as I did – can complain to George and Tom about the people around you, but you yourself are attracting the people because you need them, just as I needed the screaming row when I knew perfectly well in the depths of my mind that Mama had no intention of playing the fool with any man.'

I laughed. 'I can't imagine you in a screaming rage, Sashie. I'd love to have seen it.'

'You will see it immediately, elderly as I am now, if you don't attend to the real import of what I am trying to make you understand. What I am saying is that you write under tension or against resistance and that you yourself create the tensions and resistances. You complain to George and Tom that the world and life and people and so on are too much with you but the truth is that you can't do without them. I think I have made George and Tom understand and I have told them to take no notice of your complaints and tempers. I think I have even convinced them that they are a help to you by simply being here so that you have to cook their meals. The question is whether I have convinced *you*.'

'I think I see,' I said. 'Miss Arden said once that it was the way I wrote that made the Ladies from Sussex call. She said I was my own enemy.'

'That is precisely what I am *not* saying,' said Sashie with some vehemence. 'My point is that without these tensions you create around yourself, you would be unable to write at all and you can complain about the nuisance value of the world around you until Doomsday but you will go on attracting nuisances. But all this is by the way. What I want you very much to know, if you are not aware of it already, is that George and Tom are so proud of you that they will do *anything* to help you, even break through their reserve to ask my advice about you. And they have this beautiful phrase they use: Since *we* got into the writing business. They feel they are in it with you up to the hilt but they weren't sure that you wanted them there. I think I have convinced them that you need them and want them but I think you should try not to run the red flag up to the masthead, as Twice used to call it, quite so often in their hearing.'

'I'll try, Sashie,' I promised. 'It never entered my head that they thought I was building the barn to try to get away from *them*. Actually, I am not building it to get away from anybody.' This was something I had discovered the second before I spoke the words. 'I am building it because I don't like these poky little rooms that one can't see out of and this will be the first time since Reachfar that I shall have had a place that I feel is really my own.'

'And it is going to be exactly like your place should be, a great lump of granite with a fire in the middle. Shall I paint you a picture as a contribution to it?'

'Yes, please. Now tell me about you and why you are going to Canada, as if I didn't know you were only doing it to get up in aeroplanes.'

'No. I really have a good reason for going.' He looked down at his small hands. 'I have done a small thing, but something I never thought I would do. I— Do you remember when we went to Caleb and Trixie's wedding?'

'Could one ever forget?'

'I have turned it into a ballet. I have called it *Meeting and Parting*. A Canadian company is dancing it in Montreal and Toronto.'

'You secretive little monster. All those letters and you never gave an inkling.'

'You don't like to talk about what you are doing and

neither do I. Actually, it was really because of M. and P. that I haven't been over to visit you sooner. It is true that Don was out of action for a time and I wanted very much to come to see you but I made myself believe that I had to get M. and P. going before I came – I was creating tension, if you like.'

'Tell me about the ballet. No. That is silly. One will have to see it. You used the St Jagoan music?'

'Of course. The wedding scene comes over very well and it is more or less just as we saw it that day. That was what sparked the whole thing off.'

'Sashie, I am so glad about it.'

'So wish me luck and let's not talk about it any more. There is something else I want to talk about if you don't urgently want to go to bed. It is getting late.'

'I never want to go to bed when I am with you.'

'A doubtful compliment perhaps. I shall ignore it. Liz took me for a walk around the village this morning. Who owns those two lovely old houses round by the church?'

'I am not sure which houses you mean,' I said, 'and who owns them would be hard to say,' and I went on to tell him how property in Achcraggan tended to fall into dereliction.

'That flat I took in London is a crashing mistake,' he said. 'I must be growing senile, letting my mind set rigid in the idea that London is the only place in this country to be. London as it is now is a place to be out of, not in.'

'You mean that you would like to have a place here in Achcraggan?'

'If you could bear it, darling. I should try not to get in your way. One or two of those red sandstone houses are precisely my period, eighteenth century and all that.'

'Sashie, it would be marvellous to have you here. The man you want is Andrew Boyd.'

'Do I?'

I told him of Andrew's interest in the village. 'Before you leave tomorrow,' I said, 'we'll telephone his office in

Birmingham. Would you be able to get to Birmingham?'

'I could go there tomorrow. I have a little air taxi.'

'I thought you came up on the scheduled London flight.'

'No. I use small machines whenever I can.'

'What an addict you are.'

Breakfast the next morning was an uproar because the children had hatched a plan by which they would borrow Sir Ian's car and Sam to take them to the airport to see Sashie take off. When I vetoed this, they fell back on their subsidiary plan by which they would pool all their holiday money, borrow some more from Tom and George and hire Little John's car.

'*Some*body has to help with the asperdester,' said Liz.

'The aspidistra is not going,' I said. 'We are going to keep it until Sashie's place in this country is ready.'

The argument went on until Sashie intervened. 'It would be far better if you stayed here,' he said. 'Stay here and go down to the beach about quarter past twelve. I shall ask my pilot to fly a little circle round Achcraggan before we set off south.'

At this, their excitement could not be accommodated around the table or in the house and with large slices of toast in each hand, all three went whooping down the garden.

'You shouldn't indulge them like that,' I said.

'I am really indulging myself. I couldn't get up to Reachfar but now I hope to see it from the air.'

Shortly after ten, I telephoned Birmingham and was fortunate enough to reach Andrew. 'Andrew, this is Janet Sandison.'

'Good morning Janet. Are you all well? What can I do for you?' I told him that Sashie wanted to see him. 'Any time this afternoon,' he said. 'I'll be here all day. It will be a pleasure.'

'Janet, I do thank you,' Sashie said.

'Don't thank me. Thank Andrew. For somebody who

must have both hands and both feet mixed up in some hanky-panky all the time, he is extraordinarily accessible.'

The car drove Sashie away at eleven o'clock with the whole family as well as Miss Arden, Sir Ian and Sam waving it out of sight, after which, all of us, except the children, who were looking forward to the aeroplane, felt very flat.

'For such a little fellow,' George said over the coffee cups, 'he leaves a big hole behind him.'

'He has quietened down a bit,' Sir Ian said. 'Gettin' older like the rest of us, I suppose. But you want to keep an eye on him. Clever little devil, cleverer than he makes out, ye know.'

'How did he lose his legs, Janet?' Miss Arden asked.

'What d'ye mean, legs?' barked Sir Ian.

'In the war,' I said. 'He was a fighter pilot and was shot down in the Far East.'

'Tragic,' Miss Arden commented.

'Are *you* tellin' *me* that Sashie—' Sir Ian glared from Miss Arden to myself.

'Yes we are,' I told him, 'and the less said about it the better. If you ever let Sashie know you know you will wish you hadn't.'

'Don't be stoopid. As if I would— Dammit, to think of that little devil takin' everybody in all those years. I always thought he was *you* know—'

'I know you did. Sashie meant you to think that.'

'How long have *you* known about him?'

'Since just after Twice and I came to Guinea Corner.'

'You are as bad as he is,' he exploded at me. 'All you writin' an' actin' an' paintin' people are the same, full o' hidden meanin's an' secrets so nobody knows where they are with you.'

'You are being quite unreasonable, Ian,' said Miss Arden in a stern voice that reminded me of Sir Ian's mother.

'Well the thing *ain't* reasonable,' he argued before frowning at me again and saying: 'Often wondered what you saw

162

in him. Beginnin' to see it now. Does he write books too?'

'No.'

'I'll bet he's up to somethin',' he said as if Sashie and I, over the weekend, had been hatching a sinister plot against all mankind.

'I am going down to the bairns to watch for the aeroplane,' George said.

'And me too,' said Tom.

We all went down to the beach and quite soon the little red and silver craft appeared in the pale blue sky over Reach-far hill. Lower and lower it came until we could see two heads in the cockpit as it flew parallel with the beach before rising again and flying away south-westwards in a long sweep while the children ran along, waving the white tea-towels I had given them.

'I have never truly believed that people flew before,' George said, 'although at the same time I know that you, Sir Ian, and Janet as well have gone from here to St Jago in aeroplanes. Is that not foolish?'

'No,' I said. 'You can know things and yet not fully believe in them,' but I did not put into words my thought that we fully believe only when the heart as well as the head is involved. George had seen Sashie's head in the cockpit and a little bit of George's heart had gone with the little red aeroplane.

*   *   *

After tea that day, when everyone rose to go out to the garden, Sir Ian lingered indoors with me. 'Had a letter from Edward this mornin',' he said.

'Good. How are they?' I think this was the first time since he had come to Achcraggan that he had spoken of his son.

'Divorcin',' he said.

'What? Edward and Anna are—?'

'Divorcin' like I said. Best thing that could happen. Should never have been married in the first place.' I made no comment. 'Edward's comin' back to London. This changes things. I'm thinkin' o' goin' down meself for the winter. Not just because of Edward though. Been thinkin' of it for some time. Rosemary has a lot o' friends down there, people of about our own age. Sounds very cheery. Could come up here in the summer again.'

'That is a very good idea,' I said and added a little insincerely, 'but we'll miss you.'

'I've enjoyed meself here, me dear, the company an' that and the winter'll soon pass. 'Smatter o' fact, Rosemary an' I been thinkin' o' a trip out to St Jago but we'll see how things go with Edward first. Never liked that woman Anna. Can't think what Edward saw in her.'

It seemed useless to point out to him that Anna's effect upon Edward had been to prevent him from seeing anything at all. 'I feel sorry for Edward,' I said and this was sincere. A faint sorriness was all I had ever been able to feel about Edward.

'Ye must come to see us when you come to London,' Sir Ian said next. 'Meet the Hallinzeils an' Sir Hugh Reid again. Ye can't sit up here cookin' an' writin' all the time. Ye ought to get about a bit, meet people. It's none o' me business but ye ought to get married again, a young woman like you. Make some fellah a splendid wife.'

'I want to be a writer, not a wife,' I said somewhat sharply.

'Damned unnatural, I call it, a capable woman like you. But no offence, me dear. I'm just an old busybody but I *have* known ye for a long time.'

I did not point out that, even now, he did not know me at all, had never known what I felt for Twice which made re-marriage unthinkable or what I felt now about my writing which was the main interest of my life.

That evening, Sashie telephoned. 'Where are you now?' I asked.

'London. I liked your Mr Boyd, darling. He was very helpful and obliging.'

'I am glad.'

'He is going to see what he can do about those houses and I have the greatest faith in him.'

'You sound madly enthusiastic. Sashie, there is news. Edward and Anna are divorcing.'

'Naturally. It was bound to happen, don't you think? But do look out, Janet. You are just the right age for Edward's adolescent rebound.'

'Stop being silly, Sashie.'

'I am never silly but let us dismiss the matter of Edward. I also have news, news that will please you. Monica shall never have Mr Boyd.'

'What do you mean?'

'What I say, of course. Mr Boyd likes *you* though. Be happy, my sweet. Au revoir.'

'Exasperating little brute,' I said as I put the receiver down and went upstairs with the boys to see that they washed before bed.

'Sashie is not a little brute,' Duncan said thoughtfully, 'but he is very, very different.'

'In what way?'

'He *says* things.'

'Says things?' I repeated.

'Things that other people never tell you.'

'Like what?'

'Well, George and Tom were doing the Miss Boyds. We didn't know Sashie was there but he was behind the hedge and he saw. I asked him afterwards if he knew the Miss Boyds long ago and if George and Tom were like them. He said he hadn't known the Miss Boyds but he thought George and Tom were very like them and it was then that he said it. He said that Tom and George must have liked the Miss Boyds very much or they couldn't make themselves so very *like* them. I didn't understand what he meant.'

'Yes and then?'

'He said they must have sympathy for the Miss Boyds and know how they felt before they could be so like them. He said people can't do anything well unless they have some feeling about what they are doing.'

'I think that is true,' I said.

'So do I. I don't like maths and I am no good at them.'

'And I like them and I can do them,' Gee put in.

'I told Sashie,' Duncan continued, 'that Mum says it is wrong to imitate people and laugh about them but *he* said he didn't agree. That's how he is different again. Nobody told me ever before that they didn't agree with Mum. It was like when he said in front of everybody that you were coontermashus. *He* said that all the plays in the theatre and all the books you read are imitations of people and the things they say and do and we can learn a lot about people from plays and books.'

'You had quite a discussion,' I said.

'Yes. He makes you discuss. He is very good at telling you what he thinks but he makes you know what *you* think as well. And another thing he said,' said Duncan, 'or are you in a hurry to go downstairs?'

'No. I am in no hurry.'

'He said George and Tom were keeping the Miss Boyds alive when most people thought they were dead. He said that as long as Gee and I remembered Tom and George doing the Miss Boyds, they would still be alive.'

'Very interesting,' I said, sitting down on the bed and recalling my father's idea that Heaven consisted in being remembered with love after one was dead.

The practical efficient Duncan was already in bed, washed, teeth brushed, but Gee was still sitting on the floor where he had removed a sandal and was now absent-mindedly putting it on again.

'You are going to bed, Gee, not getting up,' I said.

He seemed to return from a distance, laid the sandal aside

and began to undo the other one. Then, dangling it by its strap, he looked up at me and said: 'Sashie discussed with me too. He asked if I wasn't fed up with people asking me what I was going to be when I grew up. How did he know that people are always asking that? He wasn't there when Mrs Henderson and Sir Ian and Miss Arden asked.'

'Sashie was a boy like you once. I suppose *he* got fed up with people asking.'

Gee took a few seconds to absorb the fact that Sashie had once been a boy. 'He makes you discuss like Dunk said, so I told him I wished people would ask what I am *not* going to be because I know that.'

'And did you tell him what you are not going to be?'

'Yes. He asked. I told him that I am not going to be a second-hand-car salesman because Dad once told Dunk and me that we could be soldiers or sailors or tinkers or tailors or anything we liked but he wouldn't like us to be second-hand-car salesmen, so I am not going to be one.'

'And did Sashie agree?' I asked.

'Yes. He said people should have nothing to do with the second-hand. But then Sir Ian came down the garden and I couldn't ask the next thing.'

'Get your shirt off. Here are your pyjamas. What was the next thing?'

'Well, what about geometry?' Gee gazed at me solemnly through his glasses. 'It all started with Euclid and gets handed on by Dad in school. Isn't that second-hand?'

My fifty-year-old mind was boggling before the gaze of seven-year-old eyes. I stood up, pulled the shirt up over his head and said: 'You can learn things at second-hand. That is the only way you *can* learn them. I think what Dad and Sashie meant was that you shouldn't sell shabby second-hand things for money. Anything you sell should be split new, like the very good food Sashie sells in his hotel or the music he writes down and sells in London or like Dad selling his own thing which is teaching children or me selling the books I write.'

'Could I sell my botany collection?'

'Yes, if anybody wanted to buy it.'

'My stamp collection?' Duncan enquired.

'Your old stamps are second-hand,' said Gee, flicking his pyjama trousers scornfully through the air.

'Stamps are regarded as works of art,' I was inspired to say in the interests of peace, 'and works of art never become second-hand.'

'Why not?'

'Because they live for ever and ever and only dead things like old cars get second-hand.' I wished that Sashie, who had taught my nephews to 'discuss', was present at this discussion which was rising rapidly over my head. 'Get into bed.'

'Then the veteran cars that Dad took us to see in the museum must be works of art,' said Duncan, 'because they are to be there for ever and ever.'

'Yes,' I agreed recklessly, out of my total ignorance of veteran cars. I opened the window and drew the curtains to keep out the long northern light and perhaps end the discussion.

'I don't think we should let the Miss Boyds get dead and second-hand,' Gee said, curling up into a ball, ready for sleep, 'as long as we don't let Mum catch us doing them.'

'What she doesn't see, after all,' came the philosophic voice of Duncan, 'won't hurt her.'

When I came downstairs, George said: 'You had a lot of blethering up there tonight.'

'It is a very odd thing,' I said, 'but when I came home to Jock's place that time, Liz seemed a lot older than Duncan and Gee was little more than a baby but he seems as old as the other two now.'

'If not older,' Tom agreed. 'Gee has a very long head on him. All of the three of them are clever but Gee can hold his own with both Liz and Duncan, young as he is.'

'Well done your namesake, George,' I said.

'They gave him my name but that's all of me that's in him for God knows I was never clever.'

'We-ell, now,' said Tom, 'there is clever and clever. I am not meaning to insult you, George, when I say that there is something in Gee that is not as strong in the rest of us except you. It is what people call cunning. There is none of it in Duncan, there is a bit of it in Liz because she is a female but Gee has even more of it than she has and that is how he can sort her when he has a mind to.'

*   *   *

At the end of August, Jock came out of hospital and two days later he, Shona and Sandy-Tom arrived at the cottage. He looked pale after the weeks spent indoors but otherwise very well. It was Shona who had undergone a complete change and had made a total return to her former self.

'Ma!' said Sandy-Tom, leading her into the house by the hand as if he were introducing us to someone we had not met before and it did seem to be a long time since we had last seen Shona. He then went to his father, hugged his leg and said: 'My boy.'

'And you are my boy,' Jock said.

'He is speaking a lot more,' I said when the hubbub of the other children died down and was suddenly aware of the sheer relief of being able to speak of Sandy-Tom in Shona's presence, just as one could speak of the other three.

When the children had gone out into the garden, Shona said in her old way: 'I hope those three have behaved themselves. It was so good of you to have them for all these weeks, Janet.'

'They have been no trouble o' the world,' George assured her. 'And it is good that you were able to come up after all.'

'School opens tomorrow,' Jock said, 'but they have put a relief man in. We'd like to stay until the end of the month if you can put up with us.'

'Of course,' I said.

'Those three will miss a month of school but it won't hurt them. They will soon catch up.'

'They are ahead of their ages in a school sense already,' I said, 'especially Gee.'

'You and I, George,' Shona said, 'will be glad of Sandy-Tom one day. He is a relief from all these intellectual academic Sandisons.'

Jock was looking at her as she spoke and I saw a gleam of pure joy in his eyes but becoming aware that he was observed, the gleam disappeared, as if the bond between him and Shona were too private and precious for even a small hint of it to be open to observation. Jock had always been very reserved, very private in his beliefs and aspirations, seldom airing his views in words, but always going his own way in action. He made it obvious now that he did not wish to discuss his illness or his time in hospital and led the conversation away to the conversion of the barn.

When Shona and I went through to the scullery to prepare supper, Jock went down the garden to join the children on the beach and some five minutes later, I saw him from the window, standing under an apple tree, holding on to a branch that was about level with his shoulder. The awareness that all was not well seemed to stab me like an arrow and telling Shona that I was going to fetch some lettuce, I tried to walk down the path at a normal pace. Putting myself between Jock and the scullery window, I asked; 'What is the matter?' He did not speak at once. He looked down at me and then up to his own hand that held the branch. That movement convinced me that I knew what he was feeling, for I remembered how, on the verandah of Sashie's house at Silver Beach, when I was convalescent and left on my own for the first time since I had been ill, the sheer panic that had made me clutch at my friend Caleb's hand as if it were a lifeline.

'I can't seem to go any further on my own,' Jock said now.

'I know.' I reached up and detached his fingers from the branch.

As I held his arm, he looked hard at me and as clearly as if he had spoken aloud I heard the plea : 'I don't want any of the others to know about this.'

'All right,' I said aloud. 'Steady now,' and gently but firmly he drew his arm free of my hand. 'Do you want to go down to the beach or back to the house?'

'The kids are coming. We might as well go up for supper.'

He seemed to be deeply ashamed of the incident, as I had been in a similar circumstance, and it was not mentioned again and once or twice I suffered a fierce glare from his blue eyes when he found me lurking near him out-of-doors. There was no repetition of the incident either but it led me to think of the strange similarities and dissimilarities between two people of the same blood. In many ways, Jock and I were totally unlike one another but in our reaction to illness it seemed that we were entirely alike.

*   *   *

By the end of September, George, Tom and I were left on our own and were preparing to dig in for the winter. I had been beginning to hope that we would spend the winter in the barn but, as the summer had gone on, it had become obvious that this would not be possible. The slaters and masons were working very slowly and carefully on the old building.

'Don't hurry them,' George said. 'Give them time to make a right job of it.'

'And us with that big cheque from our writing to pay for it all,' said Tom.

He and George, even months later, were still marvelling at the amount of the cheque which had arrived in April. It was not immense in publishing terms but Tom and George had difficulty in believing that it had been honestly earned. They tried to rationalise it in their minds in the most extraordinary ways.

'Miss Arden is a very clever lady and a doctor and all,' Tom would tell George, as if to assure him that her brother was not some poor idiot that I was robbing.

'Jock says the broadcasting people will pay people a guinea a minute just for speaking,' George would tell Tom, the implication being that someone as 'unclever' as himself could speak and that perhaps it was in order for someone who could write to be paid for doing so. Their attitude to the world of writing was ambivalent and I thought it would always be so. The publishing and financial side of it was terra incognita which they preferred to ignore but they liked to see me sitting by the fire, pushing my pen and they enjoyed the letters from the Ladies from Sussex.

At Christmas, the roads were too risky for the car, but Jock put the three older children on the train in the middle of the holiday and they stayed with us over the New Year. Their stay was dimmed a little by a 'black-tie' day when George and Tom attended, in driving sleet, the funeral of their old crony, Murdo the Ironmonger. The children were very subdued while George and Tom were out of the house and very solicitous in removing wet overcoats when they returned and as Liz poured hot water into tots of whisky for them, I thought I saw in her grave downbent face the fight against the dawning knowledge that these two men were mortal. Soon, now, she would be fourteen years old, a childish rather than a precocious fourteen, but she was growing away from her brothers into feminity and towards that loneliness that closes about all of us. She bore no resemblance now, except a slight physical one, to the hoyden she had been at eight years old and she had inherited much of her father's reserve, together with his ability to indicate silently that too close an approach, uninvited, might not be in order. Yet there were times when I felt an unspoken intimacy with her such as I felt with her father, an intimacy which I did not feel with her brothers although I felt that they had no reserves from me such as Liz had.

By way of a small celebration, we had invited Mrs Henderson, Hamish and Doctor Hay to have lunch with us on New Year's Day and while we were having drinks before lunch the telephone rang.

'The very happiest New Year, darling,' said Sashie's voice.

'Sashie, where are you?'

'New York.'

'New York? Are you out of your mind?'

'No, I am merely wishing you all a Happy New Year. Is ma princesse lointaine there?'

I held the receiver between Duncan and Gee who spoke their greetings, then George and Tom spoke, after which I put the receiver into Liz's hand saying: 'You have only a few seconds,' as George and Tom hustled the boys through to the scullery to get over their noisy excitement. I shepherded our guests to the scullery too and began to serve lunch.

'Just fancy, New York!' said Duncan, and Gee repeated: 'New York!' but Liz now joined us, her eyes enormous and said: 'Aunt Janet, Sashie!'

Throughout the meal, the talk was all of Sashie and the miracle of the transatlantic telephone, what the call must have cost, what time it must have been in New York when Sashie spoke but Liz did not join in the conversation. She was as withdrawn as if she were inside a glass bubble.

In the sitting-room, while the grown-ups were drinking coffee, Duncan and Gee got out the cards and the cribbage board, arranged foot-stools round a low table.

'Want to play first or the winner of the first, Liz?' Duncan asked.

'I don't want to play at all. You two go ahead,' she said.

Duncan shrugged his shoulders and addressed his brother: 'She is all goofy because of Sashie ringing up. She would marry him if she could.'

'It wouldn't do,' said Gee judicially. 'She is nearly as tall as he is now and she is still—'

It was as if a sudden whirlwind had struck the room. Liz came through the grown-up party, sending coffee cups and ash-trays in all directions, sending the boys' table, the cribbage board and cards flying, knocking both boys off their stools and flat on their backs on the floor before she tore the door open and went dashing through to her bedroom.

'I am sorry about that,' I apologised to our guests while George and Tom began to pick up broken china.

'Aunt Janet,' Duncan began, 'we didn't mean—'

'It is all right,' I told them. 'Pick up your cards and things. Excuse me,' I said to the others, went through to the bedroom, brought Liz back and made her apologise.

The remainder of our little occasion passed peacefully and pleasantly but I was not finished with Liz's antisocial exhibition and when the boys were in bed that evening and she had gone to her room, I followed her. She had not begun to undress but was lying flat on her back on her bed, staring at the ceiling and she tried to disarm me with a smile of considerable charm and: 'Tom and George told me I'd be for it.'

'They were right as usual,' I said. 'I didn't think much of that exhibition today.'

'I have said I am sorry,' she said, as if from an immense distance.

'That is not enough. You owe George and Tom and me an explanation. You are a visitor in our house after all.'

She sat up. 'I am not a visitor. We are all one family.'

'If you have no manners inside the family, the chances are you will have even less outside of it so explain yourself.'

'I don't know if I can.'

'Try.'

'When you get to my age,' she began, betraying the belief of all adolescents that no adult has ever been adolescent, 'people are always teasing you about who you are going to marry, like Sir Ian teasing me in the summer about Hamish.'

'I know. It's awful.'

'Oh, I don't mind,' she told me airily. 'It is just silliness. Old people and kids are just hipped about marriage, that's all. But Sashie is nothing to do with getting married and all that stuff. Ach,' she said disgustedly, 'I can't explain,' then suddenly her face brightened and she went on: 'Dad told us once about an old man, a tramp who used to be allowed to sleep in the barn at Reachfar. He said, the old tramp I mean, that he had no name, that he was just a Citizen of the World. Did you know him?'

'Goodness yes. Everybody around here knew the Citizen. Why?'

'That is what Sashie is, don't you see? A citizen of the world, flying all over the place and talking to people from New York, so it is just silly to talk about him getting married and being part of a family like us here or at home.'

'He is my best friend,' I said, 'outside of you people of the family.'

'He is *everybody's* best friend that he wants to be friends with,' Liz argued, 'the kind of friend that you don't talk silliness about. Actually, the boys don't know enough about Sashie to talk about him at all. If they really knew about him, they wouldn't be so silly. If they knew he had no legs—' She stiffened suddenly, looking horrified. 'Gracious, I shouldn't have said that. You have no right,' she accused me furiously, 'to stand there making me talk like this and say things that are secrets!'

'That is all right, Liz,' I said. 'I have known about Sashie's legs for a long time.'

She sighed deeply with relief. 'It must have been awful being shot down like that but he can be so funny and he was funny about that, even.'

'How did he come to tell you about being shot down?'

'I wanted him to come up to Reachfar with me, just the two of us. I pointed it out to him from the barn. I wanted to show him the Picnic Pond and all the places. He told me he couldn't manage to walk all that way uphill.' She pulled her sweater up over her head. 'Do you sort of understand now why I got angry today and made that fuss?' she asked from within the woollen folds.

'Yes, I think I do but I think too that you are old enough now not to make these violent sort of fusses.'

She looked at me over the folds of sweater across her chest. 'Tom and George told us once that even after you were married you threw a plate at Uncle Twice.'

'Those two should be ashamed of themselves, telling such fibs.'

'George and Tom never *ever* tell the boys and me fibs,' said Liz firmly and finally.

*   *   *

When the children had gone home, the three of us settled into our routine again but I do not want to give the impression that our life was dull. George and Tom had always had the ability to make the small events of day-to-day interesting and amusing and they were totally unpredictable. This winter, for instance, they suddenly, in their own words, took to the cooking. Having learned to make chocolate blancmange, which was one of their sweet-toothed favourites, they lost the crofting man's attitude that cookery was a mystery to be left in the hands of the women and became more and more ambitious. They still retained their crofting attitude to the baking of scones, oatbread and cakes but they would undertake anything that had to be boiled, stewed or roasted. I had quite a number of cookery books, for I had always been interested in the art and we took in a newspaper which had a weekly cookery page.

As with everything they did, they brought to their cookery an element of clownishness, as my grandmother called it. Unlike themselves, my father had worn spectacles for reading in his later years, the spectacles were still in a drawer of the sideboard and on the day the cookery page appeared, one of them would don the spectacles and look over the top of them at the printed page. This was to indicate that the cooking was a serious matter to which they were giving their full attention. Naturally, they had one or two disasters, like the first time they attempted a steamed sponge pudding – another favourite – when they put in too much raising agent so that the pudding not only burst through the paper covering the bowl but also raised the lid of the saucepan and blossomed all over the cooker in a frothy mass while they were out in the shed chopping firewood and I was writing in the sitting-room.

They also had now another new interest which they called their 'sticking-in'. When their interest in cookery developed to the extent that they were cutting recipes out of the newspaper, I provided them with a large alphabetically-indexed notebook and a bottle of glue and having learned the art of sticking-in, they extended their practice of it to the newscuttings and reviews of my books that my publishers sent to me from time to time. For this I provided them with a large loose-leaf folder which they kept meticulously. When I saw Tom cutting two lines about a book of mine out of a long printed column, which left him with a piece of paper an inch and a half wide by quarter of an inch deep, I said that this was going too far, whereupon he spoke sternly the old Reachfar tenet: 'If we canna do the job right, we'd as well not do it at all.'

They were incapable of being bored, I only now came fully to understand, because they gave their total attention to everything they did, so that nothing was reduced to the level of the chore that was a bore. On reflection, I should not have used the word 'routine' of our way of life. I myself had a mild routine of writing from after breakfast until lunch-time and answering mail in the afternoons but George and Tom would not permit routine or any kind of habit to take a grip on them. They had never done and still did not do anything unless they were in the mood to do it. They still used two turns of speech which they had used since the earliest day I could remember. 'To the devil with polishing the brass the-day,' George would say. 'I am not in the mood for it.' 'The gravel on the long path could do with a rake,' Tom would say, 'but I am not that way inclined the-day.'

Their ties with the earth were so strong that they were always in the mood for or towards the garden inclined, so that the first sting of autumn in the air would set them digging that the earth might benefit from the winter frosts and the first breath of spring would set them planting, but mood and inclination applied to all else. Frequently, they were not in the mood for dish-washing and once, in the early days, I washed up the accumulated aftermath of three meals, only to bring their wrath down upon my head.

'Wasting your time like that,' I was told. 'We would have got round to it when it came over us. Where's the harm in a few dirty plates?'

'All right,' I said, 'as long as it comes over you at least once in twenty-four hours.'

When mood or inclination was upon them, it was a pleasure to watch them work and I often baked while they did the washing-up.

'See that you wash *all* the cutlery at once,' George would tell Tom, 'for I am going to open and shut that drawer just the one time.'

'Put the cups right to the end of the board here,' Tom would tell George, 'so that I can get them and dry them and hang them on the hooks without walking about and wearing out my boots.'

They had never heard of the science of Time and Motion Study but I now discovered that its practice was in-built in them and that they had used it all their lives.

Following Jock's dictum of never asking them to do anything and never trying to prevent them from doing anything, I did not interfere or give any advice unless they asked for it. They did not do all the cooking of course, nor did they do all the washing or cleaning. On any day that was at all clement, they would take to the garden or the barn so that their very unpredictability provided that resistance against which Sashie said I wrote. I often worked my way through a writing blockage by peeling the potatoes that they would have peeled had it been raining out-of-doors.

*   *   *

After bad weather over the Christmas and New Year period, January was unusually fine and over lunch on Candlemas Day at the beginning of February, when the sunlight was sparkling on the firth, Tom said: 'I am not liking this so early in the year, George,' and went on to repeat the old rhyme:

> 'If Candlemas be bright and fair,
> Half the winter's to come and more.
> If Candlemas be dark and foul,
> Half the winter is bye at Yule.

'The bad weather is going to come late and that goes hard on the old people.'

Tom himself was, of course, the oldest man in the village if not in the entire parish but this was a fact that seemed never to have occurred to him and I did not point it out.

The bad weather came about the middle of February,

Mrs Henderson caught a chill, developed pneumonia and died within a few days of taking to her bed.

'She was a right good neighbour to Tom and me,' George said when Rory the Postman told us of her death.

'Will you two go along and see Hamish?' I asked. 'The relatives will all be coming from a distance. Tell him we'll see to the cooking of whatever meals he wants to give them and that we can lend extra crockery, cutlery, anything he needs.'

Hamish, who had been looked after in every detail by his mother for so long, while he earned the money for the household, was lost and helpless in the face of this catastrophe. He had no idea how to arrange for the funeral and the three of us were about to take this in hand when Andrew Boyd arrived on the doorstep with a cheerfully impudent air that indicated that he had not heard of the death.

'Of course I'll do anything I can,' he responded to my request, 'but you'd better come along to Hamish's place with me and convince him I won't cheat him.'

Even in these circumstances, I had to smile at Andrew's knowing estimate of his standing in Achcraggan minds.

Efficiently, he attended to everything and then disappeared into the Poyntdale hotel until the day of the funeral, which he attended, and after all the people who had come from a distance had been fed and sent on their way, he helped George and Tom carry crockery and cutlery back to our house.

'Where is Hamish?' I asked.

'Back at his place,' George said.

'Andrew,' I asked, 'will you go back along there and tell Hamish we expect him for supper?'

'What if he won't come?'

'You tell him Herself *said* he was to come,' said Tom.

It was in this way that Hamish became almost a member of our family. I discovered that, unlike George and Tom, he had never taken to the cooking and it was natural that he should have his mid-day and evening meals with us. I thought that the loss of his mother would unsettle him, that he might decide to sell the cottage and go south to some industrial district where he could earn higher pay but this did not happen. Hamish liked his home district and its land, said no word about leaving, continued to have his main meals with us and more than repaid what we gave him by the work he did for us and his contributions of game, fish and eggs. It was a neighbourly uncommercial arrangement of the kind we all liked, of everybody contributing what they could to the common pool during the days, and of very un-neighbourly and highly commercial and competitive games of Ha'penny Nap round the fire during the dark winter evenings.

On the day following Mrs Henderson's funeral, Andrew Boyd called on me again and began, 'I have to get back south tomorrow. I have been away too long as it is.'

'You have been the greatest help,' I told him, 'and thank you very much.'

'When I called the other day,' he said, pushing my gratitude aside, 'it was to tell you that I am making damn slow progress with that property your friend de Marnay is interested in. As far as I can make out, the heirs to one of the houses are in New Zealand and I haven't a clue as yet who owns the other one. Will you write and tell de Marnay I am doing my best?'

'Why don't you write yourself?'

'I have but I'd like you to assure him, sort of.' He had lost his air of sharp certainty, of being master of any situation.

'I am sure he doesn't need assuring, Andrew. He has told me that he is content to leave the whole business to you but I'll write to him if you really want me to.'

'I wish you would. Hell, Janet, it is difficult to explain but when you've been looked on as a rogue all your life, you get a sort of thing about it.' His eyes took on that cunning leer and his mouth its lopsided smile. 'I am not saying I can't be as sharp as the next one if provoked but de Marnay didn't provoke me. I want to do the best I can for him since he's a friend of yours. Besides, I liked the bloke.'

'And he likes you too. Isn't that nice?' I said, trying to joke aside the discomfort one feels when an accepted character displays an unexpected facet.

'I am serious, Janet,' he rebuked me. 'You are in the favour of this place because of what your father and your grandfather were before you but I grew up on the other side of the favour line because of what *my* grandfather had been. I don't know what my father was. I knew even as a kid that I was marked down as a rascal and I turned into something of a rascal. I'll admit that it came to me fairly naturally, though. Listen, can *you* by any chance tell me with any certainty who my father was?' he asked suddenly.

This was the side of him that I liked, this fearless facing of facts of a kind that many would try to conceal or ignore.

'I think so,' I said, replying in kind. 'My grandmother believed that your father was a man called Jock Skinner and I think she was right. I remember him and you resemble him very strongly. And your mother was not what they would have called in those days a loose woman. You were, if you like, an unfortunate accident born out of the circumstances and the climate of the time.'

'Thanks for these kind words. Oh, no apologies. I know you didn't mean to be insulting. You remember the time when I was born?'

'Clearly, Andrew.'

'What happened to my mother?'

'She committed suicide. I am sorry, Andrew. Again, that was part of the climate and the circumstances of the time. Your aunts never told you anything of this?'

'No, not a word. They always acted as if they had found me among the seaweed down at the beach.'

'I don't mean to be tedious,' I said, 'but again that attitude was typical of their time.'

'Sometimes,' he said thoughtfully, 'I admire this kind of community with its long memory for good and bad and at other times I think the anonymous way I live down south is better. I just don't know. Down south, I can face de Marnay over my desk as a friend of yours that I may be able to help in a small way but the minute I set foot up here, I get the feeling that de Marnay must be thinking I am a slick operator and that he has made a mistake in having anything to do with me at all.'

'Get that out of your head. Come to that, Sashie de Marnay himself can be as slick as operators come but, like you, he is honest when he is faced with somebody honest.' I paused and then: 'Andrew, I don't think you were quite honest with me about that barn down there. You sold it cheap. Why?'

'That takes us back to long ago again. And I didn't sell it all that cheap, you know. If I had hung on to it for another ten years, I might have got a thousand for it but what is another seven hundred and fifty in ten years?' He leered at me again, narrow-eyed. 'I'll probably turn *your* two-fifty into a thousand in five years or less. Besides, your grandmother was very good to my old aunties when I was a kid although she frightened the be-jasus out of *me*. Then your father gave me twenty quid and helped me to get away when the police were after me for a bit of thieving I didn't do. Believe it or not –' he smiled at me '– I have never *ever* stolen anything. I'll admit I have outsmarted a few here and there but it's always been legal. You believe me?'

'Yes I do and I think you pay far too much attention to Achcraggan opinion.'

'What's bred in the bone is hard to get rid of. When I left here as a youngster with that twenty quid your father gave me, I thought I would never come back but the place, as well as its opinions, is bred in the bone and when Poyntdale came up for sale, I think I'd have bought it whether I saw a future in it or not.'

'I doubt that,' I told him. 'I don't think you would invest in anything just for auld lang syne. Anyway, this isn't the Achcraggan of forty years ago. There are only about half-a-dozen people in the whole district who remember your origins and mine. But if it is of any comfort, the village doesn't see me as strictly honest either. They don't see writing as a decent way of making a living.'

He laughed. 'I find it an odd way of making a living myself,' he told me and then on a serious note: 'Janet, you and I get on. I have never had much to do with women. The aunties had put me off women for life, I thought.'

'George and Tom told me that you were very kind to your aunts,' I protested.

'I am quite kind to dogs too, in the way of seeing that they don't starve to death. That is about all it was with the old girls. They were terribly stupid, you know, even before they went completely potty.'

'Not their fault.' I defended the Miss Boyds. 'Once again, I repeat that they were the victims of their time and upbringing.'

'I suppose you are right but the thing was that I never felt they were quite human, as if there was a screen between them and the world that seemed to me to be the real one. You couldn't talk to them. But I can talk to you as I might talk to de Marnay or any other fellow.'

'Your aunts didn't get much practice at talking to people. I have had better opportunities. Sometimes my mind boggles when I think of the variety of people I have talked to in my time and no two of them have been alike.'

'Most of the people I have met have been exactly alike, all out for themselves and the main chance.'

'That was your own choice surely?' I suggested. 'You chose the money-making sphere.'

'I think you despise that sphere but it was the only one that seemed to be suited to my particular gifts.'

'I don't despise it and I admire you for putting your gifts

to use. There was a time when I thought in terms of material advancement too but I gave it up somewhere along the line. The odd thing is that I have advanced in a material sense much more since I gave up trying. This writing thing has brought in more hard cash than I ever earned in my life before, but all I want now in a material sense is that barn down there and enough to live on as George, Tom and I live here. I just want to be able to see the firth, the sky and Reachfar hill from my windows. What do *you* want, really, Andrew?'

'To go on gambling, I think, for that is all I do – just gamble and win a little more than I lose.'

'Do you ever lose?'

'Not often,' he admitted. 'At first, I set out to get fairly rich by Seaview standards and I have done that, but I am not very interested in the things that money can buy except for pictures. Like you with your barn, I have a house I like, a little old farmhouse near Stratford-upon-Avon and I intend to have a house here before too long. Maybe you'll spend a day or two at Verehampton next time you come south, by the way. I took de Marnay out there. I think he liked it,' he added by way of a recommendation.

'I know he did. He raved about it in a letter.'

'How did you meet de Marnay?' he asked me now.

I told him something of Twice's and my arrival in St Jago and our meeting with Sashie. 'It was really Monica Daviot who threw us together in the first place,' I remembered.

'Monica? Odd. Would never have connected de Marnay with Monica,' he said.

'Why not?'

'They are entirely different kinds of people. Monica is more my kind than de Marnay's,' he said, which showed his native shrewdness about people and also seemed to prove that Sashie had, for once, been in error when he had said: 'Monica shall never have Mr Boyd'. 'I mean,' Andrew was adding hastily, 'more my kind in the way of what they call aspiration. I am not laying a claim to belong to the purple.'

'It's the aspiration that counts,' I said. 'The purple doesn't mean much any more.' I rose from my chair. 'Tom and George will soon be back. They are along at the horse-racing on Malcolm the Minister's television. I'll make some tea.'

'I ought to go.'

'Why?'

'I like it here and I don't want to outstay my welcome.'

'You can't do that, Andrew. Your welcome is assured so sit down and have some tea.'

I went through to the scullery to plug in the kettle and called through to the sitting-room: 'Have you seen anything of Monica lately?'

'The weekend before I came north. I take a run to London most weekends,' he called back.

'How is she?'

'The same as ever. Looks like a million dollars.'

'She always did, even in Air Force uniform.'

By the time I had made the tea, George and Tom still had not returned and as I carried the tray in I said: 'I wonder what those two are up to today? Not that it matters. They will arrive in their own good time.'

'It was good of you to come here to look after them, Janet,' Andrew said.

'They don't need much looking after and that wasn't why I came home here. I came because this is my place on the surface of the earth. It took me a long time to find that out but I know it now.'

'You make me feel better about Achcraggan, too,' he said. 'It was the idea of you and de Marnay being here that made me decide to have a place here too.' He looked up at the wall above the fireplace. 'I like that painting of Poyntdale Bay.'

'It's by a little-known artist but I like it. Sashie was very impressed with your paintings, by the way, and Sashie does know about painting. I didn't know you were a connoisseur.'

'I'm not. I just know what I like. I got interested in pictures by accident. I bought some derelict property in Liverpool just after the war.' He winked at me, one dark eye disappearing for a split second. 'There is a supermarket on the site now. The only bit of it that was occupied was a hole in the wall where an old chap kept a pawnshop. He died and his relatives were selling off the stuff. That is where I bought my first picture. It isn't a Goya. It is an early Victorian landscape by somebody called Silver, the kind of thing that is coming back into fashion now, but I gave the people the three pounds they asked for it because I liked it. Then I discovered that the more I looked at it the more I liked it and this was something new for me. Until that time I always got sick of things instead of liking them better.'

'And, of course, paintings tend to go up in value instead of down—' I put in.

'No.' He interrupted me sharply. 'This is one area where I am not investing for profit, not financial profit anyway. I don't read much, music means nothing to me, I never go to the theatre, I am totally uneducated if you like but I am hooked on pictures, the ones I like, that is. I wouldn't give you tuppence for a Picasso but I wouldn't mind owning a Renoir before I die.'

'Quite an ambition,' I said.

The more he talked, the more I liked him but there was something strange and deep in him of which I was aware in brief flashes but which I could not identify. It was something innate in him that was escaping me, as if he had in his nature some peculiarity that was concealed, as Sashie could so well conceal his artificial legs. Indeed, in a physical way he resembled Sashie very strongly with his short slim stature, uncommon among the men of Achcraggan district, and his dark hair and eyes. He was less vivid than Sashie, the hair and eyes less black and Sashie had a quality that I can describe only as beauty, something greater and less physical than mere handsomeness, which was not in Andrew. But there was another resemblance between them that was unconnected with appearance. One of the most comforting features of the years of my friendship with Sashie was its sexlessness, a total absence of any male-female connotation which is very rare in relations between men and women and I sensed a similar attitude in Andrew, which was equally comforting in relation to myself but it made his relationship with Monica irritate me still more. In spite of all my efforts to be toughly rational, telling myself that Monica was still attractive while I had grown plainer down the years and that Andrew was well able to look after himself, I persisted in seeing him, in relation to Monica, as a victim.

*　　　*　　　*

In March, the weather, although very frosty and cold, allowed the men working on the barn to get ahead in a sudden spurt and quite unexpectedly painters were working inside and outside on the completed conversion and George and Tom had found a new ploy.

Ever since I had bought the barn, I had been visiting any auction sales that took place in the district and buying mid-Victorian furniture to supplement the pieces that had come from Reachfar and all these acquisitions were in store at the furniture shop where I had bought new beds and other items. I had arranged with the shop to deliver my purchases, stopping on the way at Jemima Cottage to pick up my books and a few other odds and ends, but George and Tom decided, for some reason that they could not or would not explain, that my books were not to travel by pantechnicon round the half-mile of road from cottage to barn.

Equipped with two shopping baskets each, they carried the hundreds of books down through the garden and along to the barn where they stacked them in a massive heap in the middle of the floor while the joiners lined one wall of the large living-room with shelves. On the day that the pantechnicon came, which was shortly before Easter at the beginning of April, I sat by the first fire to burn in the barn while George and Tom put the books on the shelves in the places I indicated. When the pantechnicon had emptied itself and gone away, I discovered that the converted dressing-table and my typewriter were still at the cottage and said to them: 'Dammit, you were in charge of the loading up there. You knew that the typewriter and its table had to come down,' and went angrily into our new kitchen to prepare supper. As I was laying the table, which was beside a large window that looked towards the cottage, a little procession began to come down the garden, Tom in front carrying a cardboard box full of stationery, George next carrying the typewriter and behind him, Hamish, with the converted dressing-table balanced on one shoulder.

'Where do you want it to sit, Mistress?' Hamish asked.

'Over at that window that looks west to Ben Wyvis,' I said.

'We weren't for trusting our books and writing things to these fellows with their big van,' George said.

'It was safer to shift them ourselves,' said Tom.

I could not think of a fitting response to the respect which they showed for the tools of my trade and I turned away and looked out of the window. At this west end of the barn, Hamish had helped them to dig what was to be the vegetable plot and now, bang in the middle of it, there grew a bunch of daffodils, pale in the dying evening light. These and the care of the books and writing equipment were George's and Tom's contribution to our new home.

When the family arrived for the Easter holidays, I was struck by one of the differences between my brother and myself. I had thought that Shona and Jock would have been glad to have more room in the cottage, to be less crowded during meals and in the sitting-room in the evenings but I discovered that from the family's point of view, the removal of George, Tom and myself to the barn meant that the children could have friends to stay. While Jock drove the car north, two girls and two boys, friends of Liz and Duncan, travelled by train and when all were gathered together on the first evening, the cottage seemed to me to be bursting at the joints and Jock and Shona seemed to be in their element in the midst of this maelstrom.

I felt guiltily anti-social at my relief in returning to the space and quiet of the barn and said as usual: 'It isn't that I don't like the young people but – I seem to get so tired.'

'No wonder,' said George, 'the way you try to listen to them all and them all speaking at once.'

'And them not listening to naybody at all, they are so keen to get speaking their own foolishness all the time,' Tom said.

'Just you go up to your bed,' George advised me, 'and take a look up to Reachfar.'

My bed faced the window and I did as he suggested, looking for a long time at the trees of Reachfar dark on the night horizon and discovered that, all my life, I had expended a great deal of ingenuity in my efforts to get away from people, to be alone, in order to find out what I thought and felt about these very people who bombarded me with impressions.

*　　*　　*

Shortly after the holidays were over, I noticed one day at lunch that Tom was having difficulty in raising his fork to his mouth and asked if he had hurt his arm. He gave up the effort to use his left hand and said: 'No, but when I wakened this morning my shoulder was sore. Will it be rheumatics? I have never had them before.'

It took two days of the pain growing worse and spreading to his neck before I could persuade him to let me call Doctor Hay who diagnosed fibrositis and said that as part of the treatment he was to stay in bed and keep warm but when George had gone to the chemist with the prescription and we were alone downstairs, she said: 'The main thing is not to let him lose interest. These old out-door men don't like being in bed. They regard illness as being something shameful and that drags their spirits down. They have been up and doing all their lives and they take it hard when they have to stop even for a week or so. They are like children in a way. They go up and down in health and spirits very rapidly. Try to keep him interested.'

After a few days, I had a despairing feeling that Tom's interest was waning. He was permanently sleepy, partly because of the pills he was taking but there was also something in him that was completely new – boredom and he hardly spoke except to apologise for the trouble he was causing. As is my way, when a situation seems to be going beyond my control, I became angry and over-energetic and I came down from Tom's room and out to George and Hamish who were working on the vegetable plot. I did not know what I intended to say but was prevented from saying anything at all by George shouting: 'Dang it, there's Willie the Tinker's old billy-goat on the loose again, Hamish. We might as well not plant this plot at all with that brute roaming about.'

While he and Hamish went away along the beach to catch the billy-goat and take it back to its tether, I had the idea that made me return to the house and telephone the masons who had worked on the conversion.

'How soon can you come and build a wall around this place?'

The masons were a man in his fifties called Donald and his son called Young Donald who had made friends with Tom and George while the work was going on and when I had explained that Tom was sick, they agreed to visit us the very next day.

'What I want,' I explained to Donald while George was upstairs with Tom, 'is a bit of action around the place. I want to get Tom really interested. Come up, both of you and see him.'

When we were all gathered round Tom's bed, George, in a depressed mood because of Tom's illness, said: 'As a garden, it is hardly worth building a wall round it. It is nothing but sand and gravel and stones and I doubt if that vegetable plot will grow a turnip in spite of all that pigeon dung and compost we put into it.'

'Ach, stop making a poor mouth!' I said and realised that I was using the words that my grandmother would have used. 'We could grow turnips on Reachfar hill and we can grow them here.'

'If I was you,' Young Donald said tentatively, 'I would pave the whole place and leave only a few little flower beds and the vegetable patch and build them up with compost and peat and stuff. You'll never be able to have a lawn or anything like that.'

'I don't want a lawn,' I said. 'I want something that will be easy to look after – just a few flowers and shrubs.'

In the end, after much argument, Tom, as George put it, was 'sitting up and taking notice' and it was only as Donald and his son were going away that I took thought and said: 'How much is all this going to cost?'

'Ach, you'll pay for it sometime,' Donald said, then laughed and added: 'When Young Donald here starts levelling the place off with this mechanical digger he made me get, the old fellow will be out of bed before you can wink to see that he doesn't knock the house down.'

And this was precisely what happened when, at eight o'clock two mornings later, I took breakfast up to Tom and the raised scoop of the digger went past his window, he said: 'Are you out o' your head, letting that young fellow run about the place with that thing? He'll have the windows in on us,' and as if unaware of what he was doing, he ate his porridge with gusto, as if a day of enjoyable activity lay before him. A few days later, he was downstairs, shouting at Young Donald from the windows and in three more days he was out-of-doors along with George, helping the senior Donald to build the garden wall.

When the family came north for the summer holidays, Jock surveyed wall, wrought-iron gates and the small flower beds between the paving-stones and said: 'It is going to look fine when the beds are planted and you have some rock plants among the paving stones but it must have cost a bit.'

'Seven hundred pounds roughly,' I said, 'but well worth it. It got Tom on his feet.'

This was how, from then on, behind the backs of Tom and George, the garden came to be known as the 'seven-hundred-pound cure', which matured into a very pleasant place. It was indeed the only kind of garden which could have been constructed on that site, right on the edge of the sea and at the mercy of every wind that blew but Sashie always argued that the reason for its construction had much to do with its prosperity.

'It was undertaken out of love,' he said, 'and not to make a show or to impress the neighbours or for any other vulgar reason. It was bound to prosper.'

*   *   *

Happiness is difficult to record. There is a fundamental flaw in human nature that makes us more deeply aware of the bad sad times than of the good happy times. Perhaps it is the tragic awareness we have that life ends inevitably in death that predisposes us to the attitude of 'getting as much out of it' as we can and we are so busy getting more and more that what we have already got goes unregarded. Whatever the reason, it is much easier to record the bad times than the good times and the summer of 1961 was a good time of Jock, Shona and a medley of young people at the cottage, Sir Ian and Miss Arden at the hotel and George and Tom busy in the gardens.

It is difficult to remember what we all laughed about, although we laughed a great deal but I recall that it was the 'Plaster of Paris' summer, which means that the young people busied themselves on the beach and in the gardens, making plaster casts of the footprints of sea birds, pieces of bark and indeed anything that could be cast. Sandy-Tom spent some of his time following the older children, some of it with George and Tom and some of it alone except for his Fly-dog who, the older he grew, looked more and more like a hairy dirty floor-cloth than any animal.

One day, the older children left their bowl of Plaster of Paris unattended and Sandy-Tom decided to make a cast of Fly-dog's hind feet, which he did by putting the feet into the bowl so that at lunch-time Fly-dog was discovered, very active about the foreparts and furiously vociferous, with his hindquarters so solidly anchored in plaster that the help of Doctor Hay had to be solicited in order to extricate him.

This was also the year that the boys caught, live, an eel about a yard long, contrived to smuggle it into the cottage and up to the bathroom where, to keep it undetected, as they thought, they put it into the lavatory cistern. Shona was unfortunate enough to be the first to flush the cistern and was sent into screaming near-hysteria at finding the lavatory pan full of writhing coils of eel before the creature disappeared down the drain to be seen no more and to come, no doubt, to an unsavoury end.

It was also the year of Kon-Tiki Two, when Liz, Duncan, Gee and their friends spent about a week constructing, after reading about the exploits of Thor Heyerdahl, a raft out of four large oil drums, planks of wood and ropes. I was a little apprehensive while this was going on, for there is a deep channel and a strong tide race out between the Cobblers to the North Sea but I kept silent, for Jock called me an old wet hen when I expressed any fear that the children could get into danger and I had to admit that they seemed to have some guardian Providence of their own. At all events, the raft was finished on a Friday evening and ceremonially named and launched by Miss Arden with a jam jar filled with weak orange juice, then anchored to a large boulder on the beach. That evening, four rough oars were made with the help of Tom and George and the next day the first voyagers were to put to sea but when the morning came and we all went down to the beach, Kon-Tiki Two was just visible in the channel between the Cobblers, well on the way to Norway all on her own.

'You silly craiturs,' said Tom into the groans of disappointment. 'This is the time o' the high tides and you left her too low on the beach.'

'And with that wind that was in it through the night too,' said George.

Suspicion coiled in my mind like the eel in the lavatory pan. There had been no wind through the night. On windy nights, especially in my room at the gable, the old barn creaked like a China Clipper under full sail and I was about to say: 'Wind, my tail!' when Jock looked at me very gravely and said: 'It is hard to realise the power of the sea and the tide until you see with your own eyes what they can do.' But I knew and so did he that neither wind nor tide had taken Kon-Tiki Two to sea and I merely wondered which of those two old rascals, with his poacher's step, had managed during the night to get downstairs and out of the house without my hearing him. But I have to admit that, as with many other mysterious happenings, I have never found out which was responsible on this occasion. On accusing them of letting the raft go, I was met with two hurt faces and the words: 'Why should you think we would be fit to do a destructive thing like that?' Jock and I knew, however, that they were fit for a destructive thing like that and things even more destructive if they thought they would be constructive in the end.

*   *   *

It is incident by little incident of the kind I have described and the trivial business of every day that constitutes the happiness of people and each little incident, each triviality overtakes the one before and causes it to slip unnoticed into the past. With Liz, Duncan and Gee and their friends around, we had plenty of incident and triviality and we also had Sir Ian and Miss Arden, Roddy and Sheila and their baby son calling on us and we must not forget the Ladies from Sussex, some of whom were gentlemen and some of whom now came from South Africa, the United States, New Zealand and points north, south, east and west. The quarter-mile of rough track from the main road to the beach deterred them not at all and I felt that many of them must have gone away with their illusions shattered. They could not have expected to find a novelist making jam or up to the elbows gutting fish that the children had caught, or reading the riot act to a gang of boys who had built a bonfire on the beach so that the smoke blew in through every window of the house. People think of writers working in isolation, not caught up in the complexities of family life.

Sir Ian and Miss Arden had breakfast and dinner and slept at the hotel but spent the rest of their time with us or driving all over the county or further afield.

'I wish they'd get married,' said Liz who, a few months ago, had said that only old people and kids were hipped on the subject of marriage.

'Why should they?' I asked.

'It's stupid to look and feel married if you're not. You might as well do it and be done with it.'

'I think Aunt Janet should marry Sir Ian,' said Duncan,

simply to oppose his sister's ideas. 'Then we'd have a Sir in the family.'

'For you that's so keen on Sirs,' Gee aided and abetted his brother.

'Shut up you little creeps,' stormed Liz. 'Aunt Janet can't marry anybody.'

'Why not?' I asked, remembering that not so long ago she had offered to be my bridesmaid.

She turned enormous horror-stricken eyes upon me. 'You wouldn't, would you?'

'No, I wouldn't,' I assured her and she swung round, embattled, on her brothers. 'If we can't have Uncle Twice any more, we don't want anybody,' she told them fiercely. 'And I am *not* keen on Sirs. When I get married it will be somebody that's just plain *some*body like Daddy being just plain John Sandison.'

'As if anybody would want to marry you,' said Duncan.

'That'll be the day,' said Gee.

'And that will be quite enough,' I added conclusively while I noted mentally another thing that is difficult to notice as it happens. As difficult to notice as happiness at the time it occurs is the growth and development of young people as it takes place. When and how had Liz come to her understanding of my feeling that 'if I can't have Twice any more, I don't want anybody'?

In such ways the summer slipped away and at the end of August the family went home and the cottage was shut up for the winter. George, Tom, Hamish and I were looking forward to the winter and busy getting ready for its onset. I had to go to London for a few days in October but now that George and Tom had taken to the cooking and Hamish was a familiar around the house, I could go away with less anxiety, while Tom and George had their own reason now for being pleased to see me go.

'When our book gets out, Tom, the Ladies from Sussex will start writing letters in force again.'

197

'Aye George,' Tom agreed and added to me: 'I hope you have put a puckle bad words in this one, Janet. There are some people that would never bother to write at all except to complain about something and it is good to give them something to complain about.'

'It is good to see the spite coming out of them,' George said, 'and it does no harm to us after all. Spite is like a bad tenant, better out than in.'

'And George and I have been thinking that you should take a day or two while you are down there whatever to go round by Andra's place and see what it is like. After all, he asked you and he is not a bad fellow and was very good when Mrs Henderson died.'

'Perhaps I shall,' I said, 'but I want to get back before Sir Ian and Miss Arden go south. I don't want to get mixed up in London with Hugh Reid and the Hallinzeil crowd.'

'What have you against Sir Hugh Reid?' George asked. 'We thought he was a very fine man when he came to Reachfar that time.'

'People grow apart,' I said repressively.

'Well, well, please yourself.'

'God knows she will do that whatever,' said Tom. 'Anyway, if the weather holds and I think it will, Sir Ian and Miss Arden won't leave the north here before the end of October so you will have plenty of time.'

*   *   *

Nowadays, I was more accustomed to the world of publishing so that the London visits were less of a strain but the London streets were a testing experience for someone acclimatised to the sound of the wind, the sea and the calling of skeins of wild geese. London was no longer the city it had been in my younger days when it had been possible to differentiate between Bond Street and the King's Road by the people one met walking along their pavements.

Perhaps in that earlier time there had been too much privilege, too much difference between the elegant women of Bond Street in their 'little' black dresses, pearls and mink coats and the shabby and sometimes eccentric denizens of the King's Road but the variety of that time seemed to me preferable to the drab uniformity of London in the early 1960s.

I think human nature, like Nature in the broader sense, needs some display of extravagance, even if it can be enjoyed by some only at second hand. A peacock in full display is an extravagant and enjoyable sight that Nature throws up as is the flaring scarlet flower of the poppy with its thousands of seeds that will never find a fertile spot on which to grow. London at this time, I felt, was suffering from a dearth of peacocks and poppies and although I was confident that these ornaments, in the sheer nature of things, would return to the scene, I could not imagine what form they would take. I did not foresee the emergence of the pop stars who would make overnight fortunes, outdo the peacock and the poppy in the extravagance of their display and thus satisfy the glamour needs of millions.

I was glad to leave London for Birmingham, where Andrew met me and drove me some twenty-five miles out of the city along a busy road from which we turned off and were suddenly in a narrow country lane, bordered by hedgerows that almost touched the windows of the car.

'What an extraordinary country England is,' I said. 'We are less than an hour's drive from the bedlam of Birmingham.'

'Bedlam is right,' Andrew said as we made another turning through a gateway in a wall and went up a short curve of drive to the doorway of his house.

It was dark and all I could see of the house was a darker bulk against the sky but the door opened to reveal an elegantly furnished small square hall from which a curving staircase rose to the upper floor. A black-coated manservant carried my bag in and shut the door.

'This is David,' Andrew said. 'If you want a cup of tea at any time or if the roof falls in on you, just shout for David and everything will be all right.'

I greeted the man who was, I thought, about thirty and he said; 'This way, madam,' and led me upstairs to a well-appointed bedroom with an adjoining bathroom. 'Come downstairs when you wish,' he said. 'Dinner will be at eight.' I thanked him, he went away and I looked around me.

The bedroom and bathroom were beautifully decorated and furnished but their individuality was uncompromisingly male, very much, I thought, in the taste of Andrew Boyd. I remembered his aunts in their younger days, with their frilly blouses and their fluttering manner and felt that these rooms were a negation of the frills and flutters, that Andrew's taste had been formed out of his rebellion against the over-ornamented, lace-doylied rooms of Seaview. Here there were no ornaments at all except for a slim crystal vase on the dressing-table which held two late rosebuds. Perhaps the colouring was most responsible for the masculine aura. Curtains, carpet, walls, bathroom fittings were all in inter-related shades of green which gave the rooms a curious air of coolness and impersonality which made me feel very much a stranger.

When I came down to a pleasant combined sitting- and dining-room, it was disconcerting to find, instead of some elegant stranger, the sharp-eyed Andrew Boyd whom I had thought I knew, and I became aware that my knowledge of him was very slight indeed.

'Andrew,' I said as he handed me a drink, 'except for Sashie de Marnay's place in St Jago, this is the most charming house I have ever seen.'

'I am glad you like it, Janet. De Marnay liked it too, as I told you. By the way, I am no further forward with his house in Achcraggan. Those New Zealanders are acting as if they had never learned to read or write.'

The walls of this room were panelled and from the dark

wood, pictures, individually lit, glowed with colour.

'I can see why Sashie raved about this house,' I said. 'How many rooms have you?'

'Upstairs, four bedrooms and four bathrooms. Down here, just this room, my office, a washroom and the kitchen places.'

'Your office in the city isn't enough?'

'I have business meetings here sometimes and I don't always have visitors like you to spend my evenings with. In fact, I have no visitors as a rule except business ones. For weeks on end, I never use this room at all, only the office.'

'I am endlessly inquisitive about how people live,' I said, 'so don't answer if you don't want to. How much staff do you need to keep this place in this degree of elegance?'

'Is elegance the word for it? I am stronger on figures than words. Staff? Only two – David and Cook. Oh, and a man who does the garden. He lives in the village. David is the king-pin, can turn his hand to anything. He is the first chap I ever employed' – he laughed – 'as a lorry-driver when I bought my first clapped-out Army lorry after the war. By the way, David is going to take you out tomorrow because I have a couple of meetings morning and afternoon but we'll have Saturday and Sunday to ourselves. Where would you like to go?'

'But Andrew, David need not take me anywhere,' I protested. 'I am very good at amusing myself. I should be quite happy around the house and garden.'

'I'd like to show you those myself. We are in easy reach of a lot of interesting places – Kenilworth, Warwick, Stratford-upon-Avon or have you seen them all before?'

'None of them. I don't know this central part of England at all. I must say I would love to go to Stratford.'

'Fine.'

'But only if it isn't a nuisance.'

'All it means is that I will take the little car in to the

office and leave the bigger one for you and David, and David will enjoy himself as well.'

So, the next morning, after breakfast had been brought to me in bed by the immaculate David, who wore a white jacket for this duty, I came downstairs to find the same David, in his character as guide-companion to elderly visiting ladies, in a well-cut tweed suit, quietly smart and inconspicuous. He opened the back door of the car.

'David, may I sit in front beside you?'

'Certainly, madam.'

'And please don't call me that. My name is Sandison but I prefer to be called Janet if that doesn't offend your sense of the proper.'

He smiled. 'Janet Reachfar, Boyd said. I found that fascinating.' We got into the front seat of the car. 'I am a Londoner. I had never thought of people being named after the places where they lived.'

I noted that he referred to his employer as 'Boyd' and noted too that although he claimed to be a Londoner, there was no trace of an accent in his voice. Indeed, it did not take long, listening to him, to appreciate that he had had more education, and education of a more exclusive and expensive kind, than his employer had ever had. He was an ideal escort, very knowledgeable on a wide variety of subjects and after an hour or two of strolling round Stratford, he said: 'I suggest that I give you lunch in one of the most vulgar places on earth. Are you interested in the vulgar?'

'I am interested in most things but I would like to give *you* lunch.'

'Thank you,' he said, 'but no. I have my instructions, you know.'

'I see. All right. Where is this vulgar place?' and he stopped in front of a large hotel.

'Right here. They have a bedroom called "Love's Labour Lost" and a lavatory called "All's Well That Ends Well" but the food is quite reasonable.'

It was a most enjoyable day and on the way back to Verehampton, I found myself glancing at the remarkably beautiful hands on the steering wheel and thinking, to my own amazement, that if I were twenty-five years younger, I should be very interested indeed in this young man. Except for the hands, there was nothing remarkable about his appearance but I found him interesting, sympathetic and simply very comfortable company.

When we reached the house, he provided me with a glass of sherry, went away and reappeared in his houseman's black coat to lay the dinner-table by the window at one end of the room. He had an air of total control of the house, the situation and even myself. I felt that any guest who was brought here was given into the hands of David, who could be trusted to do everything for that guest's comfort and entertainment, and Andrew Boyd was emerging in my mind as someone who had a taste for nothing but the best.

*　　　*　　　*

The following day, Andrew showed me over his entire domain, in which he had just pride, and the garden was only a little larger than the cottage and barn gardens put together but it was in total contrast. Instead of our four-foot wall at the barn, it was surrounded by an old wall that was about twelve feet high, so that by contrast with our wind-swept foothold on the beach with its wide views of sea, hills and sky, this garden had an enclosed privacy. And in contrast, too, with our paving, sand and gravel, it was lush almost beyond belief, with sweeps of velvet lawn and even a fig tree growing against one section of wall. Against the wall furthest from the house, there was a glass-house which was full of flowers in pots, which did not surprise me, for I had noticed that the house was decorated with pot plants, all at the peak of their bloom. In the glass-house too there were some tubs in which gardenias flourished, even showing still a few late flowers.

'Gardenias,' I said. 'Monica's favourite flower.'

'Are they?' Andrew asked.

I felt taken aback. 'They used to be. Maybe they aren't any more or she would have told you.'

'Monica has never been here,' he said, setting me right back on my heels and silencing me. 'Let's go in the back way so that you can see the rest of the house. I didn't take you in there earlier because Cook wouldn't have liked you to see the kitchen bits before everything was in order for the day.' He paused, closing the door of the glass-house. 'A thing I have always hated ever since I was a kid,' he said, 'is how little respect people often have for others, like a sarcastic teacher taking the mickey out of some poor kid and the aunts throwing away the stones I used to collect on the beach and arrange in patterns in my room. I employ people who are good at their jobs and take a pride in what they do and I try to respect their attitudes. Cook is proud of the kitchen and likes it to be seen at its best.'

'I absolutely agree with you,' I said, 'and you can certainly pick people. I admire David enormously and we had a splendid day yesterday. I hope he enjoyed it as much as I did.'

'He enjoyed it all right. I'll tell you something. If he didn't think he would enjoy it, he wouldn't have wanted to go and I wouldn't have forced him to go. I never force anybody to do anything. You don't get the best out of people by trying to domineer over them.'

He was a curious mixture of the humane and the ruthless. He tried, he said, to respect the attitudes of his employees which was humane, but he added the rider that this was how to 'get the best out of them' which betokened the ruthless profit motive. As he opened the back door of the house, I literally did not know what to make of him, or where I stood with him and I had no round vision of him as a personality.

When we stepped into the kitchen of the house, I stood

back to gaze. It was a sparkling manifestation of clinical efficiency in blue and white enamel, steel and chromium with a great deal of equipment such as I had never seen before and would not know how to use. There were chest-high ovens with glass doors, strip lighting thrown down from the junctions of walls and ceilings, a square of blue glass with gilt figures which was an electric clock on one wall and there seemed to be timing and temperature devices everywhere. The one thing I knew with certainty at that moment was that his kitchen was a far, far cry from the kitchen at the barn where the only timing device was an old alarm clock which would work only if lying on its side.

Hoping that my stunned silence would be taken for admiration, I also hoped that my preference for old alarm clocks that worked lying on their sides did not show. As I tried to find words, a man came through a doorway in a corner, a man who, I estimated, was in his fifties, large and florid and who wore the uniform of a chef, white neckerchief and all, but without the tall white hat.

'This is Cook,' Andrew said. 'His Christian name is outlandish, he doesn't like it so we call him by his surname.'

'Cook by name and cook by nature,' the man said in what I thought was the accent of Yorkshire. 'Pleased to meet you. Enjoying your stay?' I had noticed that the food served in the house was extremely good, although Andrew ate very little and that with very little apparent interest, but this authoritative figure in the white panoply was the last person I expected to find in Andrew's kitchen. I think I had expected to meet some humble country-woman who would be kept in order and out of sight by the immaculate and impeccable David.

Over the lunch table I said: 'I feel very honoured as a female to be entertained in this all-male establishment, Andrew.'

'So you should be,' he told me with his shameless leer.

'You are the first. Oh, the odd business acquaintances bring their wives with them now and again but you are the first woman to come on her own. De Marnay told me I would enjoy your company and I do. You stayed with him for quite a bit at one time he told me.'

'Yes, I did, for half a year, pretty well. I wish you would call him Sashie. I always have to blink and think twice when you say de Marnay.'

'I'll try if it pleases you but it is such a nance sort of name.'

We spoke of Sashie for a little, I on my guard as I always was about Sashie and his privacies, but Andrew seemed to have accepted him without question and asked no awkward questions now.

'And when did you last see Monica?' I then asked.

'Let me think. Not since April, I think it was. That's right, April.' His glance intensified. 'Is she a particular friend of yours, Janet?'

'Not now. She was once, during the war and for a bit afterwards but then I went abroad and well – tout lasse, tout passe, tout casse as Sashie would say.'

'French? I never took to it in my two years at Fortavoch Academy.'

'Sorry. Everything tires, everything passes, everything breaks up. People grow away from people or maybe I am just fickle and disloyal. Do you find you grow away as I do?'

'I have never had enough friends to find out. But you never grew away from Achcraggan and George and Tom.'

'I think one's family is a different category of relationship.'

'I have never had a family in the real sense so I don't know about that either. You and de – Sashie have changed my attitude to people though. Until now, I have always used people instead of making friends of them. I don't mean that you have reformed me so that I'll never use people again but you two have made me see that I *am* inclined just to use them. When you walked into the office in Birmingham that day, I felt sort of dumbfounded.'

'You didn't look it.'

'Maybe not but honestly I didn't know until after you had gone, a good few days after, in fact, what I felt and it suddenly dawned on me that I had come up against somebody who was more likely to use *me* than let me use *her* and the odd thing was that I didn't mind.' He grinned at me, that grin that was compounded of the shrewd and the sly. 'Then de – Sashie came along and I had the same feeling. You two have been something of a shock to me.'

'And we *have* used you, Andrew, now that I think of it but nobody can be used, be willing to give help, unless they want to, can they?'

'Oh yes they can. People can be used without even knowing that it's happening to them if it is done in the right way.'

'You will have to explain.'

'Well, take Monica,' he said, astounding me while he played with the cigarette between his fingers and was unaware of his effect on me. 'I sit on a board along with her brother, the Honourable Gerald, a smart enough bloke but very Eton, Oxford, ex-Diplomatic Corps. Makes no bones about the fact that he will sit on boards with types like me but wouldn't sponsor them for his clubs. I don't blame him for that. He is only acting according to his lights. But I found out that Egbert Fitzhugh the art expert was his cousin.'

'Egbert Fitzhugh?' I said. 'Is that old fish still in the land of the living, if he was ever alive at all, that is?'

'He is alive all right and more of an expert than ever. You know him?'

I told him about my one-time acquaintance with Egbert Fitzhugh and then: 'Well, what about Monica?' I asked, thoroughly enjoying myself now that the victimiser seemed to be turning into the victim.

'I met the Honourable Gerald one day by accident in a restaurant off Piccadilly and the Lady Monica was with him. He more or less had to introduce me. I had lost out on getting to Fitzhugh through Gerald but I got there through Monica although it took a little time.'

'I thought you must have met Monica over the sale of Poyntdale.'

'No. I always work through solicitors over property. I was quite surprised when I found out that Monica had been the owner.'

'And when you had got to old Eg, you just dropped Monica?' I asked after a moment.

'More or less.'

'Andrew Boyd, you are what my nephew Gee used to call absolutely bebominable but at least you are honest. I thought you were going to marry Monica.'

'No, I never had that idea but I think she had ideas about marrying *me*. Monica uses people too. I think I told you before that she and I are the same kind in most ways but she is the marrying kind and I am not.'

I looked around the elegant room. 'You obviously don't need a wife,' I said. 'This place is quite lovely, not like most bachelors' dreary barracks.'

'I don't notice the house much any more, except for the pictures, but David and I had a lot of fun restoring it and gathering the furniture together. David knows quite a bit about furniture and stuff. He comes from that sort of family.'

'He came to you first as a lorry-driver, you said? He doesn't seem to be the type somehow. I am old enough now to know that one shouldn't think of people in terms of types because nobody is typical of anything except himself but I still do it.'

'I met David in a pub in Leeds. It wasn't long before we

found out that we were both bad boys in the eyes of the people who knew us. David doesn't hold with his family's ideas. His father is an Army man and things came to a head when David would not follow in the family footsteps. David cleared out, we came across one another, we got on together and there it is. He doesn't only run the house. He is a big help in a business way too.'

'And Cook?' I asked.

'He is a more recent arrival than David. I have an interest in one or two hotels in Devon and Cornwall. Cook was chef in one of them but he developed heart trouble. We were just embarking on the new kitchen here when he came out of hospital and it seemed like sense to have him here for a bit and pick his brains. Then he just stayed on.' The grin showed again. 'Using people again, you see. You are not bored with all this?'

'No. Fascinated. I make my living by writing about people, remember.'

'You won't find much to write about in Cook. He is just a poor old devil with nobody of his own in the world.'

I was more interested in Andrew than I was in Cook. Andrew saw himself as a hard man who used people and picked their brains, he took a hard view of the world but unlike many people of this kind, he was not indulgent towards himself. He took a hard view of himself also and I think he did not even notice that not only had he made use of Cook but also had provided him with a home and the light work which was now his only capability.

'I like this house,' he said now, 'and it is handy when I have to do a bit of entertaining but I am not much of a one for possessions just as possessions, except for the pictures, that is. You said once that living was a process of discovering yourself. Since I bought this place, I have discovered that I am more interested in the garden than in the house. I had always seen myself as the big-city type but I like the garden. I know damn-all about gardening, of course, and I haven't much spare time, but I like to see the stuff growing and changing.'

As always with Andrew, the more he talked, the more I liked him.

*　　　*　　　*

When I returned home, George and Tom asked many questions about my weekend with Andrew which I answered as best I could and then George said: 'And is he still running after Monica?' so I told them the reasons behind Andrew's attentions to Monica and added: 'He is a very strange fellow altogether. I like him but I don't know what to make of him.'

'Are you sure that it is not yourself that he has a notion of?' George asked. 'You can be damn' stoopid as Sir Ian says when fellows have a notion of you.'

'And now *you* are being damn' stoopid,' I replied.

'No, George is nothing of the sort,' said Tom. 'Look at the time a whilie ago when yon wild-looking fellow that was a painter and a friend o' Guido Sidonio came north here. The whole parish except you saw that he had his eye on you.'

'A whilie ago!' I exploded. 'That was about twenty-five years ago.'

'A puckle years is neither here nor there,' Tom argued. 'We were talking about you being stupid.'

'And I am telling you that I am not as stupid now as I was twenty-five years ago. And you have got the whole thing wrong anyhow. I knew perfectly well where Bertie Stubb's eye was for *I* had my eye on *him*.'

'Then why did you run away from him like a hare with a dog at its tail and hide in the hay-loft?' George enquired.

Exasperated, I wondered if I had done a single thing in my whole life that these two did not know about. 'Oh, shut up. We are not talking about Bertie Stubb. We are talking about Andrew Boyd and he hasn't got a notion of me as you call it. Would I have gone and stayed with him if I thought he had?'

'Well,' Tom said, 'Twice had a notion of you and you went and stayed with *him* for a goodish while.'

'That was different,' I said, 'and just be quiet about the whole thing.'

In bed that night, however, looking out at the dark hill of Reachfar humped as if in sleep against the lighter sky, I realised that it was not 'that' that was different but that I was different. I was no longer interested in any man in a sexual way. I remembered how, sitting in the car with David, I had thought that I could be interested in him if – and it was a big impossible if – I had been twenty-five years younger. I was interested in Andrew as a personality, a personality who could be studied without the overtone or undertow of sex which, nowadays, I would look upon as an embarrassing nuisance.

We settled down for the winter. A writer, writing, lives inside a private world which can develop a more immediate reality than the world that lies beyond the charmed circle circumscribed by the pen-point. Christmas came and the year 1962 arrived, bringing little variation in our lives, for the weather was bad and the older children elected to stay at home to attend school parties and various functions rather than open up the cottage for a few days. The savage weather continued throughout January and on Candlemas Day in early February I said to Tom: 'This should please you. It's coming down from the north-east as if it had never blown before.' He listened to the wind, watched the snow sliding down the large window and said: 'Aye, this is what I like to see at Candlemas.'

He and George now had a new occupation. When the first letters from readers had come in in 1959 and I was replying to them, George said: 'Put the black stuff in the way you can do and make a copy of what you write back to them.'

'Why?'

'Because Tom and I are going to keep the letters. They will make fine reading on the winter nights. And if we keep the letters, we might as well keep the answers. We might as well do the job right—'

'Or not do it at all,' I finished for him. 'All right,' I agreed and put carbon and a copy sheet into the machine.

After a letter-writing session, I would give them their 'take' which they would put into a large cardboard box that they kept in a cupboard in the kitchen.

Shortly after my visit to Andrew, I came down one morning to find two mice cavorting around the kitchen and although I am not a timid or nervous woman, I admit freely that I would prefer to meet a lion face-to-face than be in the same room with a rodent of any kind. It is not fear, it is deep loathing that dates from my childhood and shuddering, my teeth chattering, I ran upstairs, opened both bedroom doors and shouted: 'Get up, you two! There are mice in the kitchen.'

'Mercy on us,' said George, 'I thought old Jean's ghost had come back.'

'Stop being funny and get these filthy brutes out of there,' I said, went to my room and climbed, fully clothed, into bed.

About an hour later, George called me downstairs, displayed two dead mice on the coal shovel and said: 'We got them but the wee booggers have been in among our Ladies from Sussex papers.'

'Throw them out,' I said.

'Of course I'm going to throw them out. What else would I do with a couple o' mice? Stew them?'

'Not the mice, the papers. The kitchen is no place to keep your old rubbish anyway.'

'We will *not* throw out our Ladies' papers,' said Tom. 'We'll clean out the boxes and take them up to our rooms.'

By this time, paper of various kinds was accumulating

in the house in large quantities and a heap of files containing publishing contracts, business letters, accounts and many more items was taking up too much room on the book-shelves in my bedroom, so I caused to be delivered a metal filing cabinet, a paper punch and a supply of file folders. I explained to George and Tom how their papers should be stored and was amazed as I always was at how they could take to something new, something completely different from all their former experience.

'I see,' George said. 'They will be like big books when we are finished with them, but a book should start at the beginning. Where, think you, is the first letter we ever got, Tom?'

Solemnly, from the drawer that held the dusters, Tom took my father's spectacles and put them on while, in my irrelevant way, I thought that in Andrew Boyd's perfectly-run house, old spectacles among the dusters would not be tolerated.

'That is going to take a bit of finding,' Tom said. 'How would yourself go about it, Janet?'

'You can sort them by date,' I said, 'but why bother? All I want is that they should be tidy.'

'If we are going to do it at all—' George began.

'All right. Take the kitchen table through to the fire and sort the stuff into a heap for each year first and then sort it into the months of the year but it will take you all winter to sort out that mess.'

'The man who made time made plenty,' said Tom and they set about their task forthwith.

It did not take them as long as I had prophesied and they became so neat and proficient that when they had filed all their Sussex papers I turned over to them all the filing that had to be done. What with their filing, their sticking-in, their mail, their cooking, their washing and their visits to Malcolm the Minister and his television, the months while the gardens lay under snow seemed to fly past.

In April, the Easter holidays came, the cottage was opened up and the older children got busy with their various activities while Sandy-Tom stumped about the gardens or on the beach, closely followed by his Fly-dog. He would soon be five years old but he still had the chubby look of a young toddler, spoke very little and was always serenely happy, whether on his own or playing with the others or Tom and George. This year, however, we discovered that he had a memory for places and events, a more detailed memory, indeed, than the older children.

The year before, George and Tom had planted early potatoes in Aunt Betsy's old bath and while the older children extended their search for buried treasure to an area of rough tussocky grass, George gave Sandy-Tom a trowel and let him dig potatoes out of the old bath. That was in the summer of the year before. This Easter, one day while I was preparing lunch, Sandy-Tom came into the kitchen, rubbed himself against me in his affectionate way, then looked with strange concentration at a potato that I was holding. 'Me?' he said. 'All right,' I said and let him have it, with which he said 'Fie-dog' and went out followed by his dog. I followed in turn and he went out of the barn garden, along the grass, into the cottage garden and straight to the old bath where he buried his potato in the earth it contained. This was the first indication he had given us of the presence of memory over a longish period and we all felt as if a miracle had happened. The little incident brought us all more closely together as we marvelled over it and it seemed miraculous indeed that Sandy-Tom, the so-called weakest member of the group, should have this power at the time when the three older, so-called stronger children were all diverging and going their separate ways at the drive of their personalities. Liz, at nearly fifteen, could be extremely difficult but Sandy-Tom could always control her tantrums with his 'Aw, come come,' and a rub of his cheek against the part of her that was nearest to him. To see this happen was part of that happiness which is so difficult to record.

I had much sympathy with Liz and her tantrums. Ours was an old-fashioned community where many ancient peasant habits of thought lingered on and the peasant preference, common to many races, for male children still floated in the air. It had been present, for instance, when George and Tom said that it would be more natural if Jock had been the writer instead of myself. In the village street, people would greet Liz with: 'And where are your brothers today?' as if, said Liz, she could not find her way along the street without them and the boys did nothing to help matters for they invariably pitted their combined wits against her. Also, she was not a pretty child, although Sashie said and I believed him, that she would have beauty later on. The hair she had worn in pig-tails as a child had been cut and now looked like a mid-brown shiny helmet framing her face and she still had her long shapely legs but she had no interest in clothes, despite her concealed desire to look pretty and strode about like a young Amazon in very short, rather dirty shorts and an old shirt or sweater.

After the holidays were over and Doctor Hay called for a cup of tea, I said: 'Shona feels she has got more than she can cope with in Liz. Shona is so gentle that she can't really understand the wild Sandisons.'

'Liz will be all right,' Doctor Hay comforted me. 'It is just that she is a girl but part of her wants to be a boy like her brothers. I have never seen such a close-knit bunch as that family. But when Liz is a little older and discovers what she has got as a girl –' she winked a mischievous dark eye at me '– your sister-in-law will really have something on her hands.'

*　　*　　*

Almost every week Doctor Hay would call for a cup of tea on her way back from her country round and never failed in her delight in the robust health of George and Tom.

'If you tested their sight,' I said one day, 'it might not be perfect but it is good enough for what they want to do.'

'Nobody can ask for better than that,' she said.

But Tom and George did not ask for anything. They were content with what each day brought and never forgot to be grateful aloud when something pleasant happened, as on the day in May when Sashie called from London to arrange a visit. When I put the receiver down, George said: 'I have said many a hard thing in my time about telephones in general but I'll say now that it brings very good news a lot of the time.'

'Aye, it does that,' Tom agreed. 'When is the wee fellow coming?'

'Tuesday. He is spending the weekend with Andrew.'

Sashie expressed himself as delighted with our new home. 'It is quite perfect, darling and exactly like all three of you, if you know what I mean,' he said when he had been shown round. 'It is not as elegant as Silver Beach or Verehampton,' I said, 'but George, Tom and I have less sophisticated and expensive tastes than you and Andrew.'

'For a writer, you are extremely careless in your use of the spoken word,' Sashie told me while George and Tom chuckled. Much of their liking for Sashie derived from their pleasure in the fact that he could 'sort' me, as they called it, that he was the one person of our family and acquaintance who did not treat me in a slightly kid-gloved way. 'Andrew Boyd may be sophisticated but I certainly am not. Do you know what the word means? Obviously you don't. It means adulterated, rendered impure in some way and I will not be accused of adultery and impurity.'

'All right, don't blow your top and you know perfectly well what I meant. How are Caleb and Trixie and Silver Beach?'

'Caleb and Trixie are as ever and sending their love but I have brought you a tiny bit of Silver Beach.'

He fetched a flat package he had left in the porch and gave it to me. It was the picture he had promised me, a painting of Silver Beach from my favourite standpoint at the west end of the house which showed the house itself and away beyond it the long stretch of silver sand, blue sky and bluer sea. I set the picture against the back of a chair and stood back from it.

'Look George, Tom, Sashie's house in St Jago.'

'My, but that is a bonnie place.'

'Aye, it is that.'

It was now that I saw what brought the tears to my eyes. In the background, which seemed to be infinite, I could see two tiny human figures, one smaller than the other, facing one another, their heads bowed forward as they looked down at their hands. They were Twice and a little girl called Percy Soames who had stayed with us once, as Sashie and I had seen them on the beach one day, in the distance, examining a shell or some item of beach trove that Percy had found. The figures were so delicately worked that, to the eye that had not seen the actuality, they might have been part of the light and shade of the rippled sand of the shore. I turned away to hide what I felt and Sashie's voice said: 'I am so glad you think it came out right, Janet,' and he then added to Tom and George: 'I wanted it to be just as she remembered it.'

When I returned from the kitchen where I had gone to recover myself, he said: 'I made a small picture for Andrew too and he seemed to like it enough to add it to that rather distinguished collection of his.'

'A Silver Beach picture?' I asked feeling, unreasonably, a little jealous.

'I painted it at Silver Beach but it is a bit of our old houses round by the church.'

'You mean you sat down at Silver Beach and painted a view of Achcraggan?'

'I always paint standing up, not sitting down.'

'But from memory?'

'I invariably paint from memory.' He indicated the painting he had given me. 'I painted that inside your bedroom at Silver Beach where I could not see the real thing. Trixie was very annoyed because I got some paint on the curtains.'

'I thought people always painted from models, looking at the actual thing,' I said.

'People have their own ways of doing things. I know a writer who wrote so secretly that she had the horrors at the idea of somebody reading what she had written.'

'But seriously—'

'Seriously, it is quite simple. If I can't remember a thing clearly enough to re-create it in paint, I know I can't make a picture of it. It is some sort of paradoxical process of filtering the subject into clarity and at the same time seeing it coloured by the light of one's mind. I am quite sure you use a similar process without being aware of it when you write. But let's not be analytical. George, how is our friend Malcolm the Minister?'

Sashie, who had rebuked me for using of him the word 'sophisticated', did lead what most of us would call a very sophisticated life at this time, flying around the United States and Europe, like what was coming to be known as 'the jet set', but not as a member of that or any other set, yet he fitted with ease into the simple life of Tom, George and myself. His interest in the activities of George and Tom was genuine, from their gardening to their Ladies from Sussex files, but especially in the gardening. To Sashie, brought up in cities, the processes of nature were as mysterious as were his own arts of painting, music and dance to Tom and George and he was fascinated and at the same time frustrated by the fact that they knew so much without being able to explain coherently what they knew or how they knew it. During the week he spent with us, I spent a great deal of time trying to interpret between the two sides. Sashie who was so very articulate could become almost furious with frustration when George and Tom failed to convey meaning to him. The fury was not directed at them but against himself and I went into the garden one day to find him totally exasperated.

Shortly after the garden wall had been built, we had planted a row of clematis along our south boundary and these plants were now sending out long shoots which had to be fixed to a trellis. 'Come here at once, Janet,' Sashie shouted. Tom and George were not tying, but untying, clematis shoots from the trellis. 'I tied them to go *that* way,' said the livid Sashie, 'and they said *they* won't *want* to go that way. Why?'

'I don't know.'

'You mean you don't know which way they will want to go?'

'They will certainly want to go that way –' I indicated the direction favoured by George and Tom '– but I am not sure why.'

'How can you be sure they want to go that way if you don't know why?'

'It is just a fact about how plants want to go. You can tie one of them your way if you like but when you come again you will find that it is not doing as well as the others.'

'But *why*? George and Tom don't know what these plants are, even, so how can they know where they want to go?'

'They are clematis.'

'But how do you know about where they will go?'

'I have never worked it out,' I said, 'any more than Tom and George have but wait a minute.' I took hold of a long trailing shoot and swung it this way and that and knew instinctively that it would want to grow in the direction that Tom and George said. 'It is partly the way the shoot leaves the stem,' I said, and then as if light were breaking in my mind, 'and most plants tend to grow towards the rising sun, like to grow in an easterly direction in this part of the world rather than in any other. This has just come to me and may be wrong but I don't think so.'

'Well,' said Sashie, satisfied, 'that makes sense. Go away, you two and let me tie mine properly now that I know why I am doing it.'

George and Tom were overawed by the multiplicity of Sashie's gifts and the enquiring nature of his mind but he was equally overawed by their instinctive knowledge and this led to that mutual respect on which Andrew Boyd had placed such high value.

*   *   *

On the last evening of his visit, Sashie and I sat up late, discussing with some malicious enjoyment, as was our wont, the affairs of our acquaintances and friends.

'We oughtn't,' I said at one point, 'to be so bitchy about Edward, poor soul.'

'Do you imagine he has a soul?' Sashie enquired. 'He hasn't come up here yet with Sir Ian and the large Herb?'

'No.'

'He will, he will, and remember what I told you. Watch out for the adolescent post-divorce bounce.'

'Oh be quiet. I am nearly old enough to be his mother.' I changed the subject. 'What a fantastic set-up Andrew Boyd has at Verehampton, don't you think?'

'Quite fantastic. After what you had told me about him, it was the last thing I expected. But I am grateful to him for trying so hard with those people in New Zealand. If they don't come to their senses soon, I shall go out there, inflict myself upon them and *then* they'll be sorry they didn't answer his letters.'

'How were you so sure that Monica would never get Andrew after you met him that first time? Did he tell you that day that he was chasing her because of Egbert Fitzhugh? I wouldn't have thought that Andrew would reveal his seedier machinations even to you on such a short acquaintance.'

Sashie frowned at me in a puzzled way. 'Who is Egbert Fitzhugh?'

'Monica's old art-dealing cousin. Don't you remember him?'

'Oh yes. I don't remember him. I have in my mind only a vague adumbration of someone I hoped to forget.'

I felt that Sashie was being elusive and evasive which he could be to an extraordinary degree but which merely made me more persistent.

'Then if you didn't know he was chasing her just because of Fitzhugh and paintings, how did you know that he wasn't simply chasing her?'

'Darling, I do wish you would use more elegant language. Chasing her indeed. You make the pursuit sound so – so unchaste.'

'Stop being not very funny. How did you know?'

'Andrew Boyd simply does not chase women.'

'Rubbish. All that stuff about not being the marrying kind. All young men chase women and some old ones do it too just as all women chase men, except that I have given it up now.'

'Not men like Andrew Boyd.'

'What's so different about *him*? His father and his grandfather chased every woman in sight.'

'Janet, you stayed at Verehampton,' Sashie said impatiently, 'for a whole weekend. Are you losing your powers of observation? Andrew is homosexual. The pleasant David is the partner. Couldn't you *feel* it?'

'Cor stone the crows,' I said when I had recovered my breath. 'Andrew Boyd! Who'd have thought it?' For I recognised at once that Sashie spoke the truth. The entire atmosphere of Verehampton now became coherent and lost the strangeness that I remembered.

'You sound shocked,' Sashie said rather sternly. 'I don't see why. It is simply another form of loving, after all.'

'I am shocked but not in the way you think. If Andrew and

David make each other happy, I am all for it. But I have this great backlog of memory about Andrew's father and hearsay from Tom and George about his grandfather so – well – it is as if those clematis out there that I expect to grow to the east suddenly turned about and headed due west.'

Sashie laughed. 'Perhaps I ought not to be surprised that you did not recognise it. It is not over-obvious, I grant you. I thought Andrew was taking a bit of a risk when he wrote me that he had invited you to Verehampton, if he did not want you to know what was going on, that is.'

'Do you know,' I said, 'I am getting the feeling that he invited me because he did want me to know.'

'That is possible. He likes you and admires you very much and in a curious way he is a scrupulously honest man, in relationships, I mean. That is why I like him so much.'

'He wasn't scrupulously honest in his dealings with Monica,' I said, my inbred prejudice dying hard.

'That was not in his sense a relationship, I should think, but more of a business deal. I am sure he entertained Monica in as lavish a way as even she could expect while he was – chasing her.'

'I suppose you are right.'

'This won't make any difference in your attitude to Andrew? If he asks you, you will go to Verehampton again?' He sounded anxious.

'Of course I will. I have never seen such a lovely place with the exception of Silver Beach. And I *like* Andrew and his David too. David took me to Stratford for a day and we had a splendid time.'

'David took you to Stratford?'

'Yes, on the Friday. Andrew had meetings and things and he said—'

'Darling, that clinches it. Andrew had every intention that you should know the situation.'

'But why should he want me to know?'

'Because he is honest, as I told you. He values you as a

friend – he told me that in plain words – and he wouldn't cheat you. He would rather lose you than let you have a false estimate of him.'

'How much more you can learn in an afternoon than I can in three days.'

'That is not precisely how it is. You spoke of your backlog of memory about Andrew's forebears but I went to Verehampton with a different backlog. I didn't know if Andrew intended that I should discover his nature. I think he took me to Verehampton because of you, really. He talked about you most of the time. But these men are extremely sensitive and seem to have an instinct for knowing who will be sympathetic to them and who will not. And then, of course, Andrew may have thought at first that I was one of his own kind. It is not uncommon for people to have such an impression of me, as you know.' Here was the similarity between Sashie and Andrew, this clear, cool amused awareness of the estimate people made of them. 'In any case, he could not know the backlog of memory I brought with me, from rattling around among dancers and actors and artists of all kinds in my young days, circles that are more liberal than most. And Andrew and David are far from obvious compared with some. But did you notice, for instance, how Andrew spoke the name David? It is difficult to define but there was that *nuance*—'

'Yes. Yes there was,' I agreed, remembering.

'I became aware of the situation as soon as I met David and the other little things I noticed were merely confirmations. But I am terribly anxious that you should not *mind* about this, Janet. People like David and Andrew need friends, people who are not of their own kind but who accept them as they are.'

'I honestly don't mind, Sashie. I like both of them very much but I am so glad that you have told me about them. I can't describe to you what I felt on that visit except that, although it was all so pleasant, I had an uncanny feeling of being out of my depth. After I left, although I had enjoyed every moment, I even hoped that Andrew wouldn't ask me again. When I was in the train on the way home, it was like looking back on a fantastic dream, as if I had spent three days in an ambience that was indescribably strange but all the uncanniness is gone now. After all, with my memories of Andrew and his origins, it *was* strange to see him against the background of that beautiful house. It is exactly your period, isn't it?'

'Yes, but I am not sure that I am now as eighteenth-century as I used to be. I didn't think I could ever like the Victorian but you have made a success of furnishing this place.'

'I didn't set out to be Victorian or any other period,' I said. 'Like most things I am involved in, it simply evolved. There were the bits and pieces of Reachfar stuff which the three of us have known all our lives. I write, so I needed something with drawers to hold manuscripts and paper and stuff and an old minister west the country advertised that desk so I bought it. I like to sew and knit and that Victorian work-table came up at auction so I bought it. Anyway, I am glad you approve and I hope you will come to see us again soon.'

*　　*　　*

After Sashie had gone, we had a few flat days, all of us very conscious of the hole he left behind him, as George called it, but soon it was full summer again, the family came to the cottage, Sir Ian and Miss Arden returned to the hotel, the Ladies from Sussex paid their calls and we were enmeshed in the family summer round.

'Edward's comin' up later on,' Sir Ian said, which made me feel a little uncomfortable, for Sashie had made me self-conscious about Edward.

'I met your wartime friend Lady Monica Daviot,' Miss Arden told me, 'at the Hallinzeils. As soon as I heard her name, I remembered your mentioning it. It is not a very common one, so I asked if she were the same person. It was most extraordinary. Nearly everybody at table that night seemed to have known you at one time or another, not just as a writer, you know, but socially. Sir Hugh Reid said that you and he were at school together.'

'That's right but none of it so very extraordinary. It was Hugh Reid who sent Lady Hallinzeil to St Jago so I got to know her and her husband a little.'

'Then there was Kathleen Malone, the singer—'

'Yes. I knew Kathleen as a youngster but it was Hugh who sent her to St Jago too. I think Hugh is at the centre of the web, not me.'

'Anyhow, you seemed to be all round the table, a sort of Banquo's ghost. Next time you come to London, you must renew your acquaintance with all these people.'

'I don't think so,' I said. 'It would be like the suffragettes' dinner you told me about once. They belong to my past, so many Banquo's ghosts.'

'You will certainly meet Lady Monica again. She and Edward have been going everywhere together during the last few months and Edward is coming up here in August.'

'I shall look forward to that,' I said truthfully and with inner relief. Why had it not occurred to me that, in that London circle of dinner parties and exhibitions of paintings, sooner or later Monica would come across Edward who was the ideal prey? He was reasonably personable, extremely rich, a little younger than Monica but she looked younger than her years.

'Ian hopes they will marry,' Miss Arden was saying.

'And you?' I asked, noting the frown on her forehead.

'It is none of my business but between ourselves, dear, Lady Monica has seven children which seems a bit of an undertaking for any man and Edward doesn't strike me as a very family sort of person.'

'Some of them aren't children any more. Two of them are

steps – Monica married a widower – and they must be getting on for twenty.'

'Quite the worst age,' Miss Arden announced pessimistically, 'when they are neither one thing nor the other, but people will do as they please.'

And Edward will certainly do as Monica pleases, I thought but I did not say it aloud.

'Did you ever meet Edward's first wife, dear?' Miss Arden was asking. 'Ian can become quite apoplectic about her but he does exaggerate so.'

'Even Sir Ian couldn't exaggerate the awfulness of Anna,' I said. 'I think she was the nastiest creature I have ever met. I don't know what got into Edward about her.'

'My dear, men have so little sense,' said Miss Arden.

Miss Arden treated Sir Ian very much as she treated her brother Aubrey, in a brusque yet affectionate sisterly way which he seemed to find very comfortable. I think he found in her something of a replacement for his mother, Madame Dulac, at whose imperious beck and call he had lived for so many years. I found a similarity in their relationship to the relationship that had developed between Hamish Henderson and myself, for just as Sir Ian would say: 'What d'ye think, Rosie?' Hamish would not commit himself to a new shirt or suit without saying: 'D'you think it's all right, Mistress?'

*   *   *

When Edward and Monica arrived, Edward was once again in the dazed besotted state that Anna had once induced in him and I could hardly wait to write the news to Sashie, who replied by return.

'Darling, isn't Providence wonderful how it removes pitfalls from your way? As you know, I regard Monica as something of a bitch but she is a more intelligent one than Anna and will keep Edward in a very pretty and comfortable cage and feed him lots of sugar and everybody will be ever so happy ever after but don't expect me to come over for the wedding. Now to a topic of much more interest. Andrew has at last received some response from those New Zealanders and will be up your way fairly soon I should think—'

In the event, Andrew did not come north until late October, when all our summer visitors had dispersed and we were about to settle in for the winter and this time, which I found significant, he brought David with him.

'Goodness, we are glad to see you both,' I greeted them. 'All our summer people have gone and we are missing them. George and Tom, here is Andrew and this is David – sorry, I don't know your other name.'

'It is Welton but David will do very well,' he said.

Andrew looked around the room. 'You have made a right job of this old place, Janet. What d'you think, David?' He and David no longer appeared as employer and servant but as close friends.

'And Janet was telling us that you have a right fine place too, Andrew,' George said.

'David here saw to most of it,' Andrew said. 'He knows more about the restoration lark than I do. That's why he came up on this trip. I wanted his verdict on these houses.'

'You really have got Sashie's house?' I asked.

'We've got both of them. Sashie can have his choice. The owner of the second one turned up quite suddenly, in Wales of all places, an old retired sea-faring man.'

'We have even got the keys,' David said. 'Dug one out of a solicitor's office in Inverness and the other out of an office in Dingwall. They are out in the car, weighing down upon the springs. I think they must have been made by a blacksmith.'

'Listen,' said Andrew, 'let's all go round there and have a look.'

We all piled into the car and drove to the other end of the village where we had to fight our way through a rusty gate and up the overgrown path to the steps in front of the first house.

'So it's these two places you have been talking about,' George said. 'Tom and I thought it was them over there,' and he pointed to two Victorian semi-detached villas.

'This is old Cleek's house,' Tom said while David struggled with the large key in the rusty lock. 'Maybe we had better stop outside, George, in case Cleek's ghost comes after us and sends us for whisky.'

'Janet, have you one of those paper hankies about you?' George asked and I gave him the tissue. 'Here, lad,' he said to David, 'get a little o' your engine oil on this and bring me a spanner or something.'

He coated the key with oil, put it in the lock, put the spanner through the large ring handle, gripped the ends of the spanner and the lock turned.

'The first move in house restoration,' Andrew told David, 'is to know how to get in.'

There was a teasing affection in the words and I felt that this was how they normally behaved and not as they had done when I was at Verehampton.

Both houses were in the last stages of dereliction, Tom and George said quite plainly that Andrew was mad to have bought them, I myself was appalled by the smell of damp and rotting woodwork but neither Andrew nor David were in the least dismayed.

'Verehampton was far worse than this,' David told us.

'Who used to live in this one?' I asked in the hall of the second house while Andrew poked around in the attics and David, accompanied now by young Lewie the Joiner and his ladder, climbed over the outside of the roof.

'The Princess,' said Tom.

'Princess?'

'That was her byename,' George said. 'I canna mind on her real name now but it will come back to me.'

*   *   *

That evening, after Andrew and David had gone back to the hotel, I said: 'Look here, you two, you always say I have a good memory but I don't remember those two houses at all when I was a kid, although Sashie says they must have been there since about the 1780s.'

'That is not to be wondered at,' Tom said. 'All your time in Achcraggan was spent in the church or down in the Fisher Town among the herring guts with Bella Beagle.'

'Or holding the horse outside The Plough,' I reminded him. 'Who was old Cleek? That a byename too?'

'Aye. His real name was Donald Sinclair,' George told me. 'He had been a sea captain but he lost a hand in some accident at sea and had a big steel cleek – a hook, ye know – instead of a hand.'

'I know that a cleek is a hook. I haven't forgotten all I ever knew.'

'He was a devil of a man,' Tom went on. 'He was about six feet six with a big black whisker and a belly so big he could hardly walk. We were all frightened of him. He used to be at the corner o' the church when we were running past to school and he would reach out with the cleek and get you by the jersey and send you to The Plough for a bottle o' whisky. Then, at the finish of school, he would be there again and somebody would get cleeked and sent for another bottle. Do you mind on him, George, or was he before your time?'

'I mind on him fine,' George said, 'but I never got cleeked. He was past it by the time I came to the school. He used to be in his bed at the window on the left o' the front door with his bottle on the windowsill. Donnie Boatie got a penny a week for fetching whisky to him.'

'It was said that he was a fairly rich man when he came here but he must have drunk every penny before he died.'

'Like the Princess,' George said.

'Who was she?' I asked.

'She was a breed o' the Monros o' The Heights,' George told

me, 'and I am minding on her name now. It was Vandaleur.'

'Very lah-di-dah for Achcraggan,' I said.

'Aye, that is how she got the byename. That and the place where she was born and the way she used to dress herself.'

'The place where she was born?' I repeated.

'Aye. It was an island somewhere about Canada, where there was a military barracks. God knows I should be able to mind on the name of it if I had ever been able to learn anything. She was for ever preaching about it from her window when we were passing back and fore to the school. Something to do with royalty.'

'Prince Edward Island?' I suggested.

'That's it. What it is to have brains.'

'Never mind that. How did a breed of the Monros of The Heights finish up as a Vandaleur on Prince Edward Island?'

'One o' the Monro lassies was a lady's maid to some General's wife or another. The Monro lassies were all bonnie and this one took the eye o' some officer o' the name o' Vandaleur on Prince Edward Island and the upshot of the thing was the Princess. We are talking of things away back in His Old Self's time, ye know.'

'People said she was illegitimate when she was brought home here to the old Monro granny,' Tom said, 'but people are everlasting scandalising about people. She had the name of Vandaleur and not Monro, whatever, but the poor craitur was a cripple with what they called infantile paralysis although she was a cripple to her dying day as an old woman and no longer an infant.'

'His Old Self,' said George, 'used to tell of the to-do in Achcraggan when the lawyer came and bought that house and moved the old granny and the baby into it and how the banker from Dingwall used to drive down once a month to see them. Monro had drunk himself to death and the son had taken over The Heights and had shoved his old mother into a wee single-end. The old granny was dead long before

I went to the school but I mind on her story because I like stories where the scandalisers get green with envy o' the one they have been scandalising about.'

'She was dead before myself went to the school,' Tom rejoined. 'Indeed, when I went, the Princess herself would have been about fifty maybe but it was hard to tell, with all yon feathers and lace and veils she had about her. Herself and Cleek kept Achcraggan in things to speak about until the day they died but that was away back long before you were born, Janet. Why are we speaking all these old yarns?'

'Sashie will like to know all this.'

'Oh then, how much more can we mind on, George?'

'Were the Princess and Cleek friends?' I asked.

'In a manner o' speaking they were,' said George, 'until they got drunk and then there would be bonnets on the green. The Princess could walk and no more and she had a crutch and Cleek had his cleek. They would start off by visiting one another, then get drunk and then they would fight, real vicious fighting with the crutch and the cleek.'

'It doesn't bear thinking about,' I said.

'Ach, but people were neighbourly in those days.'

'Neighbourly?' I repeated.

'What George means,' Tom explained, 'is that the fights always started about the same time o' the day, about seven in the evening as a rule and they started with the empty bottles getting thrown out o' the window on to the street. As soon as the neighbours heard the noise, a puckle o' the men would go in and separate them. Many a time my mother warmed my lug for watching the men dragging Cleek down the Princess's steps and along the street and up the steps into his own place.'

'Stirring times,' I said. 'Can you remember when they died?'

'No, that I canna mind.'

'I can,' said George. 'Cleek died when I was in the Fourth Standard at the school. I mind on it because Dougie

Mackinnon and I got a leathering for slipping the school the day after he died because Hector the Spout had a bit of a still in a cave behind the Cobbler and he gave Dougie and me twopence each for getting all the empty bottles that Cleek hadn't broken out of his back shed for him.'

'That would have been in the late 1880s,' I said.

'You and your dates. Tell me, Tom, when was the Battle o' Waterloo?'

'Never mind that. Did the Princess die before Cleek or after?'

'After. After I left the school,' George said.

'That would have been the early 1890s likely. And who lived in the houses after that?'

'I don't know.'

'Nor me either,' said Tom. 'We were both out of the school and working and not taking much notice o' the village here. But whoever lived in the houses, if anybody lived in them at all, they must have been quieter people than the Princess and Cleek for there were no more fights that I mind on.'

On the following day, I wrote down what I had heard and sent a copy to Sashie and another to Andrew. Both were interested in the story but Sashie wrote: 'You have made me make up my mind, sight unseen, which house I want. The gifted David has sent me rough plans of both and they seem to be much alike and both equally poor in condition. On the title deeds, he tells me, they are called Church House and Highland House. Church House is not in the least suitable for my place of residence and I think letters addressed to S. P. G. de Marnay, Highland House, would look a little bizarre. I *could* change my name to MacTavish but I really prefer not to so I intend to ask for the one that belonged to the Princess and commemorate the colourful lady by re-naming it Princess House.' This led to my having to draw a rough plan of the houses and the area, walking round there with George and Tom, having them point out to me which had belonged to whom and sending the resulting sketch to David.

* * *

This year, the three older children decided that they would spend most of their Christmas holiday at the cottage because, Liz said, the boys she met at school, Boy Scout and Girl Guide parties were a lot of pimply creeps while Duncan said that the girls he met were just plain silly and Gee said that all parties were strictly for the birds anyway. Liz had a very poor opinion of the Girl Guide movement in general.

'I had to be in the Guides,' she said, 'when I was a kid at Daddy's school because the Dominie's kids were supposed to be Guides and Scouts and it was all right then but now that they want me to lead a patrol, I'm giving up. It's all so corny, Aunt Janet. Probably you don't like me saying that. I suppose you were a Guide yourself like Mum was.'

'No, I wasn't,' I said.

'They didn't have such capers up here when Aunt Janet was young,' Tom said.

'But didn't they have them at Cairnton when you went to the Academy?'

'I believe they did, now that I think of it, but I never was one.'

'Your Aunt Janet,' said George, 'would never have done for that kind o' thing, being among a big gang o' people and taking orders and all the like o' that.'

'That's enough. I spent six years in the WAAF during the war among a lot of people and I took quite a lot of orders.'

'And Tom and I have always said that if the government had just sent you over to sort Hitler on your own there wouldn't ever have been any war.'

'The only Guides I have ever known,' I said, ignoring this, 'were the ones I met in the WAAF and they were a dead menace. They all had double-barrelled names, were terribly hearty and chummy and their mothers used to send them birthday cakes made from black-market rations as if they were at boarding-school instead of at a war.'

'What was I telling you?' George asked. 'She fought with the Guides without ever being in them.'

'I got put out of the Scouts,' Gee said suddenly, looking up from his book and gazing at us all solemnly through his spectacles, 'or not put out exactly but the Scout Master said it wouldn't matter if I never came back.'

'Mercy on us,' said George.

'It was when the frying pan caught fire and burned down the cook tent at camp,' Gee said and returned to his book.

'That was only the last straw, the tent, I mean,' Duncan explained. 'Gee is just not the scouting sort if you see what I mean.'

'And are you?' I asked.

'I think it's quite fun for one night in the week. Ours is the Culdaviot Troop, you see, so I meet different chaps from the ones I meet at the Academy.'

Duncan was growing more and more like my father as he grew older, turning into the social friendly man who could get along with all sorts and conditions of 'chaps', while Gee was more like a great-uncle, now dead, on his mother's side. This man had been a highly skilled engineer with a bent for minor invention and Gee was beginning to show something of his benevolent good-humoured eccentricity. The differences of individuality and the traits of heredity in the young people never failed to fascinate me.

On the day after Boxing Day, while Liz and Duncan were playing pop records at deafening pitch to George and Tom, while I prepared lunch in comparative peace behind the closed door of the kitchen, Gee came wandering in, his book in his hand. He picked up a carrot which I had scraped, took a bite from it, then scratched his head with what was left and said: 'What am I doing in here?'

'How should I know?'

'Oh yes. You are wanted on the telephone.'

The record-player was still blaring and not having Gee's ability to do anything, much less read, in the midst of such a din, I shouted: 'Turn that thing down!' and then said: 'Yes?' into the telephone.

The first sound to come from the other end was laughter and then: 'Janet, this is Mark – Mark Alexander.'

'Mark, where are you?'

'Inverness. I tried to call you on Christmas Day from Liverpool and last night from Glasgow—'

'We've got the young people here. We were out. Look, take a taxi. You can get here from Inverness in an hour.'

'I have a car. Are you sure it is all right to come like this with—'

'Of course it is. We'll all be delighted.'

'Mark who?' Liz asked.

'Mark Alexander.'

'Same name as you, except that everyone says Sandison now?'

'That is how we became friends,' I said. 'We met on the ship that brought me from St Jago. He was the Second Engineer.'

Down the years since 1959, I had had a few short letters at long intervals and from various points on the globe from Mark but I had begun to think that it was one of those relationships that would tail off into silence and that I would probably never see him again. With this attitude of mind, it was like meeting a stranger when I first opened the door to him but a warm feeling of familiarity soon returned. He was nearly thirty now but was outwardly very little changed and his charm took effect immediately upon the family.

'And where are you doing your ship-building?' I asked. 'It seems to me you have never stayed in one place for long enough to build anything.'

'You are quite right. I gave up the ship-building idea after nine months. I found the drawing-board side of things just plain dull. It seems the sea got me during that voyage to St Jago and I have gone back to it. I've got my ticket now and I am sailing Chief with a line of tankers.'

'And that is what you really want to do?'

'Yes. At times I think I am potty, living miles from land in cramped quarters but about a month ashore is the most I can stand so I might as well settle for the sea.'

'How old were you,' Gee asked, 'before you knew you wanted to be a sailor?'

'Nearly twenty-seven, I am afraid.'

'So I have plenty of time,' said Gee, who was a curious mixture of the absent-minded dreamer and the extremely practical. 'I can't make up my mind whether to play football for Scotland or be a professor of mathematics.'

'You'd better wait for Scotland to ask you,' said Liz scathingly.

'Mathematics phooey,' said Duncan.

'Our great-grandfather on the Sandison side was a sea-faring man,' Liz informed Mark with pride.

'On the *distaff* side of the Sandison family,' Gee, now in his professorial role, corrected her. 'His name was Reid.'

'I hope you have no professors in ships at sea, Mark,' George said. 'They can be a fearful nuisance at times.'

Gee, accustomed to teasing of this kind when he became over-precocious, took this in good part but got something of his own back by saying: 'She might as well get it right if she is going to say it at all.'

Pointedly ignoring her brother, Liz turned to Mark. 'Where is your home?' she asked.

'I was born in Ireland but my only home now is my ship.'

'Mark's people are dead,' I said, 'and he has no relations. You complained to me once that relations only muddle things up with all their different ideas. I wonder what Mark thinks?'

'I think it must be rather good to have relations and a

236

family,' he said, 'even if they do muddle things up a bit at times.'

'I can't really imagine not being part of a family,' Liz said, looking at Mark with sympathetic eyes, 'but then we are a terribly familial family. I think it all started with Reachfar.'

'On board the ship coming from St Jago,' Mark told her, 'your aunt became known as the Reachfar Lady, because she used to tell stories about Reachfar to a little girl who was on board.'

'Why did you do that?' Liz asked me and although she would soon be sixteen, her tone was childishly indignant. 'The Reachfar stories are *our* stories.'

'I do not think you have the right of things there, Liz,' Tom said. 'The stories belong to Aunt Janet in the first of it and she can tell them to whoever she likes.'

'And God knows there's enough of them to go round,' George added.

'What I think is,' said Duncan suddenly but quietly, 'that even if Aunt Janet told the little girl about the ferret in Miss Tulloch's shop, it would be different to her from what it was to us. This little girl was from England, you said, and she has never seen a shop like Miss Tulloch's or even a ferret likely. The person that hears the story makes it different.'

I looked at the boy with admiration. 'Sometimes,' I said, 'I think that Duncan is the only one in this family who has any real sense. Of course the person who hears the story or reads the story contributes just as much to it as the person who tells it or writes it.'

*　　*　　*

The next day, when Tom and George had gone to watch some sporting fixture on television and the children had gone out walking, I said: 'I hope you are not sorry you came, Mark. There is absolutely nothing to do here.'

'I only wish I had more than four days,' he said. 'I wish

now that I had come long before this but when I read about that success you had with your writing, I got scared, thought that you wouldn't want to be bothered—'

'You silly ass. You might have known I was too old to change, too old and thrawn a tree to be twisted, as George and Tom would say.'

'What a pair they are and those kids are real characters. As Liz says, you are a very familial family.'

'Sometimes I think that we are too much so. I know that Liz and the boys fight like fiends some of the time but they always prefer to be with each other than with any of their friends in the last resort. I suppose they will outgrow that, though.'

'I hope they never outgrow it entirely. It must be a wonderful feeling, that sense of belonging.'

He sounded wistful and I said: 'You must know by now that you are welcome to belong here if you want to.'

'Yes and I do want to. After Dad – my grandfather died, I thought it was terrific to be free but during that nine months when I was studying marine engineering I found out that that sort of freedom can mean just loneliness. Sometimes at sea I feel like throwing my colleagues overboard but I know now that it is better to be irritated than to be absolutely on your own.'

'I know what you mean,' I said.

'And there is another thing I have found out. It is probably not very profound to you,' he said diffidently. 'I have discovered that one has to have what one might call a home port. I used to feel that home was a sort of prison, that if only I could get free of all it meant, everything would be better. I never want to see that house or even Ireland again but I feel now that there has to be somewhere, with people you can think of as your own. Little Helga used to pass on the Reachfar stories to me, you know. I often think about Reachfar and about that estate in St Jago where my father worked and although I have never seen Reachfar and was only on the estate for about two hours, they are more real in a way than the place where I grew up.'

'I think it is very wise of you,' I said, 'at your age, for you are not all that old yet, to have come to know that nobody can live in isolation. In time, you will establish your own home port but if this family will do in the meantime, you are welcome, as I said. By the way, the young people will probably want to drag you up to what was Reachfar if some of the snow melts before you go and you may lose an illusion.'

'I doubt that,' he said. 'My Reachfar has no relation to the physical place. It is a country of the mind.'

*   *   *

Liz, Duncan and Gee did indeed take Mark on an expedition to Reachfar and came back, as they always did, with thermos flasks filled with cold water from the well on the moor.

'They are right,' Mark said. 'It tastes like no other water in the world.'

'And is extra good with a little whisky in it,' said George.

'And we brought this,' Liz said, unzipping her anorak and producing a twig about two feet long with two long thin roots at one end. 'Dunk says it's a rowan.'

'It is a rowan right enough,' George agreed, 'but you were very foolish to take any plant out of the ground in weather like this.'

'I told them that,' Duncan said, 'but it was three to one.'

Liz, Mark and Gee looked chagrined. 'Mark said he wanted to give Aunt Janet a present,' Liz explained, 'and was asking us what she would like and we told him that what she wanted most was a rowan tree to keep the witches away from the barn and this was growing in a crevice in the Old Quarry face and Mark got it out with his knife. It isn't going to die, is it?'

Holding the little sapling between my hands, I remembered what Sashie had said about the walling and paving of

239

the garden. 'It was undertaken out of love. It was bound to prosper.'

'No, it isn't going to die,' I said.

'Aunt Janet is very hard to give presents to,' Gee was explaining to George and Tom. 'Everybody knows that. Book tokens are the only thing but Mark wanted something more special than that. Mum is easy for presents. Every Christmas we just club together and give her one more of these plates she is collecting for the dining-room wall but you can't hang plates in this place because the walls are mostly books and windows, so I voted for the Reachfar rowan tree.'

'And we'll go out and plant it right now. At least there is no frost,' I said.

'If it is to keep the witches away,' George said, 'it has to be on the north side of the house.'

'Aye,' Tom agreed solemnly. 'The witches always come down on the north wind.'

'George and Tom are only clowning,' Liz explained to Mark. 'They don't believe in the witches any more than the rest of us but I like old Highland customs and most of the houses here have a rowan tree on their north sides so Aunt Janet and I want one for the barn, don't we?'

'Yes we do and there couldn't be a better present,' I said and we all went out into the cold slushy garden.

While George fetched his spade from the shed, I chose a spot by the north garden wall and when George turned out the first spadeful of sand and pebbles, Tom said: 'This is what Robert Burns meant, Mark, when he wrote about Highland scab and hunger. Come west here a bittie, George,' and he indicated a spot with the toe of his boot, 'this feels a little more like the thing.'

George did as instructed, took out another spadeful, where-upon Liz pounced at the hole saying: 'Look, a Christmas dumpling threepenny bit!' She held up the little coin, so worn that the head of Queen Victoria could only be des-cried and no more. Now George straightened his back, leaned his spade against the wall and began to examine some black rags that fell to shreds between his hands until all he was holding was the rusty metal clasp of an old-fashioned purse.

'It's Mrs Bull's buried treasure!' Gee shouted.

'Go to the shed, Duncan and bring me a hand-fork,' George said while I explained to Mark how Mrs Boyd had buried things long ago.

In all, we found three of the little silver coins and it was growing dark before the children gave up the search for more and Duncan began to pack the cold gravelly soil round the roots of the little rowan sapling.

'You should give it some manure,' Gee said and Liz agreed with: 'Yes. When the Sergeant at home plants the garden, he always puts in lots of manure.'

Duncan ignored them and went on filling the hole.

'What do you think, Duncan?' I asked. 'There is plenty of compost in the pit.'

Duncan looked up at his sister and brother. 'Will you two ever learn any sense?' he asked. 'This tree came out of a slit in the Old Quarry face. You go and stuff it up with manure and it would get indigestion and die.'

'That is Reachfar speaking,' George said to Mark. 'Duncan is quite clever at the school but he is just a crofter at heart.'

George told the children that they might have a coin each and while they were washing them at the kitchen sink I said: 'These coins really belong to my friend Andrew who sold me the barn.'

'No. When you buy the ship, you buy the cargo,' said Duncan with a lewd giggle, 'as Willie Beagle said when—'

'That will do!' I said sharply and instantly remembered that the words were those of my grandmother when I produced some of George's and Tom's less refined lore over the supper-table.

And now, as we sat down to supper, Liz said: 'To think of all that digging we've done, looking for that treasure. I am sure we must have dug at the rowan place because we dug just about everywhere.'

'Things can be very thrawn at times,' Tom told her. 'You often come on a thing you are looking for when you are just *not* looking for it.'

'If Sashie were here,' I said, 'he would say that it was Mark who found the treasure.'

'Me?' Mark questioned. 'I didn't even get my hands dirty.'

'Why would Sashie say that?' Liz asked.

'He would say that it all started with Mark wanting to give me a special present, with Mark not looking for something for himself but thinking of somebody else.'

There was a strange silence round the table while everybody considered this idea before George said: 'And it seems to me that Sashie could be right,' and all the heads nodded in concurrence.

* * *

After Mark and the children had gone away, I watched the little rowan tree day by day and tried hard to keep my faith that it would survive but January turned into February and it looked more and more lifeless. At the end of February, a mild month which had brought the garden well forward, I began to ignore the rowan tree while, at the back of my mind, I tried to go on hoping that one day it would surprise me by suddenly showing some sign of life. March came, with the crocuses ablaze among the paving stones and the clump of daffodils in the vegetable plot showing the green spears of buds, when the aftermath of the mild February took its toll of the village. Little John the Smith's grandfather died and then an old lady whom we did not know but George and Tom, as was the custom, attended both funerals.

'They are a remarkable pair,' Doctor Hay said. 'Just what age are they?'

'We don't recognise birthdays in this house,' I said, 'but

George turns eighty-four some time this year and I have no idea what age Tom is except that he is older than George. But I thought you might know with all the bureaucratic records you keep nowadays.'

'I inherited my records from Doctor Mackay and he was not given to any paper work that could be avoided. Not that it matters. Age and illness don't necessarily go together.'

'My own totally uninformed opinion,' I said, 'is that illness is as much a state of mind as a physical thing. I have been really ill only twice in my life and both times it was mostly because I was unhappy.'

'I wouldn't say your opinion was as uninformed as you claim,' she told me.

Shortly after this, there was a minor crisis in the house one morning. Before breakfast each day, George and Tom cleaned their black leather boots so that they shone all over the top and across the insteps between heels and soles underneath. When I was a child, the boot-cleaning used to be done after supper in the evenings but now that they were retired and at their leisure, as they put it, the job was done in the morning. In their methodical way, Tom was putting on the the blacking, George was polishing and while Tom laced his own finished boots, George was polishing his own, except that they would not take a polish.

'What the devil is wrong with them?' George asked.

'Mine are just fine,' said Tom and skipped smartly away from the kitchen to the porch, porch to garden while his voice came back to us: 'Hunt the Gowk!' and now we saw that there were two tins of blacking on the floor, except that one of them held not blacking but a sticky mixture of lard and soot which Tom had applied liberally to George's boots to celebrate All Fools' Day. I need hardly say that, about five minutes later, Tom returned to the kitchen to help George wash the boots with hot water and soap, while I was told to get out of their way, go to the living-room and get on with my writing.

I have said already and it cannot be repeated too often that happiness is difficult to recognise except in retrospect and difficult to define even when recognised. Spring with us was always a happy time as we sowed and planted, looking forward to the Easter Holidays and on to the summer and autumn when what we had sown and planted would come to maturity.

This April was a beautiful month and on Good Friday, at breakfast, Tom said: 'The north end o' that vegetable plot o' ours is so close to the firth that the ground is fine and warm. What about putting in a row of early tatties the-day, George? It will be a fine surprise for Jock tomorrow when he comes up from that cold hill in Aberdeenshire.'

'I was just thinking much the same thing,' George agreed and they went out to the garden.

It was about an hour later that George came into the house, his step unusually rapid along the paving-stones outside the window. 'Janet, will you come out?' he asked. 'Something has come over Tom.'

I ran to the vegetable plot where Tom was lying on his side. Death has a terrible serenity and authority that are immediately recognisable. Tom's tweed cap had fallen off and his thin white hair was silver beside the gold of the daffodils that he had helped to plant, while his ruddy skin was already growing pale against the black earth that he had helped to make fertile. I stood up and turned away from George, trying to raise my eyes and look away to the sea and the hills but my glance was suddenly arrested. The little rowan tree by the wall was covered with green buds.

*   *   *

In the days that followed, George was stronger than any of us, although his sense of loss must have been greatest of all. Jock arrived that afternoon, bringing Duncan with him, which led me to protest: 'You shouldn't have brought the

244

boy, Jock. He is as white as a sheet. He is only twelve, after all.'

'He is their elected representative, Janet,' he told me, 'and as you know, we all have to learn to face these things sometime. Roddy will be up for the funeral on Tuesday and then we'll all go home. You and George will be better on your own for a bit.'

I wandered about the house, trying to do what was required and anything that was asked of me and when the undertakers came that same afternoon, I went out into the garden with Duncan. When I saw again the plot with the daffodils at its centre, I could neither speak nor move for a moment and the boy put a hand on my sleeve and said: 'I think you should send a telegram to Sashie, Aunt Janet. He ought to know.'

'Yes. Yes I will,' I said and went to the telephone. Somehow, it was a relief to dictate the words: 'Tom died' to the operator. It was like speaking the words to Sashie himself. 'Tom died funeral Tuesday think of us' was the message I sent which brought comfort and although I knew that it might have to be relayed back to Sashie from St Jago to New York or Milan and might not reach him for some time, I felt that this comforting contact had been made.

When the undertakers were almost ready to leave, the senior man asked for the date of Tom's birth that it might be engraved along with the date of his death and his name on the plate of the coffin. George, Hamish, Jock, Duncan and I all looked round at one another, bemused, for until now, Tom's age had been a family joke, with George telling the children: 'At the time Tom was born, the people up here wore blue paint instead o' clothes,' and Tom himself saying: 'A whilie back, when I was the half-hundred—' 'Just a minute,' George said to the undertaker and to me: 'Come, Janet.'

We went up to Tom's room where he lay serenely on his bed and George opened the big wooden 'kist' or chest which was a common possession of all men of their generation and our district. We had blankets stored in the main part of it but at one end there was a built-in section with its own inner lid. George now opened this and it contained a bank book, the silver cup that Betsy the filly had won at the horse show some fifty years ago, a pair of Pinchbeck ear-rings of Victorian design, one of them broken and a folded yellowed birth certificate. It named his mother, Mary Forbes, no father was named but Thomas, a male child, the immaculate faded copperplate handwriting informed us, was born on twenty-first April, 1868. Tom had been within two days of his ninety-sixth birthday.

George replaced the certificate beside the cup and handed the bank book and the ear-rings to me. 'Tom would have wanted you to have these, Janet. The ear-rings would have belonged to his mother.'

The funeral was timed for three o'clock on Tuesday after-noon and on the Monday evening, Andrew Boyd telephoned me from Poyntdale. 'No good saying I am sorry, Janet. Rice told me what happened and David and I came up. Anything we can do?' It struck me that Andrew used the phrases: 'What can I do for you?' and 'Anything I can do?' very frequently, something I had not noticed until now. 'Just come to the funeral, both of you,' I said.

Duncan was spending most of his time out-of-doors in the garden or on the beach. He did not go far from the house but seemed to derive comfort from the growing plants or the wash of the water on the shingle. After breakfast on Tuesday morning, he went out as usual and I went up to my room, wishing now that three o'clock would come so that all might be over. I had not been there for very long when Duncan tapped and put his head round the door.

'Aunt Janet, I think Sashie is coming in over Reachfar!'

'It isn't possible,' I said but from my window I could see the little aircraft coming low over the hill and turning east.

'He is flying over the churchyard,' Duncan said and we

246

ran downstairs and out of the house, the others following us.

'Duncan and I think it is Sashie,' I told my brother. 'Yes, it is,' I added as the aircraft dipped low over the house, then rose again to head south-west towards the airport.

'I have never met Sashie,' Jock said as the aircraft disappeared from sight, 'and I have never quite believed all that the kids said about him but – now—'

An hour later, Sashie was in the house, very small in stature compared with Jock and Hamish, only a little taller than the twelve-year-old Duncan, yet he seemed to dominate us all. He spoke no words of sorrow or sympathy but merely shook hands with each one of us and then said : 'Do you need that car and driver I have out there or shall I dismiss him ?'

'We have all the cars we need, thank you,' Jock said and Sashie went out.

He did not return to the house immediately but began to walk slowly round the garden, looking down at the spring flowers and when I went through to the kitchen, Jock followed me.

'I believe the kids now,' he said quietly. 'Meeting that fellow is more like encountering a cosmic force than meeting a human being.'

'What they call star quality,' I said.

'Janet, what is there between you and him to make him come all this way ?'

What *was* there between Sashie and me that I could put into words ? 'The flip answer,' I said, 'would be that he likes me and he just *loves* aeroplanes, but I can't find words, Jock, for what is really between him and me. I like him and admire him because he is the sort of person I would like to be if I could but I have no idea why he came to like *me*. Yet he is always on hand when my spine needs stiffening, like now. I was surprised when his aircraft came over but I ought to have known he would come.'

Shortly before three, the people began to gather in and

around the house. But for the hearse and a few cars to carry older people, it was to be a walking procession the short distance up to the churchyard and Jock said: 'Do you want to walk or drive, Janet?' I did not want to go to the churchyard at all but was prepared to go if it was expected of me and as I hesitated, Sashie's voice came from behind me: 'If it is all right, Jock, Janet and I will stay here after the house service is over.'

'Of course it is all right,' Jock said.

The service did not take long and the six bearers, George, Jock, Andrew, David, Roddy and Hamish carried the coffin to the hearse while the dark mass of mourners formed in a long column behind Duncan, the representative of the new generation, who carried a bunch of the daffodils that Tom had helped to plant.

'Come inside, Janet, and sit down,' Sashie said when the long procession had moved away from the garden gate.

'He is everywhere in and around this house,' I said, 'and he is in the very fabric of all the years I have lived.'

'And he always will be,' Sashie told me.

'Always,' I repeated. 'When I was a child, Sashie, the word always meant to me the people and things I had known since I was old enough to know anything at all. Reachfar, my family, the kitchen clock, the routine of the days and the seasons were all part of what I thought of as always. If anything strange happened, I was afraid of it, like the time I told you about when I made a scene, because my father was late for supper. But now I see for the first time that always doesn't only come down from the past. It extends away into the future too. Tom will always be part of always. Thank you for coming, Sashie. Now, will you get the drinks out while I get tea ready?'

'Certainly, darling. People. Drinks. You are so right to accept that life goes on ... always.'

*   *   *

248

Only the coffin bearers returned to the house and they did not stay long. As Roddy, Duncan and Jock were leaving, Jock said to me: 'You and George will arrange with the masons about putting the name on the gravestone?'

'Yes,' I said. 'We'll see to it,' and after supper, when Hamish had gone, I sat down at my typewriter and said: 'I might as well write to the masons now about engraving the stone. The sooner the better.' I began by typing on a separate sheet the words to be engraved and had written 'Thomas Forbes' when George, from behind me, said: 'Sandison'. I looked up at him. 'You had better leave that for now and come over here to the fire with Sashie and me. There is a thing that I want to tell you,' he said.

'Shall I—?' Sashie began.

'Not at all. Sit down, man,' George said and turned to me. 'I didn't bother about the plate on the coffin for that was going under the ground whatever and I would have had no chance to explain to you about this, what with all the people coming and going but I want Tom's proper name to be on the stone, the name he is entitled to. Tom was my half-brother, the son o' my father by Mary Forbes.' I made a gulping noise and he smiled and went on: 'Go on and laugh, Janet. Tom would have liked you to laugh.' He turned to Sashie. 'By the time Janet knew my father, her grandfather, he was an old man and looked like the pictures o' Moses that used to be in old Bibles, with his long white whisker and all. In fact, he was like many people's idea o' the Almighty Himself and terrible good and strict and holy with his way of it and would come down on one like thunder from Ben Wyvis for a bit o' poaching over Poyntdale or taking a fish out o' the river at Dinchory. He seemed to have forgotten that when he was a young man he was no better than most and worse than some.' His voice became more grave now. 'You will mind that Her Old Self lived for just a day after your grandfather died? Your father was the apple o' your grandfather's eye, Janet, and he looked on Tom and me as a couple o' good-for-nothing lazy devils most o' the time but I think that myself was Her Old Self's favourite, next to your mother, that is.'

'Yes,' I agreed. 'You were, in spite of all the scoldings about being a clown.'

'The evening your grandfather died, she took me into the milk-house and shut the door and then she told me about Tom being who he was, but I wasn't to tell Duncan, your father. "Duncan thinks the world of his father," she said. She told me that she wanted me always to look on Tom as my brother, although there was no need for her to tell me that for I had looked on Tom that way all my life. It was Her Old Self that brought Tom to Reachfar when his mother died and left him all alone as a boy just out o' the school. Her and your grandfather met and were married up in the west when he went up there to graze winter sheep for the Laird. It seems that after they were married and she came to Reachfar, she heard a few rumours about your grandfather and Mary Forbes for people scandalised then just the way they do now. The one thing I would have liked,' and George chuckled now, 'is to have been there when she tackled your grandfather about Tom being his son. I'll bet you she fairly sorted him and no wonder he looked like Moses for the rest of his life.'

'There was an old man in Culdaviot who said Sandy-Tom resembled Tom when I took the pram up the village,' I said almost to myself.

'Your mother must have been a very generous-minded woman, George,' Sashie said.

'She could be as wild as the heather up in the west where she came from,' George told him, 'and had no respect for what they call the law but she had a few laws o' her own and God help anybody that went against them.' He knocked out his pipe on the bars of the grate. 'Now, we'll have a dram as Tom would have liked, Janet and you can see to the letter to the masons in the morning.'

At eleven o'clock, George knocked out his pipe again and announced that he was going to bed. 'It was good of you to come all this way so quick, Sashie, to be here with us. How long can you stay?'

'I have to be in New York by Saturday.'

'Dear me. You know I doubt if Tom was ever further than Inverness in all his life.'

'He was a fortunate man,' Sashie said, 'to know so well his own nature and where he wanted to belong.'

'Aye, maybe.'

'You will miss him very much, George, won't you?'

'No,' George said. 'Tom wouldn't have liked us to miss him and go about with long faces being sorry for ourselves. What he would like is that we should *mind* on him and be thankful that he had such a good long run and came to the last without being any bother to anybody, like he would have wanted. Tomorrow, Janet, we will plant these early tatties if we are spared and go on just as usual. We'll be busier than ever, now that there's just the two of us, what with the gardens and the sticking-in and one thing and another and before long it will be the summer and the Ladies from Sussex.'

When George had gone upstairs, Sashie said: 'In a physical sense, there are only two of you now but, nevertheless, every time I think of this place, I shall see you here as I have always seen you, in the company of your friends George and Tom.'